"A brilliant journey from the harsh realities
of making the grade in the English Premiership,
via the A-League and onto the sobering realities
of football corruption in Asia – 9/10"
Trevor Treharne, *Australian FourFourTwo* magazine

"Being an old West Ham boy who grew up in
East London and played in Malaysia, it's clear to me that
Neil Humphreys knows this world. *Match Fixer* paints
a vivid picture—colourful, exciting and unpredictable.
It really is a fascinating book."
Tony Cottee, former England, West Ham,
Everton and Selangor striker

"Knowing Singapore rather well, and now that I find
myself working in the game, I think *Match Fixer*
has an intriguing insider's perspective of both worlds.
It's an engrossing look at the Asian football scene."
Nick Leeson, Galway United CEO
and author of *Rogue Trader*

NEIL HUMPHREYS
MATCH FIXER

mc Marshall Cavendish
Editions

© 2010 Marshall Cavendish International (Asia) Private Limited
Reprinted twice 2010

Cover art by OpalWorks Co. Ltd

Published by Marshall Cavendish Editions
An imprint of Marshall Cavendish International
1 New Industrial Road, Singapore 536196

Other Marshall Cavendish Offices
Marshall Cavendish Ltd. PO Box 65829, London EC1P INY, UK • Marshall Cavendish
Corporation. 99 White Plains Road, Tarrytown NY 10591-9001, USA • Marshall
Cavendish International (Thailand) Co Ltd. 253 Asoke, 12th Flr, Sukhumvit 21 Road,
Klongtoey Nua, Wattana, Bangkok 10110, Thailand • Marshall Cavendish (Malaysia)
Sdn Bhd, Times Subang, Lot 46, Subang Hi-Tech Industrial Park, Batu Tiga, 40000
Shah Alam, Selangor Darul Ehsan, Malaysia

Marshall Cavendish is a trademark of Times Publishing Limited

National Library Board Singapore Cataloguing in Publication Data
Humphreys, Neil.
Match fixer / Neil Humphreys. – Singapore : Marshall Cavendish Editions, c2010.
p. cm.
ISBN-13 : 978-981-4276-29-0

1. Soccer players – Singapore – Fiction. 2. Gambling – Singapore – Fiction.
3. Organized crime – Singapore – Fiction. I. Title.

PR6108
823.92 – dc22   OCN441572963

Printed in Singapore by Craft Print International Ltd

for Chris Newson

acknowledgements

Chris sat me down in a Singapore coffee shop and bought me a hot chocolate that lasted four hours. The conversation started with "do you remember all your daft theories about football corruption?" and ended with an outline for *Match Fixer*. Thanks for the idea, Chris.

The outline and daft theories are mine so I take full responsibility. Shawn and Mei Lin then encouraged my sex, drugs and football conspiracies further, and helped me bash them into shape.

We've all read stories about corrupt footballers and watched football matches that were corrupt. This book would not have been possible without either. Long live The Beautiful Game.

MATCH FIXER

This is a work of fiction and the characters portrayed do not exist. It is a story about an aspiring footballer from East London who ends up in Singapore; it is not a book about football. Any similarity or apparent connection between the characters in the story and actual persons, whether alive or dead, is purely coincidental.

 **one**

TIGER grabbed his mask. The mid-afternoon heat was particularly stifling and he could already feel the sweat trickling down his temple. This was not a particularly astute idea, but he had no choice. Whacking an S-League footballer behind the knees with a baseball bat in front of a security guard outside a condo was not a wise career move at the best of times, but to do it off Orchard Road, the busiest shopping district in Singapore, was nothing short of career suicide. But he had no choice. Orders were orders.

Dressed head to toe in black, Tiger wiped his forehead again and reached for his bat in the passenger's seat. He knew what to do. He prided himself on his professionalism. Over 20 years in the job and not a single minute spent in a Changi jail cell. That wasn't an achievement in Singapore; that was a miracle. But then, Tiger had always been meticulous because he genuinely loved his job. When he left school in Toa Payoh and started drifting towards the teenage gangs around Chinatown, he was the one who always got away. And while the other kids just threw styrofoam cups of tea or splattered paint across the apartment, he was methodical. He would calculate how much tea or paint to use depending on how much money the gambler owed his boss. They were usually gamblers. Tiger preferred dealing with gamblers because they were invariably scrawny, weak Chinese guys who sobbed on their doorstep every week as he nailed a pig's head to their door and scrawled "OWE MONEY, PAY MONEY" across their bright, pastel-coloured apartment walls. The weak-minded imbeciles watched him vandalise their homes and did nothing. Some actually *thanked* him for not beating them up. He had no qualms about taking their money and still didn't, although he hadn't made an actual house visit for years. He employed his own teenage school dropouts to carry out his *Ah Long* jobs now. Tiger was an entrepreneur now. Like a productive Singaporean, he had dutifully upgraded his skills years ago.

Tiger had no issue with the job itself. The baseball bat routine was honed and polished years ago, and he recalled a similar job about a decade back when another S-League footballer required a lengthy spell on the injury list. The footballer was incapacitated, and Tiger was across the Causeway and into the Malaysian countryside before the traumatised security guard had a chance to react and pick up the telephone in his little box. Condo security guards were a joy to work with. Tiger didn't even have to bribe them anymore. He had to in the early days; his boss always insisted on it as they were mostly Singaporean then. But today's security guards were Indian or Bangladeshi guys earning $600 a month. They never wanted any aggravation. They never wanted to be interviewed by the authorities. They just wanted to keep their 'green cards'. Globalisation had worked wonders for Tiger's business interests. Besides, Tiger knew that this Indian security guard would see nothing.

The difference with this particular job was, Tiger liked Chris Osborne. He was all right for a white man, a decent *ang moh*. Of course, Singapore had given him the tanned Malay girlfriend, the Orchard Road apartment and the odd TV appearance on the Super Soccer channel with his *ang moh* mates—all for playing in a shit football league. All of that was a given. But Chris was still relatively humble despite his modest success. There was something retained from Tiger's strict Chinese upbringing that made him look for that quality in another person. Tiger could still see Chris' humility. Despite his wealth, Tiger still treated every gambler, punter, bookie's runner and prostitute exactly the same—with complete indifference. But he couldn't help himself; he liked Chris. Chris was everything that the middle-aged, plump, balding Tiger was not and yet modest about all of his attributes. And he could play, too. He could really play. Tiger hadn't bothered with local football since Singapore were booted out of the Malaysia Cup in 1994. The S-League made him a decent living and he attended the odd game for work purposes, where he would spend the entire 90 minutes organising bets over the phone. Until Chris came along. He danced around defenders in a way that reminded Tiger of those halcyon days of black and white portable TVs showing flickering images of Kevin Keegan and Trevor Brooking. Tiger particularly liked Brooking. He played in that unique, effortless fashion that only the true mavericks could master—Cantona, Zidane and even Le Tissier—showmen who were slower than their opponents, but always two steps ahead. Chris Osborne wasn't in their class, but he was in that category of entertainers and he came from the same world as Brooking, too. Tiger always liked that. Brooking was Tiger's favourite player in the early 1980s and Chris reminded Tiger of Brooking. Chris had achieved something that Tiger had always thought impossible— he made Tiger watch local matches for pleasure again.

Now Tiger was going to break Chris' legs.

CHRIS stepped out of the condo lift. Caucasian, blond, tanned and athletic, he could only be one of two things in Singapore—a sportsman or a banker. Chris hated maths at school. The only time he ever showed any interest in a maths lesson was when his mate Colin organised a fantasy football league. Chris chipped in two pounds to join on one condition—he could sign himself for West Ham United. Even then, Chris was never short of confidence when it came to his playing ability.

But he was never allowed to be arrogant. His father always reminded him that there was a subtle difference between arrogance and confidence. Each time Alan Shearer stepped onto a pitch, he expected to score every time he collected the ball around the penalty box. That wasn't arrogance; that was an innate self-belief in one's skills, his father always said. But if Shearer went on *Match of the Day* bragging about his goal-scoring capabilities … now that's arrogance. Chris always understood the difference.

He needed his self-confidence today. As he walked through his condo's manicured gardens, Chris thought about the club meeting that had been hurriedly organised after training and considered his options. His coach and manager, who both appeared to have no idea of what had happened, wanted him to stay, and he knew the fans, all 5,000 of them, appreciated him. But questions were being asked after the last match and he wasn't sure he had the right answers. Would any answer suffice? Besides, his contract talks were the least of his worries. He wasn't sure his sanity could take another season in Singapore. Back in England, there had been some casual interest from Leyton Orient, but if he was going to leave Singapore, he needed something more concrete than that.

Chris took out his wallet when the Indian security guard stepped out from his post.

"Hey, Chris, how many you gonna score today?" the guard asked excitedly. "I'm going to Singapore Pools later."

Chris smiled. The man said the same bloody thing every morning.

"No, I'm not playing a match today, mate. I'm just training, like a warm-down session. It's the end of the season now. I don't have a match until …"

Chris felt a stabbing sensation behind his knees. His legs buckled and he suddenly felt fear. Instinctively, he rolled forward and tucked in his legs. Years of being kicked from behind by slow, lumbering defenders had taught him to jump forward, tuck in his legs and roll quickly along the turf. Slow-motion replays always made the rolls look more theatrical and an obvious attempt at simulation, but most forwards were conditioned to move away as quickly as possible to avoid a second kick. But this wasn't turf; the concrete path hit Chris on the back of the head and neck hard, and he suddenly felt nauseous. His fingers reached around and grabbed the back of his head, and he knew the warm, trickling sensation was blood.

He felt a crack on his right knee and screamed out in a combination of pain and terror. His trembling fingers tentatively moved towards his knee and he felt the edge of a bone. Chris was overcome with the urge to vomit when a second blow struck his shattered knee again. Dizziness was overwhelming the fear and, in a sudden moment of lucidity, Chris rolled on to his back and opened his eyes. The image was so surreal, it was almost comical. A flabby Asian man clad in black shoes, trousers and a sweater was standing over him, wielding a bloody baseball bat. Most strangely, his face was covered in a black balaclava with the eyehole knitted shut. This was equatorial Singapore with 30-degree heat and 90 per cent humidity. Chris couldn't believe the absurdity of the situation. He smiled. And then he giggled.

The masked man in black raised his baseball bat again and suddenly Chris understood everything. Everything became clear. He knew exactly who was behind the mask and why his legs were being hammered. As the bat whistled through the air towards his right knee, Chris calmly accepted that he was fucked.

 **two**

HE looked like a total dickhead. Chris prayed that none of his friends would turn up for a kickabout. There had to be a more effective training exercise than this. He was standing in the middle of Parsloes Park with a Darth Maul slipper on his right foot and an Adidas Predator boot on his left.

"Try not to be too self-conscious about it," he heard his father shout.

How can I not be self-conscious about it? Chris thought. I'm a 14-year-old teenager standing in the middle of a Dagenham park wearing a fucking Star Wars slipper on my right foot. Chris peered at his father. A tall, well-built man, his enthusiastic old dad stood in their improvised goal—a tree trunk and their coats acting as goalposts—and waved at him to shoot. Chris smiled. He adored his father.

From an early age, Chris knew his dad wasn't like other fathers at the football matches. He simply watched (or analysed, as he liked to call it), always reminding Chris how the old West Ham bosses Ron Greenwood and John Lyall never ranted from the touchline at Upton Park. If you were screaming from the sidelines, his father reasoned, you would inevitably miss something. You wouldn't rant and rave during a science lesson, would you? That was another one of his dad's favourites. It was this type of comment that set him apart from the other Dagenham dads. He wasn't a "Dagenham Dave". That singer Morrissey had written a fairly crap, superficial song about the stereotypical moronic Essex geezer and named it Dagenham Dave; and now every dad who wore an England shirt, white trainers and a sovereign ring was called "Dagenham Dave" (although Chris did seem to know a disturbingly high number of men called Dave).

That was the other strange thing about Tony Osborne. He never wore an England shirt, not even when he went down the Captain Cook pub in Barking with his mates from work to watch local boy Tony Adams. Chris had noticed that every other dad wore an England shirt or, more commonly, a West Ham shirt, particularly at their boys' Sunday morning matches, but his own father didn't even own a West Ham shirt and he worshipped the Hammers.

"Why would I wear a West Ham shirt?" he once told Chris, who had finally plucked up the courage to broach the subject with his father during a *Super Sunday* clash on Sky Sports. "I never played for West Ham, did I?"

"But you nearly did. Steve Wallis' dad told me that you had a trial for West Ham and you nearly got in."

"It's like a near miss though, isn't it? There's no such thing, mate. It either goes in or it doesn't. It didn't go in for me, but who knows? The way you're playing, it could go in for you."

"And if it doesn't?"

"Well, that's why you don't rant and rave during those science lessons, right?"

Chris nodded and pretended to listen to Richard Keys and Andy Gray on *Super Sunday*. That's why his father was different to all the other dads. He always seemed to say the right thing at the right time.

Chris stared down at his slipper again. He was too old to

even own a pair of Darth Maul slippers and no one was going to believe they were a misguided present from his oblivious nanny Rose in Forest Gate. Darth Maul slippers should neither be seen nor heard in his living room. But wearing those bloody things out in public in Dagenham on a Saturday morning? He might as well wear a sign saying, "I'm a dickhead. Please kick my head in."

"Are you gonna take this penalty or what?" Tony said. "West Ham kick off in four hours."

"Yeah, all right. Can I take it with my right foot? I could curl it into the bottom right hand corner with my right foot, even in my slipper."

"I know you can. That's why you've got to take it with your left foot. In the old days, this is what they always did. Boot on the weaker foot, slipper on the good foot. You keep kicking with the weaker foot, use your slipper foot to stand on and before you know it, you don't have a weaker foot anymore. Remember this time last year? You couldn't even trap the ball with your left foot, now you can dribble and feint with it. All you've got to do now is shoot with it. This could really help you tomorrow, you know."

"But if I get a penalty, I'm going to take it with my right foot, aren't I?

Tony grinned at his son. He enjoyed Chris' straightforward logic. He secretly savoured their Sunday afternoon discussions about football, school, politics, girls and the general state of the world far more than he ever let on. Chris' intellect made his father immensely proud and he never understood why his mates were dismissive and, at times, embarrassed when their children ever displayed any academic potential. His own father, who spent 40 years covered in grease on Ford's assembly line, was little different. He had toiled in a glorified sweatshop to provide for his family and he saw no reason why his son shouldn't do the same. Our people can't push pens for a living, he always told Tony, but we're not too proud to build the cars for those who do. With more than a little reluctance, Tony followed his father down to Ford at Dagenham Docks. Dagenham kids were not overburdened with choice in the 1970s, but things would be different for Chris. Chris had the academic potential to break the cycle of drudgery. That's how Tony always explained it to his son. The working classes knew their station in life and took a pathetic sort of pride in always getting off at the same stop. Not Chris though. He knew what his daft old man was going on about. He always understood. That's why he was different to all the other kids.

Ironically, Tony was fully aware that his son also had a slim chance of breaking the cycle by taking the only escape route usually open to the working classes—sport. Chris was now only a competent left foot away from being one of the most promising teenage strikers in London. Everyone in Dagenham knew it. But Tony had recognised the talent first. From the moment he stood upright, Chris was blessed with a hand-eye coordination and a sense of balance that was altogether freakish. Chris had his father's height and basic ball control and a natural athleticism. He stayed stick-thin and ran like a whippet. His mates at school stayed back at lunchtime just to watch him play.

In one primary school match against particularly inferior opposition, he collected the ball straight from kick off and dribbled it around every static, clueless kid who foolishly attempted to block his path. Every parent standing on the sidelines, including those cheering on the opposition, gave Chris a spontaneous round of applause. Except Tony. He shoved his hands deeper into his pockets and stared down at his scuffed shoes.

Chris' euphoric team-mates asked him to do something else, anything else, to humiliate their outclassed opponents. Thinking quickly, Chris dropped back into midfield to collect the ball and dragged his labouring marker out to the right flank, where he danced around the ball repeatedly, sending his befuddled opponent in the wrong direction time and again. Then he did something that he'd seen his father's favourite player, George Best, do to one of his confused and exhausted opponents on an old black and white video from the 1960s. Chris took his right boot off and mockingly offered it to the panting boy standing beside him. His team-mates and their parents laughed loudly. The wheezing opponent blushed and, in a desperate bid to avoid anyone seeing the tears welling up in his eyes, made a final, half-hearted lunge at the ball. With an effortless step-over, Chris skipped over the tackle and flicked the ball off to a team-mate. The parents from his school roared with approval.

Tony continued to stare down at his shoes as they kicked at an invisible blade of grass. He waited until the ball was over the other side of the pitch and walked slowly and unobtrusively over to the school's PE teacher. Tony politely asked the teacher to substitute his son. The teacher said he had no cause to withdraw the team's most accomplished player. Tony whispered that there was one pertinent reason—if Chris wasn't pulled off now, this would be his last game for the school. Chris was substituted. And he never offered his boot to an opponent again.

Tony watched his son methodically replace the ball on the penalty spot and gently place his weaker left foot underneath the ball, find a comfortable position right above the laces and then take his usual three steps. Chris stood with his hands on his hips as his eyes darted instinctively from left to right to make it more difficult for the goalkeeper to guess correctly.

"You're gonna miss! You're gonna miss! You're gonna miss!" Tony screamed.

Chris trotted towards the ball. Tony swayed from side to side repeatedly and flapped his arms in the air.

"You're gonna miss! You're gonna miss! You're gonna miss!" Tony screamed.

But Chris did not miss. He never did.

TONY was quietly confident. Dagenham Schoolboys had turned over Newham Schoolboys, with Chris scoring two and laying on the third. But it was the *way* that he had played—that's what pleased Tony. The intelligence, the quick look up before he received the ball rather than after, allowing the ball to run across his body to give him a head start on his marker—everything was there. The first two yards really were in the mind and Chris had glided away from his opponents. Tony always prided himself on his objectivity, but he was having some difficulty taking a step back today. It was a startling performance. Someone had to be watching.

As he watched Chris collect the district cup from some dignitary in a suit on the pitch, Tony made a point of checking that both father and son were keeping up appearances. He observed the other dads, all beer bellies, white Umbro England shirts and black leather bomber jackets, bouncing along the touchline and hugging each other, gleaming like their sovereign rings. He applauded both teams politely and kept an eye on Chris at all times. His boy was making a point of shaking the hands of his defeated opponents, plenty of affectionate pats on the backs, arms across the shoulders and all that. Good boy, son, Tony thought.

A plump, red-faced man in an ill-fitting suit sidled up to Tony. He was the only spectator not applauding. Tony immediately knew what he was, but couldn't yet work out who he was.

"Great game today, wasn't it?" the perspiring man said, wiping his forehead.

"Yeah, it was actually," Tony replied. He meant it, too. "I was very impressed with the coaching on both sides. The boys kept the ball on the ground and it was mostly two-touch football."

"You must have been impressed with your boy," the man said, examining Tony's face for any discernible reaction.

"Yeah, he did OK. He brought other players into the game and was happy to take the ball on his left foot. How do you know he's my son?"

"Oh, I'm sorry. My name's Bob. I do some part-time scouting in the Essex area and I'd heard a lot about your boy, but I wanted to wait until the district final so I could see him against some half-decent opposition."

"And what did you think?"

"Oh, I'm sure you know what I think, Mr Osborne. I think I've found a genius."

Tony never reacted. Calm exterior. He stared across the pitch at his son celebrating on the field with his team-mates. Someone emptied a water bottle onto Chris' head. Tony smiled as Chris playfully chased after the culprit.

"Call me Tony, please. Well, that's very kind of you to say. Who are you scouting for, Bob?"

"From what I can gather from some of the other dads, Tony, it's the team you and your boy have been waiting for. I represent West Ham United."

Tony slowly clasped his hands behind his back. He had calculated that he might look foolish, but he needed to hide his arms. He didn't want Bob to see the goosebumps.

 **three**

THE petite, attractive nurse was typical of most Singapore hospitals—she was Filipino. She picked up the clipboard at the foot of Chris' bed and ticked a couple of boxes. She looked at Chris and checked her watch. The white man had been asleep for too long. Gently peeling off the sheets, she examined the bandages covering Chris' knees. Some blood had seeped through, but that was to be expected and certainly not reason enough to change them so soon. Lateral meniscus tears always involved some blood loss, not much, but they would take months to heal properly. The pain must be excruciating, the nurse thought, as she re-tucked the sheets into the mattress. But then, the meniscus tears really were the least of this guy's problems. And she had been told he was a professional footballer, too. Until he was wheeled in yesterday afternoon, screaming that his football career was over, she hadn't even known that there was a professional football league in Singapore. She only came down from Manila five years ago.

"Oh, hello, Rosito, didn't see you there."

Rosito looked up and saw the blond, *ang moh* footballer yawning. He offered her a boyish, toothy grin. He was rather handsome, for an *ang moh*. She understood why the other nurses in the ward found him attractive.

"Oh, hello, Mr Osborne. Sorry, I didn't mean to wake you."

She did.

"That's all right. Don't be silly. It's nice to have a pretty face to wake up to."

Chris wasn't being polite. Rosito was stunning. She was short, slim and blessed with an olive skin that pasty, peeling British white women barbecuing themselves on Spanish beaches could only dream of. Her dark skin also served to accentuate her warm, inviting smile that, in some quarters, might be misconstrued as submissive. It wasn't, but Chris had met enough blokes pursuing the Western white man's dream of an exotic, submissive Asian partner to know that dear old Pinkerton lived on after Madame Butterfly.

He had been one of them.

"How are you feeling today?" Rosito asked, ignoring the compliment completely. She heard it all the time. "How are the knees doing?"

"They only hurt when I'm awake."

Rosito laughed in spite of herself. This *ang moh* was actually a good guy. Some of his other footballer friends were not. The fat, loud one who was always on TV was a real asshole. He had visited twice in one day and was clearly agitated. Even Rosito and the other nurses knew that this hadn't been a random assault. Baseball attacks in the middle of the day in front of a security guard just do not happen in Singapore; in Manila, perhaps, but not Singapore. Besides, the injuries were calculated and specific. When Rosito had changed the dressings for the first time, she was shocked at how specific and targeted the damage was. There was not a bruise or cut anywhere else on the body except around the swollen knee area. They had both been smashed, but each blow had been precise, not frenzied, and the violence was not prolonged. Rosito had seen similar assaults that had left the victims confined permanently to wheelchairs, but Chris would certainly walk again. In fact, there was a better-than-average chance that he would play again. The attacker wanted to stop Chris' career, but not end it.

Rosito had her theory for the attack and it was neither profound nor original.

Kelong.

The word was buzzing around the hospital ward. Rosito already knew what it meant.

Fixed.

Kelong was the Malay word for 'fixed'.

She knew that a *kelong* was used as a trap to catch fish. But in local slang, in Singlish, the term meant something else. It meant football corruption. If the *kelong*'s nets are ripped, then the fish leak through. So the analogy goes that if there are '*kelong*' nets in football, the goals leak. The score is fixed. Rosito had no idea that Singapore's only professional football league had existed since 1996, but she was aware of match-fixing. She was from the Philippines. Everyone in Southeast Asia knew about *kelong*.

She had overheard the doctors talking about Chris' attack in the cafeteria. He was bashed just a couple of days after some really important game, so it had to be *kelong*, the doctors said. Football was always *kelong*, wasn't it?

"It's good to get plenty of rest," Rosito reassured. "That'll help to manage the pain. You've got to lie still and give your knees a chance to heal after all the surgery."

"Are you serious? It's my line dancing class tonight at the community centre. I never miss a class and tonight we're doing 'Man, I Feel Like A Woman'."

They both laughed.

"Ah, you've got to laugh, haven't you?" Chris said, pulling himself up and propping his back against a pillow. "As long as you've got your health, you've got something to smile about. My dad always says that."

Chris pulled back the sheets and looked down at his bandaged knees.

"You see, as long as you've got your health."

Rosito smiled nervously. Chris started to turn red. He felt a restrictive, burning sensation at the back of his throat. He wiped a tear away from his eye quickly.

"Ah, for fuck's sake," he said. "I'm really sorry about this."

"Don't be silly, really. It's normal to be emotional. You've been attacked and you're in a lot of pain."

"I still feel like a complete dickhead though."

"A complete what?"

"Oh, it's an English … doesn't matter. What time are the visiting hours?"

EVERY Asian male and Western expat knew Danny Spearman. He was the most popular football pundit in Asia. From his very first appearance on the Super Soccer channel, which beamed from Singapore to Shanghai and everywhere in between, Danny was a hit with the viewers, and not only because his percentages as a tipster were the highest on the show by some distance. He told it straight. He was Asia's Brian Clough, Malcolm Allison and Andy Gray all rolled into one, a football commentator who didn't toe the line, didn't hide behind bluff and bullshit despite the fact his studio was the exclusive broadcaster for the English Premier League in Asia. Other pundits were wary of biting the hand that fed them. Danny didn't give a shit. It didn't take long for the studio's executives, the guys who made the PowerPoint presentations, to draw an obvious conclusion on all their graphs: the more controversial Danny Spearman was on air, the more viewers tuned in to see who was going to be the sacrificial lamb targeted by "The Spear" the following week.

As his popularity grew, Danny modelled himself on Brian

Clough. Love him or loathe him, everyone knew Cloughie. Only football fans knew Brian Clough. But every housewife and old granny in Britain knew Cloughie. So Danny Spearman wanted to be known as The Spear. The salivating executives at the station used it ceaselessly to flag Danny's sections of the show with lame titles like 'The Spear's Transfer Targets', 'The Spear Hits Out' and, of course, the omnipresent 'The Spear's Betting Tips: The Hits and Misses'. Danny's betting tips was such a ratings success that the segment had five product sponsors of its own despite being no more than 10 minutes long. The S-League reporter Billy Addis had pointed out that it took 30 seconds of the allotted 10 minutes just to name all the product sponsors.

Danny's team-mates always called him "Spearmint", suggesting he should be banned in Singapore. Like the chewing gum.

Danny played along with the dressing room banter, but he was not particularly keen on the Spearmint nickname. He was never sure if his team-mates were taking the piss or not. Despite playing in Singapore for several years, and Malaysia before that, the Yorkshireman had never fully come to grips with Singlish, the local vernacular, because no one really spoke Singlish at the Singapore Cricket Club. It was called the Singapore Cricket Club, but few Singaporeans were members. Western expats, on the other hand, practically lived there. Sometimes they took their women to the club. Sometimes they even took their wives.

Danny meandered slowly through the hospital ward. He always took his time in public places; it gave people a better chance of recognising him. He was also a little heavier than usual. When he wore a suit in the studio, the weight gain was less perceptible, but in a T-shirt and Bermudas, there was no place to hide the expanding girth. His thighs had always been broad, and in the humidity they were starting to chafe around the groin area, which was never a positive sign for a professional footballer. Not that there had been much S-League football this season. Danny played less than half of the fixtures and attributed it to a debilitating ankle injury, publicly at least. That bastard journalist Addis had pointed out that Danny had spent more minutes sitting in a Super Soccer studio than out on the pitch. The cheeky fucker even had a sarcastic line graph made up, showing a correlation between Danny's dramatic loss in form and his rise as a TV pundit.

"Hey, Spear, it's you right?" a voice cried. "Can you sign my arm?"

Danny noticed the young Chinese guy sitting up in a hospital bed with his left arm in a sling and his right hand reaching over for a pen on his bedside cabinet. Danny headed towards the bed and quickened his stride. He loved being spotted.

"Sure, mate, can lah," Danny replied, in a painfully stilted attempt at Singlish. "What's your name?"

"It's Xavier," the guy said excitedly as he watched Danny sit beside him and write "You've been hit by The Spear" on his plaster cast.

"Thanks, man. That's great."

"No problem, Xavier. Hope your arm gets better soon, mate."

Danny got up to leave.

"Wait, wait," Xavier said quickly. "Who do you think will win the league this season?"

"Well, it's only just finished, right? But I'm sure the usual suspects will be up there again. It'll be either us or Orchard FC."

"No, I didn't mean the S-League. I mean the real league, the English Premier League. Who's gonna win that?"

"Oh, I see. Right. Well it's not original, but you can never rule out Manchester United for me."

"Thanks, thanks. How much you think I should bet? One thousand can?"

"Hey, come on, mate. That's not for me to say, is it?"

Danny winked at Xavier and Xavier winked back, bursting with pride. Xavier believed he was now part of some unspoken secret society, a member of Danny's clique, the inner circle that always had the gambling inside track on the latest team news and the best betting tips. Danny would forget Xavier the instant he left his bedside.

"It's OK, man. Understand, cannot say how you know right, but you just know," Xavier said. "Hey, is it true that Chris Osborne is in this ward? Are you going to visit him now? Do you think he'll sign my arm too?"

"See ya, Xavier," Danny said. "Take care, mate."

DANNY noticed Chris talking to that fit Filipino nurse who had changed his dressing yesterday. I'd give her one, Danny thought. Even from across the ward, Chris' appearance alarmed Danny. His weary face was more haggard and sickly than yesterday. The black rings under his eyes were deeper and darker, probably exacerbated by his ghostly pallor. Danny had always secretly envied Chris' youth and good looks. He didn't today.

"You're looking well, you old bastard," Danny boomed across the ward. "She's obviously treating you well."

Chris forced a smile. Rosito muttered something under her breath.

"They must be feeding you all right in here then," Danny continued. "I could do with a week in here. They say the camera adds 10 pounds on screen and I keep telling them to stop using so many cameras on me."

Chris pretended to laugh for Rosito's benefit as Danny pulled out a chair beside his bed. Danny had told him the joke several times.

"How are you doing today, nurse?" Danny asked. "Why are

you wasting your time on this reprobate?"

"I'll leave you two guys alone," Rosito said.

"Thanks, Rosito," Chris said. She smiled back at him. She ignored Danny, who watched her walk away.

"You've landed on your feet here, mate," he said. "Look at that arse. She looks even better today. I swear that uniform is even tighter than yesterday."

Chris glanced around the ward. Apart from a couple of dozing patients, the place was deserted. He leaned in towards Danny.

"What the fuck has been going on?" he hissed.

"What are you on about?"

"Don't fuck me about, Danny. Something's obviously happened because you shouldn't even be here. Something should've happened by now."

"How do you mean?"

Danny was whispering now. The cocky, genial disposition disappeared the moment Rosito left the ward. He was terrified.

"Don't treat me like a mug. You should be in here with me, sitting in the next fucking bed."

"Ssh, keep your voice down."

Danny checked the ward again before continuing.

"Things have moved on pretty quickly. One or two deals are being made I think and ..."

"Since yesterday? Don't be ridiculous."

"This is Singapore, remember. They like a smooth surface, calm exteriors and all that."

There's a first, Chris thought. Danny sounded like his father, a comparison that would've disgusted his dad.

"But you were there, too. You're involved. We're banged to rights. We both are. We've got no chance."

"Well, things got a bit crazy after you got attacked. There's been lots of speculation, at every bloody level you can imagine, and some deals are about to be made."

"What about Billy Addis? I can't believe it, but the wanker was still threatening to go public with the lot. And Yati was there, too."

"Who knows? This is Singapore. The country doesn't like to lose face, especially when it comes to foreigners. Those two will probably be taken care of, too."

Chris struggled to focus on the bowl of fruit at the foot of his bed. The image blurred. He felt light-headed.

"Fucking hell," he muttered weakly.

"Yeah."

Chris glanced at Danny.

"What happens to me now?" he whispered.

"Er, well, I had a chat with the club and I think Mr Teck is going to help you out with the hospital bills, transport and all that. He said it was the least the club could do."

"Thank God for Mr Teck then, eh?"

They sat in silence for a while. Danny waited impatiently for Chris to ask the question he dreaded answering. He kept his eyes trained on Chris' tired face, seeking any indication. It proved to be a mistake. Danny accidentally made eye contact with Chris. Telepathy did the rest.

Chris spoke slowly.

"What about Tiger?"

Danny fidgeted in his chair.

"That's the funny part," he said with a forced jocularity, his face betraying his real emotion. There wasn't anything funny about it at all. "No one seems to know where he is."

"He hasn't been caught?"

"No. He's, er, kind of disappeared."

Chris grabbed the wash basin beside his bed and threw up.

 **four**

THE training ground had always looked rather incongruous. Surrounded by council houses that had been garishly covered in pebble dashing after being sold off by Margaret Thatcher, West Ham's training ground in Chadwell Heath did not typify the average Premier League facility. It bore closer resemblance to an Essex halfway house for chavs.

As a kid, Chris enjoyed examining the latest squad photo that came out every pre-season. The Hammers were always framed by the red roofs of old council houses around Chadwell Heath. Houses just like Chris' in Dagenham, which was next door to Chadwell Heath. Chris often wandered around Chadwell Heath with his best mate Ross during the long summer days of pre-season to play Hammer spotting. On one unforgettable morning, Chris and Ross were sitting on a bench when Julian Dicks stepped out of a newsagent in front of them. He was reading a copy of *The Sun*. Ross shouted out "Terminator" and the West Ham skipper came over and asked them if they wanted to watch the training session. They couldn't, because Ross had to get home and look after his little sister, but Chris never forgot Dicks' kindness.

Chris pulled his car into the training ground car park, waved at Wally on the security gate, and found a spot for his Ford among the Ferraris and Bentleys. Remember, people with real wealth

never display it, his dad had always said. It's only the Dagenham
Daves and the lottery winners who get in touch with Rolls Royce
and lay the foundations for their helipad. That's great, Dad, Chris
thought. But I haven't got any fucking money.

More than six years at West Ham and he was still driving a
Ford. He had not kept his initial promise to Harry Redknapp; he
had not made it by his 21st birthday. Chris inked his signature
for the first time as a West Ham player in Redknapp's office two
weeks after his 16th birthday. Redknapp had asked him where he
wanted to be five years on.

"Driving around the East End in a Ferrari," he had replied.
Redknapp took an immediate shine to the cheeky youngster with
blistering pace and an unerring right foot. The East London old
boy from Poplar saw something of himself in the scrawny kid
from Dagenham. Redknapp even made Chris a promise. If he
could do half as much for Chris as Ron Greenwood had done for
Redknapp and Chris made steady progress, then the boy would
make his England debut before his 21st birthday.

The *Dagenham Post* devoted its entire back page to Chris that
week. Chris toasted his sudden elevation to teenage celebrity by
taking Ross to Faces Nightclub in Gants Hill. It was the classiest
venue in Essex and a popular hangout for soap stars, eliminated
Big Brother contestants and the odd footballer. Ross and Chris
went on the "bras optional peroxide party" night. Being tall,
blond, athletic and reasonably acne free, Chris was certainly not a
virgin. He was a Dagenham boy after all. But he was no lothario
either. His father had told him to focus on one set of balls for now.
He was right, but not at Faces. He was a professional footballer
now, a bona fide Hammer. He was an Essex rock-and-roll star,
a playground superstar.

So he did what he had to do in such tempting circumstances.
Nothing. The shiny, happy peroxide people came to him.

"Excuse me, babe, are you that bloke in the *Dagenham Post* today?"

Chris smiled. He stood at the bar with Ross and never bothered to turn around. He did not have to.

"Yeah. Why?"

"Chris Osborne, right? I reckoned it was you. It's that blond hair. It makes you stand out, don't it? My mates said it weren't you, right, but I said it was, so they dared me to come over and see if you'd buy me a drink. D'ya know what I mean, babe?"

Chris looked up at Ross, who glanced briefly at the woman. She wore ripped khaki pants over a pair of white trainers and a white crop top. Her push-up bra shoved her heaving breasts under her chin. Ross guessed that she was around 18 or 19, definitely pretty, definitely up for it. He turned back to Chris and nodded. Chris faced the girl for the first time.

"Yeah, I'll buy you a drink," he said. "What's your name?"

"Joanne. You're much better looking than your photo in the paper, aren't ya?"

"Well, I don't know. That's not for me to say, is it?"

"Oh, look, babe, you've got the stamp on your hand like me. That means you can go out of the club and come back in again, doesn't it?"

"Yeah, I suppose so."

"Yeah, me too."

"Yeah."

Joanne took a swig from her bottle of Becks.

"So d'ya fancy a blow job in the car park then?"

CHRIS walked through the training ground car park. The prestige cars lined up like West Ham's forward line. That one belonged to Marlon Harewood; that one Bobby Zamora; that one Carlos Tevez—the better the player, the better the car. It was a point of principle within English Premier League football clubs. When he was a kid, Chris read about West Ham goalkeeper Ludek Miklosko being sponsored to drive a Skoda around. Skodas were shit cars even then. Miklosko was now back at the club as a goalkeeping coach and Chris had been desperate to ask the Czech if he still owned the Skoda. But then, Miklosko worked almost exclusively with the first team and Chris rarely saw him.

Chris stopped by the manager's car. He saw more of his bloody car than he did the actual man. There was an unwritten rule in football that if a manager had anointed a "Chosen One" during his regime, then his successor would invariably consign him to the scrapheap. It was a point of principle within English Premier League clubs. Chris was Harry Redknapp's boy. In Upton Park circles, Chris was "one of our own". Redknapp was taking another famous punt on one of the academy kids, and Chris Osborne had been earmarked to follow Michael Carrick, Jermain Defoe, Rio Ferdinand, Frank Lampard and Joe Cole off Harry's production line.

Six weeks after Chris signed professional forms, Redknapp left the club. No one saw it coming, least of all Chris. There were all kinds of rumours, but by the time they had filtered down to the youth team they had been distorted beyond recognition. There was a brief period when Chris believed he was somehow connected to Redknapp's dramatic exit from Upton Park. He was certain that his first contract and Redknapp's departure were too close together not to be linked. His father's common sense eventually prevailed. Paranoia sufferers did not make for dedicated professional footballers.

The door to the manager's office quickly became a turnstile. Glenn Roeder, Trevor Brooking briefly, Glenn Roeder again, Trevor Brooking briefly again, Alan Pardew, Alan Curbishley— the names above the manager's parking space changed constantly.

Chris hardly spoke to any of them. The longest conversation he was actually involved in with any of the first-team managers barely allowed him a chance to participate. He introduced his star-struck father to Brooking and the two kindred spirits chatted for 20 minutes about 'the-slipper-on-the-stronger-foot' trick.

Chris had plugged away for more than six years. He was 21 years old and the closest he ever came to the Upton Park turf with the first team was a solitary appearance on the substitute's bench in a meaningless League Cup second-leg clash against Wycombe. West Ham had a two-goal cushion from the away leg, which quickly became a four-goal aggregate lead at Upton Park, and still Chris waited for the nod that never came. The match programme said he was likely to get a start and the *Dagenham Post* gave him another full-page write-up. Even the national tabloids mentioned his name. Everyone did. Except his fucking manager. He wanted that first appearance more for his father than himself. As he sat on the bench pretending he wasn't shivering, he peered up at his father sitting in the West Stand. Tony smiled encouragingly at his son, but he had already accepted that this wasn't going to be his son's night. It broke Tony's heart to acknowledge the possibility that Chris Osborne might not be a West Ham player after all.

THE manager's car, obviously freshly polished by Wally this morning, suddenly angered Chris. He had been at this club longer than the damn car and it was treated with more respect by the staff. Chris was in danger of being consigned to scrap. Fuck it. Enough's enough, he thought. Being the top scorer in the youth team for two seasons, 10 goals in the reserves last year and another seven this season had to count for something. Perhaps his goal-scoring consistency had dropped off after being promoted to the reserves, but there had to be a period of adjustment. Chris accepted he might not be in the same league as Carlos Tevez. OK, he knew he wasn't. From the moment Tevez dummied him in a training session before chipping the goalkeeper, Chris realised that all the hours spent with his dad at Parsloes Park could never teach him the tricks that real magicians were born with. It was not a happy day and one that Chris preferred not to dwell on.

But Chris could still play. He might not be another Tevez, but no one else in the West Ham squad could say that either. There was only one Tevez and there was only one Chris Osborne, and they both deserved regular, first-team football.

Chris jogged across the training pitch in his boots. The pitch was more boggy than usual, which made life even more difficult for Chris. With his back to goal, his lanky frame turned much slower than the likes of Tevez. He noticed Mick handing out bibs to the other players. Chris loathed Mick. The man represented everything that was fundamentally wrong with the English Premier League.

Mick Peters only joined West Ham three months ago as part of a new three-man management team. Based on the continental model, Mick was a member of the mighty triumvirate, which divided the responsibilities of talent scouting, transfer deals, contract negotiations, team selections and daily training routines between the three coaches. There was only one drawback with this profound system of checks and balances—no one knew what the hell they were doing. As a No. 2, Mick's duties consisted of taking training every morning, agreeing with the boss and screaming at underperforming players during half-time that they were "not fucking fit to wear the fucking shirt".

He was also a massive fan of Prozone. Mick could not get enough of Prozone's pointless stats and figures. There was even a room at Chadwell Heath devoted to Prozone. It was full of charts, graphs and computers, and there were half-baked, self-help philosophies plastered up all around the room. If Chris farted three times during the 90 minutes, Mick would always be on hand with his Prozone stats to point out where, when and how he had broke wind.

Brooking, the master that he was, said it best about Prozone: Who cares about a workmanlike plodder who successfully executed 10 passes backwards to his defender? Where is the artistry in that? By his own admission, Brooking's Prozone statistics as a player would have made for grim reading. His bold vision might have led to only two passes out of 10 being successfully pulled off, but if they had led to two goals then they were priceless compared to a dozen back passes to the goalkeeper. Brooking was a genius; Chris and everyone else at the club knew that. That was why he wisely avoided a full-time coaching position. Unlike Mick "Prozone" Peters.

"Morning, Mick," Chris said brightly. "Is the boss about?"

"No. Take one of these bibs."

Mick never acknowledged Chris.

"Is he coming in for training? I was hoping to have a word with him."

"I take the training."

"Yeah, I know that Mick, but I just wanted to have a chat with him."

"You can have a chat with me."

Mick continued to hand the bibs out. He refused to make eye contact with Chris.

"Well I'd rather talk to the boss."

"The boss isn't here."

"Yeah, I know that, Mick. But if he was he might at least put the bibs down and fucking look at me."

Chris heard his heart pounding. The other players stopped warming up and stared at Chris and Mick. In the distance, a train pulled out of Chadwell Heath station. Normally, the players never heard the trains. Mick managed a half smirk. Chris considered punching him. The image delighted him, but he could never face his father again. Mick moved half a step towards Chris and gazed at him.

"All right, Chrissy boy," he said softly. "I'm looking at you now. What do you want to say?"

Chris shifted his feet uneasily. He never planned to do this here, not in front of his mates and certainly not in front of the first team. Six years in the stiffs had stripped away his dignity so this was not about pride. Chris had swallowed that about 18 months ago. This was about being pragmatic. After six years of languishing in the youth team and the reserves, Chris was minutes away from ending his West Ham career.

"Why haven't I played for the first team yet?" Chris blurted out.

Mick turned away and smiled.

"Don't laugh at me," Chris continued. "Who are you to laugh at me? What the fuck did you ever do in your career?"

"You've got no idea, son, all right. I've worked with more players at more clubs than you ever will."

"Yeah, 'cos you got sacked from them all."

Chris pouted like a petulant child. His team-mates glanced nervously at Mick.

"Yeah, that's right," Mick said firmly. "You're right there, son. I was given the boot at a few clubs. I can't argue with that. But I've had a career. You've had nothing."

"That's because you and the boss won't give me a chance."

"And do you know why?"

"Of course I do. Because you lot didn't sign me; Harry Redknapp did. And you're still scared of Harry's shadow. And those bloody ridiculous stats of yours tell you that my fucking goals-to-chances ratio—or whatever they're called—are not as good as the other players."

"It's not that."

"No? So what the fuck is it then?"

"You just don't have it, all right," Mick shouted. "You can shoot, turn, run and hold the ball up, but you just don't have 'it' to make it at this level."

Chris' stomach muscles tightened.

"What's 'it' then?"

"It! It! Who knows what 'it' is? You can't bottle it and you can't teach it; you can only buy it on the transfer market. You and Tevez can both bang in hat-tricks in training, but when it matters, he's got 'it' and you don't."

Chris peered over at Tevez who blushed and turned away. Chris paused, scrambling to find some words.

"I was the top-rated junior when I joined this club," he croaked.

"And so was Lee Sharpe at Man United. He was like you— confident, quick, and had an eye for goal. Some saw him as a better prospect than Giggs. Look at Giggs now. And where's Lee Sharpe today?"

"Lee Sharpe won Premier League trophies."

"Yeah, he did, you're right. But if you compare the two, he was never quite as good as …"

"Ryan Giggs, right?" Chris snapped. "Just as I'll never be a fucking Tevez."

"Look, there's no need to let this thing spiral. The boss wouldn't like that. Things get said on the training ground every day, especially this training ground. We can still sit down with the boss later and …"

"Bollocks. Tell him to expect a call from my dad today."

CHRIS liked having his father as his agent. The working relationship never impinged upon his personal life and there was no better counsel than his dad. Besides, the job meant Tony had a more direct involvement with the professional game, if only on the periphery, and allowed him to finally reduce his hours at Ford. Not that Tony had much say in the matter. The Dagenham plant had been downsized so drastically in recent years, it was practically irrelevant. Dagenham was once a proud Ford town, but now it was a housing estate with an industrial ghetto beside the Thames.

Tony always impressed upon Chris how the parasitic agents were sucking the lifeblood from his beloved game and Chris only managed to pacify him by insisting he took on the role in a part-time capacity. Besides, it wasn't much work. Chris was struggling to make a name for himself in West Ham's reserves so the name Tony Osborne was not keeping IMG executives awake at night. There was the obligatory boot deal, an apparel sponsor, a column in the *Dagenham Post* that paid less than a night shift at Ford, a couple of straightforward playing contracts and an ill-advised swimwear shoot for the local Tesco. The job involved nothing more than the occasional phone call and was so scandalously easy that it underscored Tony's belief about the precarious state of the modern game. But he kept those thoughts to himself. He cherished the memories of standing in the manager's office at Chadwell Heath, watching his son sign a contract he had helped to negotiate. Just like those endless kickabouts at Parsloes Park, he still enjoyed working with his son.

But not today. Tony wished he was back down the docks assembling a Ford Fiesta. He dialled his son's number. He had no idea how this phone call would pan out. Tony had tried to stay positive when Chris came round and asked him to find him another club, but he was disappointed. Yes, the thought of his son never running out in the claret and blue at Upton Park hurt. Tony was only human. But it was the manner in which Chris walked out that disappointed. That wasn't like Chris. Tony had felt responsible and guilty. Not for foisting his unrealised West Ham ambitions upon his son because he had been careful not to do that. But he hadn't seen it coming. Chris' failed attempt to earn a first-team appearance had obviously driven him to the brink, and Tony had missed it. He was determined now to get his son's career back on track.

"Hello, Chris. It's me. You all right?"

Tony hoped he sounded breezy.

"Yeah, I'm fine, Dad. Just been out for a few beers with Ross."

That wasn't the response Tony had hoped for, but this was not the time for reprimands.

"Ah, yeah, good, good. Did you, er, have a word with Mick?"

Chris sighed.

"Yes, Dad."

"And, er, did you apologise?"

"Yes, Dad."

"All right, mate. I'll leave it at that."

Tony had rehearsed his next couple of lines and paused to make sure they did not come across as flippant.

"How do you fancy a trip to Australia?"

"What?"

"Australia. You know, kangaroos, koalas, Kylie Minogue."

"Are you serious?"

"Yep, I got you a trial with Melbourne Victory. They are one of their top sides over there in the A-League."

"Sounds like a Mickey Mouse league to me."

"Nah, it's not. It's on the up. Remember Dwight Yorke went over there."

"Yeah, yeah, that's right. I do remember that. Some time after he shagged that Jordan, right? Yeah, that sounds familiar."

Chris perked up a little.

"And Terry Butcher was a manager over there, too."

"How did he get on?"

"He was sacked."

"Oh, nice one. Sounds like a great place."

"No, come on, just think of it as a stepping stone. You're still only 21. You bang in a few goals over there and I'll have you back in London next season."

"Really?"

"Yeah, look I probably shouldn't tell you this. Queens Park Rangers are quite keen, but they insist you get some first-team games under your belt first."

"Bloody hell, that sounds all right."

"Exactly. So get yourself over to Melbourne. Get a suntan, score some bloody goals and get back over here where you belong."

"Yeah, yeah, all right then."

Chris paused.

"Do many Aussies even play football over there?"

 **five**

CHRIS saw the Docklands Stadium through the carriage window. He stood up and made his way to the door as the train pulled in to Southern Cross Station. That was the station's name, but every bloody Australian in Melbourne referred to it as Spencer Street Station, which caused Chris no end of confusion. They also called the Docklands Stadium the Telstra Dome, which confused him all the more. The journey had taken just over an hour. Thanks, Dad, Chris thought, as he made his way towards the train door.

Chris had asked for the Aussie cliché, or at least the British perception of the Aussie cliché. He wanted to rent a house near the sea with a barbeque. It had to be in a court, or a banjo as it was known in Dagenham, just like Ramsay Street in *Neighbours*, and preferably in a quaint little town where the bells still rang above the shop doors. As a child, Chris had grown up watching *The Sullivans*, *Neighbours* and *Home and Away* and he thought he could live in all three. The best Tony could come up with was Geelong. The seaside town was the second biggest in Victoria after Melbourne, but still had a relatively compact population and there was a barbeque in the yard of the house in the court. Chris needed to be close to Melbourne. On the map of Australia, Geelong and Melbourne practically touched each other. On a train, they were a bloody hour apart.

But Docklands Stadium looked magnificent. Chris was told that the venue had been designed primarily for football—the other football, that Aussie Rules football. Chris had watched some on the Qantas flight coming over and saw highlights from a game at Docklands Stadium. A club called Collingwood, which was nicknamed the Magpies and looked suspiciously like Newcastle United, was playing Geelong, where Chris was going to live. The game was certainly fast, but ludicrous. The teams appeared to score over a dozen goals each because they were kicking between empty posts. There were no goalkeepers. There were no bloody goalkeepers. And the best part was, the ball spent most of the time in the players' hands. This was the national football code of Australia and yet it was played with a rugby ball, which was rarely kicked, and when it was, it was into an empty goal. The English Premier League must be shitting itself, Chris thought. No wonder Harry Kewell and Mark Viduka escaped as soon as possible.

Chris stood on the platform at Southern Cross. The cavernous building had a funky, wave-shaped roof, but the station still reminded Chris of all the famous stations around central London, albeit with fewer people and less pigeon shit. Nevertheless, Melbourne had the scruffy, slightly decaying feel of a city. It smelled like London. Chris liked that.

A MASSIVE security guy in a suit and wielding a walkie-talkie like a Neanderthal's club met Chris at the top of the steps in front of Docklands Stadium's main entrance.

"Are you Chris Osborne?" he asked.

"Yeah, I've got a football trial with Melbourne Victory today," Chris replied. His nervousness surprised him, catching him off guard.

"No, you haven't. You've got a soccer trial," the security guard said smugly. "If you had a footy trial, mate, there'd be a lot more people waiting for you than just me."

He led Chris through a tunnel towards the pitch.

"Is that right?"

"Ah yeah. This is a footy town, mate. Soccer will never take over from footy in Victoria."

"Really?"

"Yeah … nah, soccer's all right when the Socceroos are in the World Cup. That was massive. But that's about it. Was straight back to footy as soon as they lost to Italy."

"What about Tim Cahill and Lucas Neill and all the others?"

"Nah, not interested. Paid far too much to roll around on the bloody ground. Viduka's all right. He's a good bloke. He's a Melbourne boy, a Collingwood boy, like me."

Chris stopped and stared at the security guard.

"So what about Melbourne Victory then? I've read that they get over 20,000 at every home game. Someone must be watching them."

"Ah, it's still wogball, mate. All the Greeks and the Italians and the 'skis', mate. You'll probably be the only one there who isn't a 'ski'."

"A what?"

"Every bloody player has got 'ski' at the end of their name. They're all Croats and Serbians and all that. They're the only ones interested in soccer. Oh, and the housewives. The bloody soccer mums love your game. They don't want their little boys playing the Australian game, a man's game, and getting hurt in marks and tackles. You'll have plenty of those housewives at your games."

"Sounds terrific."

"That's Melbourne, mate."

Chris stepped out into the Docklands Stadium and expected to see Russell Crowe wrestling CGI tigers. The arena was shaped like the Coliseum. Chris craned his head to take it all in—the retractable roof, the massive replay screens and the corporate boxes. At West Ham, he trained in the middle of a housing estate. The Docklands Stadium was right up there with Old Trafford. He knew that Melbourne Victory usually trained somewhere else, but still, the boys played their home games here. His father had told him that over 50,000 would cram in here when Melbourne faced Sydney FC. Let's have some of that, Chris thought.

Chris examined the pitch. It was oval. That was disconcerting. Cricketers played on oval pitches, not footballers. That annoying security guard was right. Melbourne may be the sporting capital, but it's a whole new world for football. Chris vowed never to call his beloved game 'soccer' for anyone. Football, *his* football, was the world game. Australia had to get its head out of its arse, not the other way round.

"So you must be Chris Osborne then, boyo."

The accent was Welsh. A hand tapped Chris on the shoulder, which annoyed him. It always felt condescending. He glanced over his shoulder and saw a trim, grey-haired man with ruddy cheeks wearing a Melbourne Victory tracksuit that was clearly one size too small. He worked hard at maintaining such a physique in his late 40s and wanted other people to be aware of it. He offered his hand to Chris.

"My name's Eddie McDonald," he said. "Now I know that sounds Scottish, but it's actually Welsh. I also know that your dad, who I'm told is a lovely fella, organised the trial with the previous manager, but things change very quickly in the A-League. I'm sure you'll see that for yourself … if you impress me at the trial."

Eddie McDonald talked fast and never stopped moving. It was a sign of over-caution, rather than over-confidence. Eddie did not allow the chance for others to contradict or correct him.

"Yeah, of course, Mr McDonald," Chris replied. "I just want to …"

"There's no need to call me Mr McDonald," the Victory manager interjected, with another condescending hand on the shoulder. "Just plain 'gaffer' will do. Everyone else here calls me the gaffer and it just seems to have stuck, you know."

Eddie had an inferiority complex. Chris realised that now and understood. He had read that Melbourne Victory were the most successful football club in Australia. The A-League only kicked off in 2005, and in a distant country where the only football codes that mattered were Aussie Rules and rugby league, the league was given little chance of succeeding.

Then something unexpected happened, something that caught the nation off guard and terrified the Aussie Rules establishment. The Socceroos qualified for the 2006 World Cup finals. If there were two things the average sports-mad Australian lived for, they were a half-decent national side on the world stage and an underdog who could serve as an antidote to their tall poppy syndrome. The Socceroos gave them both. In Melbourne, Perth and Sydney, Australians gathered in their city centres in the chilly early hours of the morning to watch the Socceroos battle the world's best. They hadn't seen anything like it since The Ashes.

Melbourne Victory were the first A-League side to fully cash in. Being the only franchise in Australia's sporting capital certainly helped, as did the healthy population of European immigrants in the multicultural city. But Melbourne Victory were actually a decent, attacking side who scored plenty of goals to pacify those supporters raised on the scoring system of Aussie Rules.

Eddie McDonald couldn't lose, which was a unique situation because he had managed to lose with considerable aplomb as a journeyman coach travelling around the lower leagues of the world. Chris had never heard of him. Nor half of the clubs he had guided to mid-table obscurity. Suddenly, after decades in the sporting wilderness, Eddie found himself leading the most popular, and best, team in the fastest-growing football league in the world. No wonder he had some insecurity issues. This did not bode well for Chris. Insecure managers rarely indulged in creative, unpredictable mavericks. Such players lacked consistency and uniformity in a results-driven business. Most of all, the fast dribbling showmen reminded these journeymen of the kind of player they never were. How do you manage a player whom you both know can do things with a ball you could only dream of?

"OK then, gaffer," said Chris with as much chirpiness he could muster. "What do you want me to do?"

"Well, there's no point seeing what you can do with a ball at this stage, if you're not fit enough to get to it. I'll introduce you to the lads and then we'll get you all running."

Eddie outpaced most of his players. He was fitter than many of them and took great pride in goading them as they puffed their way around the edge of the enormous oval pitch at Docklands Stadium.

"Come on, Chris, you're not at West Ham now, son," Eddie barked. "This is a real bloke's world here. We're not interested in reputations here. We've got no time for Ferraris or Mercedes Benzes here."

That's because you can't bloody afford them, Chris thought.

"You're gonna have to build up your muscles, Chris," Eddie shouted. "Look at your team-mates, Chris. Look at those biceps. Our sportsmen look like real sportsmen here, son. Real blokes."

Eddie had been in Australia too long. He sounded like the security guard.

"How are you feeling, Chris? You look knackered, son," Eddie said, slowing down to run alongside Chris. "The West Ham superstar looks fucked, doesn't he lads? It must be all that commuting from Geelong."

The other players giggled. Eddie looked around the playing

group and smirked at Chris.

"If you're a West Ham superstar, Chris, you might not be able to stay in Geelong very long. You'll be mobbed everyday down there in sleepy hollow, son."

The players laughed loudly. Chris giggled, too, and thought he should make an effort and join in with the banter.

"So is Geelong kind of like Wales then?" he said. "It's at the arse-end of England and everyone's a sheep shagger. They produce a lot of wool in Geelong, too. Maybe that's how they do it."

Chris laughed. Eddie stopped running. The rest of the training camp followed suit. Clearly, they did not need to be told. With his hands turned backwards and clutching his hips, Eddie stood in front of Chris.

"Is that how you spoke to Mick Peters at West Ham?"

Chris stammered for an answer. The mention of Mick Peters' name horrified him.

"Ah, you didn't know that me and Mickey Peters knew each other then? You didn't know that me and Mickey Peters had three very productive seasons together at Wrexham when we were a couple of kids not much older than you. You didn't know that I went to Mickey Peters' wedding then?"

"Er, no."

"And even if I didn't know Mickey, did you really think that I wouldn't check up on you first? Some kid from West Ham quits the club just when he was about to make his first-team debut. Mickey Peters told me you were just weeks away from your debut."

The lying bastard, Chris thought. Mick Peters really wanted Chris Osborne out of the club.

"So I have to ask myself, why would a boy who's about to play in the English Premier League want to come to Australia instead? Could it be because he has something to offer the A-League? Or could it be because he wants some experience so he can fuck off back to England as soon as a better offer comes in?"

The Welshman didn't appear to have much time for Englishmen, or the English Premier League for that matter. Chris sighed.

"I just want to play football, mate."

"I'm not your mate. Not yet. I'm the gaffer."

"But you're not my gaffer, though, are ya, mate? You're just a little Welsh bloke with a chip on his shoulder who seems to have a problem with the fact that my last club wasn't Mickey Mouse United."

Eddie smiled and started running again.

"Come on, lads," he said. "Three more laps to go."

Chris watched the other players go by. None of them bothered to look at him.

CHRIS saw the funny side. He was only 21 years old and was working his way through more clubs than Tiger Woods. He sat by the phone in his bare Geelong house and found himself recalling the day his father had given him an old computer. It was called a Sinclair Spectrum 128K, which meant nothing to Chris. Everyone else had Nintendos and Playstations, and he had been lumbered with a computer the size of a suitcase.

"What am I supposed to do with this, Dad?" he had asked incredulously.

"Just watch."

Tony played a cassette and the TV exploded with a series of hisses and crackles as wavy lines ran up and down the screen. After several minutes, two words finally appeared. *Football Manager*.

"Forget all the modern computer games. This is the only one you'll ever need to play," Tony said.

"Why?"

"Because it's fair. If you manage the team right, you really will progress. There are no hidden computer bugs or anything like that. It's not like these stupid new ones where if you're a computer geek, you can win the title. You have to understand football tactics in this game and you have to play fair."

"Yeah, but the graphics are crap, Dad."

"Forget the graphics. This is the closest football manager game to reality. You'll get rewarded for loyalty. If you stay at the same club, like say, West Ham, you'll improve as a player because you are a settled player. If you jump from club to club, you'll get more money, but your player rating will not improve automatically. Just like in real life. The best footballers—Trevor Brooking, Bobby Charlton or Ryan Giggs—are the loyal footballers. Honest footballers. Which is the most settled club in the world? Manchester United. They're untouchable. That's what it's all about. Honesty and stability."

Chris wondered what his player rating would be now. Two clubs in one year and not a first-team appearance for either of them, Chris' market value on his old football manager game would be negligible. Honesty and stability. What a load of bollocks, he thought. Wonderful virtues for a professional footballer in a computer game, but where had they gotten Chris? Being an honest pro had made Ryan Giggs the most decorated footballer in Premier League history, but it had made Chris club-less, country-less and penniless. Honesty and stability—since when did one ever lead to the other in football? His father was an idealist, but he had never played the game at the highest level. Chris worshipped his dad, but he was out of touch with the modern game. He still revered the values of Brooking and Charlton, but the game had moved on to Beckham and Ronaldo. His dad waffled on about the core virtues of a shitty computer game, when kids a third of his age played football in their living rooms with Nintendo Wiis.

Tony Osborne still watched his football on VHS tapes.

During their kickabouts at Parsloes Park, Chris' father had always said, "Do you want to be a footballer who is remembered for his football or a footballer who is remembered for all the clubs he played for, all the money he pissed up the wall and all the women he shagged?"

Chris just wanted to be a footballer. But he wasn't sure if his nostalgic dad was capable of getting his head out of the 1970s to make it happen.

The phone rang at 7 p.m., as always—8 a.m. in London, 7 p.m. in Geelong—regular as clockwork. Chris took a deep breath and picked it up. Here come the daily rejections.

"Hello, Dad. How are you?"

"Good, good. Listen, don't worry about Melbourne, because I think I've got something in the pipeline," Tony replied.

This was unexpected. After three weeks spent climbing the walls of a house he had foolishly paid two months' rent for, Chris expected to leave Australia in a straitjacket.

"Really, that's great," said Chris. "We've been knocked back by so many clubs I didn't think there were that many left."

"No, no, boy. We could be on to something."

"OK, good. What is it?"

"Right, well, you know I went for a few of the leagues nearer to you while you were out there? Well, finally I got a bite."

"Not the J-League is it, Dad? I'd love to play in the J-League. That's where Lineker ended up going. And Zico."

"Er, no, they weren't too keen on you. I thought I'd focus on Southeast Asia."

"Oh, right, yeah. We talked about that before. Thailand's all right. And Peter Withe was doing something out there, wasn't he?"

"Yeah, he was with their national team, but their economy is a mess at the moment after all this stuff with that Thaksin. No, I was thinking more of Malaysia actually."

Chris rolled his eyes.

"Malaysia, Dad? Really? It's all corrupt over there, isn't it? That Grobbelaar and Fashanu corruption thing. That was from Malaysia, wasn't it?"

"Yeah, it was, but that doesn't matter because …"

"And the floodlight thing. That had something to do with Malaysia too, didn't it? Charlton … or was it West Ham? They did something to their floodlights to fix the result."

"Yes, but it doesn't matter now, because they were not so keen anyway. They've cut right back on their foreign players now. I thought Malaysia would be a winner because Tony Cottee went out there and …"

"He wasn't there for five minutes, was he? He went back to England."

"He still won silverware in Malaysia. And David Rocastle, God bless him, was a massive success over there at a club called Sabah. They loved him there, paid him well and still speak very highly of him. So I gave them a ring and they asked for a video, but can't make any promises."

Chris resisted a sudden urge to smash the phone through the coffee table.

"So that's it then? I've got to wait for them to watch the video before they make a decision. That could take months, Dad. I've been rejected by England, most of Europe, Australia, and now you're telling me that Japan, Thailand and Malaysia don't want to know either. We've already scraped the bottom of the barrel. There can't be any other league left in the world."

"There is. I've found one. That's why I've got you something else in the meantime. I was talking to some of the guys at QPR about your predicament and they said you reminded them of

Michael Currie."

"Who's Michael Currie?"

"He was a young QPR lad in the late 90s, about your age, a YTS boy and they wanted to get him some first-team experience. They showed me some pictures. He was even built like you. Tall and slim with blond hair, and he had a bit of pace, too."

"That's a great story, Dad. I've got to go back to England and sign on in a fortnight."

"Shut up, you cheeky bastard and listen. They sent him to a fairly new league and the fans loved him over there, turned him into a bit of a celebrity apparently. The money wasn't great, but the place was fabulous."

"What league?"

"The S-League."

"The S-League, Dad, really? That's fantastic."

"Oh, you've heard of it then?"

"No. Where is it?"

"Singapore."

Chris did not know whether to laugh or cry.

"Singapore? Are you having a laugh, Dad?" he replied. "Don't you remember what happened to Gazza when he went over there? He cracked up and flew back. Why the hell would I want to go and play in China?"

 **six**

CHRIS stared out of the window. The landscaped gardens outside were manicured, not an orchid or blade of grass out of place. Very Singapore. Early morning rain had given the gardens that humid, misty sheen that Chris loved. It always reminded him of how far he was from Dagenham. He needed a reminder this morning. Last night, he had slept fitfully and his knees were only partially to blame. His old nightmare recurred. Whenever his career hit the crossroads, the dream popped up again.

In the dream, he was not a Raffles Rangers striker. He was a long forgotten West Ham reject languishing in the reserves. In a training session that never ended, Chris was running. There was no football; Chris never kicked a ball once. It was just running—endless, monotonous, running. Mick Peters and Eddie McDonald stood together in their wedding suits, holding stopwatches and a clipboard. They never said stop. The most infuriating aspect of the nightmare was that Chris' reality was his dream. As he ran laps of the damp, foggy Chadwell Heath pitch, Chris fantasised about playing for Raffles Rangers and being the S-League's top goal-scorer. Then he realised that his Singapore career was all just a dream and he had been stuck in the West Ham reserves all along. That was when Chris always woke up in a cold sweat.

Last night's dream was different though. Chris continued

to run laps through the murky, pea soup-like fog, but he had a training partner this time.

Tiger ran beside him.

"ARE you feeling OK to see some visitors today?"

It was Rosito. God bless Rosito. Her daily check-ups were the highlights of Chris' day. They were the only highlights. She had a certain quality that captivated Chris. After several days in hospital, Chris had finally worked out what it was—she wasn't on the hustle.

She was Asian. She was beautiful. She was slender and petite and had an overall exoticness that white men simply did not encounter in the checkout queue at Tesco. Most of the women Chris had been introduced to in Singapore had shared similar qualities. The difference with Rosito was she didn't want anything from Chris. She wasn't interested in his particular profession (unusual, but not uncommon), she had no interest in his bank balance or his monthly salary (simply unheard of) and, most of all, she had no interest in his skin colour. If Yati had been blessed with a similar quality, he might not be lying here.

"Yeah, why not, Rosito," Chris said, sitting up and flattening his bed sheets. "Who are our contestants today, Rosito? What are their names and where are they from?"

"They said they were both journalists."

Chris stopped fiddling with the bed sheets.

"Ah, that might be a problem. I know you weren't here when I came in, Rosito, but I asked the nurses not to allow any journalists in to see me. It's only because I don't want them to photograph me looking like this. I hope you understand."

Rosito nodded. Chris had become a convincing liar recently.

"It's no problem," Rosito said. "I'll tell them you are sleeping."

"That's why I love ya, Rosito. Here, you know what they call 50 journalists at the bottom of the ocean, don't ya?"

"What?"

"A start."

"A start of what?"

"A start. You know, a good start. A good beginning. Something to build on, like a, you know ... what were the journalists' names anyway?"

"The guy said his name was Billy and the lady was called Yati."

Chris leaned back on his pillow and stared at Rosito.

"I suppose I can see those two for a few minutes," he mumbled.

"What did you say, Chris?"

Chris cleared his throat.

"I think I had better see them, Rosito. It's all right."

"Only if you are sure. If they make you uncomfortable, just let me know."

Chris smiled. It's a bit bloody late for that, he thought.

BILLY Addis and Yati sat beside Chris' bed. No one spoke. Chris gazed at both of them as they shuffled uneasily in their chairs. Yati turned away. Billy smiled awkwardly and glanced out of the window. Chris smirked at him. He might as well savour their discomfort. He was annoyed to see Billy looking so well. Skinny and tanned, Billy had obviously been dragged up and down the East Coast Park jogging paths. Yati would have him rollerblading next with all the other expat twats. Wearing her usual *sarong* and white tank top, Yati still turned heads. Chris watched her work the crowd when she strolled effortlessly into the ward. Her hospital audience consisted of an old Chinese uncle with kidney stones and a Malay kid who'd fallen off his scooter, but she couldn't help herself. She was gorgeous. She always was and she always knew how to use it to manipulate others; that was usually the problem.

Yati forced a smile.

"You're looking well," she said.

"No, I'm not," Chris retorted.

Chris and Yati glared at each other. Billy glanced at both of them and waited for a reaction.

"This is ridiculous," Billy said finally. "We're all in this together. We're all fucked so there's no need to be at each other's throats now, is there?"

Chris rubbed the bandages on his knees.

"Some of us have been a bit more fucked than others though, haven't they?"

"No one saw that coming."

"Yes, you did. You had an idea right from the start. You had been working on it. You knew what was going on."

Billy nodded towards Chris' bandaged knees.

"But I never knew anything like this was going to happen, Chris."

He meant it, too. There had been sources—his growing number of 'deep throats' and a few tip-offs over late-night *roti prata* in Geylang and pork rib soup in Balestier Road—but he had never expected reprisals like this. Not in Singapore. No one did.

"Well, it's not finished yet, is it?" Chris snapped. "That bastard is still out there, isn't he? Isn't he, Yati?"

Chris stared at Yati. She peered down at her sandals.

"I don't know. I really don't know."

"Fuck off."

Chris spat the words out, making no attempt to hide his anger. He loathed this woman. Billy watched them both nervously.

"I really am sorry, Chris," Yati muttered.

"It's a bit fucking late for that."

"Look, Chris, there's really no need for that," Billy interjected. "We're all up to our necks in this, too, you know. Even Spearman's not answering his phone at the moment. All of us are in the shit."

Chris laughed.

"Ah, poor you. What's gonna happen? No S-League coverage for a few weeks? No photo in the paper for a couple of days? Are you gonna be sent to Kallang to cover netball for the next few Saturdays? What a tough life. I'd hate to be in your shoes."

"Look, Chris …"

"Just look at me, will ya? Look at my legs. I'm fucking crippled. You can still write, but look at my legs. I'm fucking finished."

"I thought you were going to be OK. You should make a full recovery and be able to play again," Yati said quickly.

"What are you, Florence Nightingale now? I thought you were just an SPG, Yati. Can you be both? Is it possible to be Singapore's number one Sarong Party Girl and Florence Nightingale? Because I didn't think it was."

Yati bowed her head and wiped her eyes.

"You always were a good actress," Chris muttered.

"All right, Chris, that's enough now, all right," Billy said, his temper rising for the first time. "I know what happened to you was right out of order, but don't take the piss. We've got our own problems, too."

"Really?"

"Yes, fucking really. I've been called up for a meeting at the end of the week, we both have. Once all the facts have been put together."

Billy sarcastically punctuated the word "facts" in the air with his fingers.

"A meeting with who?"

"Who do you think? The boss. So don't think you're gonna be the only one on the next plane back to England, and I won't have a sugar daddy like Mr Teck to bail me out either."

Billy clenched his fists and stared out of the window. He stared at the monsoonal rain lashing against the window. Bloody weather, he thought. Yati gently reached for one of his hands and held on tightly. Chris noticed that she really was crying.

"Will you go with him or will you stay at *The Newspaper*?" Chris asked her.

Yati took a piece of tissue paper from a box on Chris' bedside table and wiped her eyes. Chris saw that she was shaking.

"I don't think I'll have much of a choice," she whimpered. "He's got that video somewhere, hasn't he?"

Chris slumped back on his pillows and watched the raindrops dance around the window pane. He could not speak.

"You see, I know we didn't get our legs smashed and we're really sorry about that," Billy said slowly. "But we're all finished now."

 **seven**

BILLY Addis swivelled slightly on a chair in his new sports editor's office and examined the walls. There was the obligatory photograph of the sports editor smiling with the family he never saw. Every editor that Billy had ever worked for had a cuddly snap of his family somewhere in his office. Maybe it alleviated the guilt. Maybe it was a transparent attempt to convince the editor's underlings that he really wasn't a masochistic bully addicted to newsroom politics, but the reporters never fell for it. Billy had only ever worked with two types of sports editors—those who were feeding a genuine, lifelong passion for sports and those who were climbing the next rung on the newspaper's ladder. Billy wondered who he had been lumbered with this time.

Beside the staged family photograph was a Polaroid shot of the sports editor standing next to Muhammad Ali. The great man was clearly way past his Rumble in the Jungle phase but not yet in the vice-like grip of Parkinson's, so Billy figured the photo was taken in the early 1980s. That boded well. His new sports editor loved the real legends and had been in the game for at least 25 years. Either that or he was a sports faker posing with the most recognisable pop culture icon of the 20th century. Billy would know once his editor bothered to put in an appearance.

Billy checked the time on the Manchester United clock on

the desk. His new boss was now 15 minutes late. That was not a good sign and neither was the Manchester United clock. This guy was increasingly looking like a dedicated follower of established franchises. Beside the clock, Billy noticed one of those gold-plated, desk plaques that read "Peter Chan, sports editor". Oh god, he needed to remind others (and possibly himself) of his lofty position. The bad signs were piling up.

"Hello, sorry I'm a bit late."

Peter Chan breezed into the room. His appearance surprised Billy. He looked like a slimmer, taller Jackie Chan. Dressed in dark, well-pressed trousers and the white Ralph Lauren shirt that seemed to be de rigueur in Singapore, Peter had that thick black hair that Chinese men were blessed with (and Billy rather envied), but it was parted and styled in a big, bouffant style popular with Hong Kong actors. Perhaps Peter Chan fancied himself as one of the Heavenly Kings of Cantopop. There was certainly a touch of Andy Lau about the hairstyle. On a white man's head, it would look ridiculous and far too reminiscent of *The Sweeney* and *Starsky and Hutch*. But Chinese men made it look retro and cool.

"Oh, that's all right. I was just admiring your photograph with the great man," Billy said.

Peter smiled at the photograph. Every visitor to his office commented on that photograph.

"Ah, yes, me and Cassius. I've met a few greats in my time, but there was only one Cassius Clay."

Billy already had Peter Chan down. He was a sports faker. No one called Muhammad Ali 'Cassius Clay' anymore.

Sports fakers were the worst kind of sports editors—appalling news sense, a taste for the trashy and too tabloid in their thinking. Billy knew it was only a matter of time before he was being assigned to write features on David Beckham's best hairstyle.

"Anyway, as much as I'd love to talk about The Greatest, I've got to go for another meeting soon, so we'd better get down to it," Peter said.

"Absolutely."

"Right, Billy, I know you've got plenty of experience in England, but you've never really worked in Singapore before so it may be a bit of a culture shock. But I'm a big believer in throwing my reporters in at the deep end."

"Great, that's how I like it."

"You'll be mostly covering the S-League. Now don't get excited because it's no English Premier League and most people think it's *kelong* anyway."

"*Kelong*?"

"Fixed. You'll hear that a lot in Singapore. Ask around about it. I've got two assignments for you. The first is *kelong*. The second probably will be in about six months or so."

"They're about corruption?"

Peter laughed and adjusted his sports editor's plaque on the desk.

"Don't be ridiculous. This is Singapore football. Nothing is corrupt in Singapore," he said.

"Oh, right," Billy replied. He was thoroughly confused now.

"You see, Singapore is all about its image," Peter said as he sat back and forgot about his upcoming meeting, savouring another opportunity to pontificate to another rookie reporter.

"Singapore is polished, clean and, where possible, green. Did you read your Singapore Tourism Board brochure like a good foreign talent when we hired you?"

"Er, yeah. I flicked through it, sure."

"It was all Stamford Raffles, Singapore Slings, Long Bars and Chinatown, right?"

"Pretty much, I suppose, yeah."

"Of course, that's the image Singapore presents to the world.

It won't tell you about the hookers or the transvestites around Geylang and Desker Road, but they're there. It won't tell you about the Bangladeshi illegal immigrants, but they're there. It won't tell you about the Africans on football visas in Bencoolen Street who've never kicked a ball in their lives, but they're there. It won't tell you about all the maid abuse that goes on in the housing heartlands, but it's there. And it won't tell you about the national gambling obsession, but everyone on the sports desk has to work alongside it and, to a certain extent, nurture it, just like you will have to."

Peter paused for dramatic effect before continuing.

"Tell me, why did you apply for this job?"

"I love sports, particularly football. But I love all sports."

"So do I. And so does every one of the guys out there on the sports desk, but the average football reader doesn't give a shit."

"Really?"

"He cares about winning or losing, whichever pays out more. That's sports in Singapore. That's life in Singapore. Betting funds the Singapore Pools. Singapore Pools funds many of the major sports events in Singapore, including the S-League. Have you seen the Theatres on the Bay at the Esplanade yet?"

"Yeah, of course."

"Singapore Pools helped to build them. Sports gamblers helped to pay for them. It's everywhere and you can't escape it."

"Sounds great."

"I'm only telling you because I know you've probably come over here with your idealised *ang moh* views about The Beautiful Game. Well, that does apply for some Singaporeans. I've got a dozen of them working on the sports desk. But for the rest of them, if they can't bet on a game, then it's no game at all."

"Blimey."

Billy stared through the glass partition of Peter's desk at the other sports reporters, copy editors and sub-editors working on the day's early pages. He spotted a page layout on one of the computer screens. The headline mentioned Manchester United. Singapore headlines usually referenced Manchester United. Ironically, Billy felt a long way from East London.

Peter watched Billy and smirked. He savoured the moment as he always did. Destroying the ideals and principles of wide-eyed, naïve journalists, particularly *ang moh* journalists, always gave him a cheap thrill. Peter knew that the big bosses had thrown him out to pasture on the least important desk in the newspaper, so he'd take his kicks where he could get them.

Time to go in for the kill.

"And that's only the legal side of the game," Peter continued. "At least, there's nothing illegal about sticking the mortgage down on this week's Man U game at any Singapore Pools outlet. Singapore Pools took $500 million in one month during the 2002 World Cup and that's nothing. In betting terms, that barely protects the rice bowl. Outside bookies took billions. They might account for 60, 70, 80 per cent of all football gambling—no one really knows for sure. It's not like these guys file tax returns. Most importantly, these buggers will always give you credit. They want to give you credit, especially now. They want to make as much money as they can before the big cash cows really arrive."

"What are they?"

"The two casinos. You think *Ah Longs* are doing well now, wait until those casinos open."

"*Ah Longs?*"

"Loan sharks. *Ah Longs* are loan sharks. Listen, Billy, you've really got to pick up the local terminology, the basics of Singlish and some Malay if you're going to mix with the local footballers here. They're not all Cambridge graduates."

"OK, yeah, sure."

"Which brings me to my last point. This isn't the EPL. Footballers aren't paid much here. Some of the S-League kids are paid a fair bit less than you. So there is a risk of being tapped all the time. Go back and check some of the daft results of the past couple of seasons. Look for high-scoring games. Bookies love high-scoring games because they pay more and they're easier to fix. Only need to take care of the goalkeepers. So always be mindful of this when you cover the games. Yes, I expect you to be professional at all times. But you are going to see some soft goals, terrible goalkeeping and some really strange penalties. God, the S-League must have the highest penalty rate in the world. Watch the replays and poke your nose around. That's the kind of journo I want here, OK?"

"Yeah, sure. Sounds intriguing."

"OK, now bearing all that in mind, I've lined up two interviews for you today. After next week, you should arrange all your own interviews and build up your own contacts and sources. You've got an advantage actually, because *ang moh* footballers talk far more openly than local footballers. Singaporean footballers are just not conditioned to speak freely. And white footballers will always prefer to talk to another white man."

"Yeah, sure."

"Right, you're going to Stamford Stadium, home of the reigning S-League champions, to speak to two Raffles Rangers players. The first one is Danny Spearman. You might have seen him on TV last night. He's setting up some soccer clinics, but we're not interested in that. Give it one paragraph at the end of your story. He was called up to speak to the CPIB last week and I want to know why. I know you don't know what CPIB is, so read all our previous stories about him to find out."

"OK, will do. And who's the other player?"

"Oh, some kid on trial. He's an *ang moh* from London like

you. Something Osborne. Find out why he's here, what his plans are, whether he likes local spicy food, all the usual fluff that readers want. Give him a 200-word sidebar. That's all he's worth."

BILLY stepped out of the taxi, which rejoined the traffic by swerving across two lanes the moment Billy closed the door. He craned his head to take in Stamford Stadium. The setting was incongruous to say the least. Flanked and hidden on all four sides by restored shophouses selling everything from baby clothes to wall paint, the stadium suddenly rose up behind the bustling shop façades—a permanent tribute to the ugly, grey architecture of the 1970s which celebrated concrete in all its drab glory. This stadium wouldn't look out of place in Leytonstone, Billy thought. And yet it had surrounded itself with elegant, art deco Peranakan shophouses, which served no other design function than to underscore its ugliness.

Billy walked through the entrance of the stadium and noticed a couple of middle-aged Singaporeans limbering up against the wall. At least a dozen others were jogging on the athletics track around the pitch. Billy smiled. This just doesn't happen at Old Trafford or Stamford Bridge; perhaps it should. When he was a kid, Billy used to wander into Upton Park or even Highbury during the school holidays just to sit in one of the empty seats and stare at the pitch. No chance of doing that now.

The pitch appeared to be in a decent condition and the grass was reasonably lush, but the terracing was shocking. There were a handful of plastic bucket seats in the middle of one of the stands, presumably for VIPs and the media, but everything else was endless, deep rows of concrete. Billy sat on the edge of one of the concrete rows (at least it was cool) and waited for the players to turn up. The perspiration was already trickling down the back of his Ralph Lauren shirt. The humidity was relentless. Eager for any sort of distraction, Billy checked his notes again.

Peter Chan was right. He might not know his Muhammad Ali from his Cassius Clay, but he had to be right about Danny Spearman. He was either the luckiest footballer of all time or he had extremely generous, anonymous benefactors. Danny had arrived in Singapore a couple of years earlier, after decent spells in Malaysia and Australia's old National Soccer League. That was Danny's level. Several stints at various clubs in England and Scotland had failed to secure a regular first-team place, so Perth Glory must had been an easy offer to accept. According to the match reports, Danny was a midfield grafter, an old-fashioned fetch-and-carrier. He had Roy Keane's voice and temperament, but not his game. He was closer to David Batty in style, only at a lower level.

His game suited the National Soccer League, but not the more illustrious A-League, so Danny was relieved to answer Singapore's call. The S-League proved to be a perfect fit. Singapore's players were not lacking technique or touch—years of playing *chapteh* and *sepak takraw* on the housing estate hard courts took care of that—but they did sometimes lack what Danny always called "a bit of bottle". That was Danny's thing. Where others feared to go in feet first, he went in head first. Singaporeans were instructed to stay on their feet; Danny slid his away across every bone-dry pitch on the island. He had "a bit of bottle" and always made a point of picking out players who didn't on his TV show. They were often English Premier League superstars, blessed with a talent that Danny could only dream of, but they never had *his* "bottle". It made him feel better. It also took several months for his Asian audiences to work out what the hell "a bit of bottle" was.

After several non-compromising performances for Raffles Rangers, Danny got the inevitable call to appear on the Super Soccer channel. The cable channel beamed across Asia, taking advertising dollars from the various beer, car and razor companies in Vietnam, Cambodia, Thailand and Malaysia to fund the different football highlights packages and panel shows. All this from a studio tucked away in nice, secure Singapore, the safest, most affluent haven in the region. It was win-win for the mostly expat presenters and producers.

Danny's success on the show was immediate. He slagged everybody off. In interviews, he had said that no one remembered the politically-correct fence sitters working at the BBC or Sky Sports in England. They remembered Brian Clough, Malcolm Allison, Andy Gray and Alan Hansen. They were real men with real opinions, men with "a bit of bottle". Danny never recognised the obvious irony. All of those pundits' words carried greater weight in football circles. They could all actually play.

But Danny never let a mediocre playing career get in the way of a bit of bluff and bullshit. From red cards to controversial referees, offside goals, unruly crowds and leg-breaking tackles, Danny always had a relevant anecdote about his own playing career in England. No one knew for sure how many first-team appearances the midfielder actually made at the higher levels in England, but it was barely in double figures. And yet the anecdotes just kept on coming, week after week. Danny must have had the most action-packed, incident-filled dozen games in English football history. Nevertheless, his guest appearances rated through the roof and he was eventually given his own show. That was when the rumours started.

Billy heard some noise and peered over at the players' tunnel. The Raffles Rangers squad strolled towards the pitch, their boots clattering on the athletics track. None of the joggers or power walkers paid any attention. Two elderly Chinese women performing *tai chi* nodded at the players as they loosened up on the touchline. Billy stood up and took in the whole stadium. Raffles

Rangers were the reigning S-League champions and Singapore Cup holders, and their training session had an audience of one. Himself.

Billy spotted Danny. He was the last out of the tunnel and walked slowly. He had his arm around a lanky, blond kid. That's got to be Chris Osborne, Billy thought. This skinny geezer needed to get a few curries down him if he's going to make it, even in the S-League. Billy had seen several photographs of Danny back at the newsroom, but he was still shocked by his expanded waistline. If Danny had the wherewithal and the experience to carry that belly around for 90 minutes without being humiliated, then the S-League really was dire.

Danny Spearman noticed the journalist in the stand. The journalist was white. That was not a good sign. He might ask some genuine questions. Singaporean journalists were always more professional and often more accomplished writers, but they never challenged in press conferences, never queried or answered back. Danny never forgot the crappy exhibition match he played a couple of years ago at Kallang. He was part of a Singapore Selection taking on Manchester United at the National Stadium. Inevitably, the match was a joke. The United boys refused to tackle in a meaningless pre-season marketing exercise, and the Singapore Selection boys couldn't tackle. The shameful game ended 3-0, which was no disgrace, but Danny had hated every minute of it. Sir Alex Ferguson played most of his kids and the older pros changed positions for no other reason than they knew they could. When their reserve goalkeeper was allowed to play at full-back and the naïve crowd actually applauded the move, Danny lost it. He ran to the United bench and screamed, "Why don't you just tie their fucking legs together and make a real game of it?"

The United bench laughed and gestured towards their

opponents' dugout. Danny was substituted. As he warmed down on the touchline, a Chinese fan in a United shirt shouted, "Hey, can ask your team to let in two more goals? I bought five goals. Can or not?" The crowd laughed. Danny stopped caring and started thinking about soccer clinics and early retirement.

In the post-match conference, the British media ripped into the players and managers from both teams. A fat, red-faced bloke from *The Sun* insisted the match was a shirt-selling exercise and nothing more. Another hack from the *Daily Mirror* claimed United's pre-season preparations had been disrupted by wasting time against such inferior opposition. Danny had watched from the top table as the British tabloid hacks interrupted, heckled and shouted down Asian journalists from the hosting country. Most of the Singaporean journalists said nothing until the end of the press conference, when they asked to have their shirts signed.

That was why Danny preferred Singaporean journalists. Preoccupied with 'saving face', they were more reverential and rarely asked probing questions.

Danny waved at the journalist and gestured for him to come down to the pitch. The journalist was young, sweaty and wearing all the wrong clothes for the climate. Danny bit his bottom lip. This geezer hadn't adapted to the climate here yet, both literally and metaphorically. He would ask questions.

"Hello, mate. Danny Spearman," he said quickly, offering his hand. "Bloody hell, you're sweating a bit there, mate. Ralph Lauren makes lovely shirts, but you're gonna waste them wearing them anywhere here that isn't air-conditioned."

Danny rarely perspired in the oppressive heat so he took every opportunity to make fun of those who did. On this occasion, he had an ulterior motive. He needed to intimidate this kid.

"Yeah, I know it's a nightmare. I'm Billy Addis," Billy said.

He smiled and stared directly at Danny. He was a good-looking, confident bastard, Danny thought. He might not be able to overwhelm or shout him down like he could an Asian journalist.

"I'm gonna have to buy myself some more polo shirts once I settle in properly," Billy continued. "I'm bloody soaking under the armpits already."

"Yeah, I struggled with the heat when I first arrived."

They were playing poker, neither wanting to show their hand too early. Danny stretched his arms upwards to warm up. That exercise helped to tuck in his stomach.

"And you never get used to it," Danny said. "Don't let anyone tell you differently."

"Yeah, I reckon you're right. I've already seen some locals fanning themselves in Orchard Road."

Danny smiled at Billy. He decided to go first.

"So which papers were you at before? How the hell did you end up here? Singapore's never going to win any prizes for its free press, is it?"

Danny was nervous. Billy spotted his apprehension far too quickly. The big man had played his cards too early. He smiled back at Danny.

"I started off at a couple of papers around East London, *Newham Recorder* and the *Hackney Gazette*, but I was actually covering news. There were no sports jobs going, and then I heard about this one online and thought I'd give it a go."

"Sounds great. And how long have you been covering the S-League?"

Billy laughed.

"This is my first assignment."

"Oh, I'd better impress you then. I don't want you ruining my career."

Danny bent down and fiddled with his bootlaces. The eye

contact was lost. He had offered Billy a way in.

"Well, as I think you know, Danny …"

"Call me Spear, everyone else does."

How the fuck can I call you 'Spear' and say what I've got to say, Billy thought.

"OK, Spear, sure," Billy continued. He sounded ridiculous. "I've been asked to have a chat with you about two things. The soccer camps you're working on with the Singapore Sports Council and that thing with the CPIB recently."

Danny adjusted a bootlace and craned his head back to look at Billy. His eyes squinted in the sun. He had messed around with his boots long enough to clear his head and get his story straight. The Spear was ready now.

"Yeah, I know. I spoke to Peter on the phone," Danny said quickly. "He's a good bloke, your editor. I've had him on my show. He did all right. Sweated a lot and got a bit tongue-tied, but he did all right. I could get you on once you've settled in, if you think you'll be all right in front of a camera."

"So it's up to you, Spear, which one you want to talk about first."

"Let's save the best to last, eh? Let's get this CPIB stuff out of the way first."

This CPIB stuff. This Corrupt Practices Investigation Bureau stuff. Danny certainly had balls. This CPIB stuff had sent other footballers to prison. Singapore took tremendous pride in being one of the least corrupt countries on the planet. Every year the proud media trumpeted the latest international Corruption Perception Index figures and Singapore was usually in the top five. The Corrupt Practices Investigation Bureau made it possible. No one was entirely sure what their officers did, least of all Billy. He read through their website, checked previous stories, asked other reporters and learnt there was a fair bit of surveillance and undercover work involved, but it was all cloaked in secrecy for the benefit of internal security.

These boys got the job done though. On the rare occasions when the CPIB surfaced to interrogate a high-profile sportsman, the chain reaction was immediate and decisive. Arrests swiftly followed, local syndicates were dismantled and the calm exterior returned. And the CPIB officers disappeared again.

Match-fixing was their rice bowl, their bread and butter. Almost every case Billy read about involved match-fixing. Illegal bookies, footballers, coaches, managers and even one or two club chairmen had been linked with the scourge of Southeast Asian football. Corruption was a cancer in this part of the world, eating the game from the inside out. There appeared to be more stories about bent matches than genuine ones. Some of the local quotes from the punters beggared belief. The average Singaporean thought the S-League was fixed, that the English Premier League was probably fixed, and that the World Cup might be fixed. How else could you explain South Korea in 2002 or Andres Escobar in 1994? They both had to be fixed, right? The cynical thinking made no sense to Billy. He had backpacked around poor European countries with hardly any recorded cases of football corruption, and here he was in one of the richest, safest, cleanest countries and its only professional sports league was known locally as the "Kelong League".

The CPIB had taken on a hydra. Every time a betting syndicate was smashed, another two mushroomed in its place. Some had connections in every major Asian city with bookies' runners dashing from one end of the continent to another. Asian crime families coveted the English Premier League more than Russian oligarchs. Football betting paid more than drugs during major tournaments, and the business transcended competition and rival territories. There was more than enough money to go around. It was the world game after all. Most importantly, no one in Singapore ever got hanged for match-fixing.

Billy watched Danny re-tie a bootlace that did not need re-tying. He recalled a common thread that ran through every article, feature and comment piece he had read earlier in the afternoon that touched on CPIB investigations. The officers were never wrong. Each recorded case of a suspect being interviewed by the CPIB led to criminal charges somewhere along the line with no exceptions. The mud had always stuck. Until now. Danny had been the exception.

"Two weeks ago, I think you were called in for an interview with the CPIB," Billy said. "And then last week, the CPIB confirmed to us at the paper, in a public statement, that you had been called in for a second interview and may be called upon at a later date to help them further with their enquiries."

"That's right, mate."

"Can you say what happened in those interviews?"

Danny stood up and tucked his shirt into his shorts.

"No, you probably know I cannot do that. Anything said at the CPIB has to stay inside CPIB."

"But you promised my editor a statement in exchange for a plug about your soccer clinics?"

Danny peered at Billy's notebook.

"You don't mess about, do you? OK, here's my statement," Danny stopped and watched his team-mates warming up on the pitch.

"OK, say that I was called in, on two occasions, to assist the CPIB. They needed some clarification on a couple of things and I was more than happy to help. I said they could call me any time if I can help them again, but I don't think I'll be needed anymore. That should be the end of the matter."

"If you don't mind me asking, Danny, there has been talk that some of Raffles Rangers' recent results were a bit unexpected. You dropped a few easy points and there had been some really high-scoring games on days when the odds for more than five goals scored were higher than usual."

"That's football, mate. You know that."

"And the other key game was the six-pointer against Orchard FC last season. That one was seen as a must-win for both sides and Raffles went in as clear favourites, but you pulled out injured at the last minute."

"Yeah, I had trouble with an old ankle injury. It does flare up from time to time. As you can see, I've been blessed with tree trunk thighs and meaty calves, but I've got a little girl's ankles."

"But it's flared up four times in the last couple of seasons, Danny."

Danny brightened suddenly.

"Which is why I've got to think about the future with my soccer clinics with the Singapore Sports Council. My dream is to find a player good enough to play for Singapore within the next 10 years and you can definitely quote me on that."

"They sound great, Danny, they really do. Do you have any backers for the clinics?"

"Yeah, everyone's come on board. Some of the lads at the Super Soccer studio are on board and the club's main sponsor here, High Teck Construction, may sponsor some kits and boots for the kids."

"That's perfect, Danny. Thanks, mate. I've got more than enough."

"OK, Billy, no problem. Try and give my soccer clinics a good plug, if you can. I'm always good for a story for you later on if you need one."

"Yeah, sure."

Danny turned towards his team-mates.

"Oi, Chris, get your arse over here," he shouted across the pitch. "This reporter's a Cockney just like you. He'll make you a star."

"Thanks for that, Danny," Billy said.

"Nah, this Chris Osborne kid looks like a decent player. He started off at West Ham. They reckon he's got a bloody good right foot."

Billy watched the lanky striker jog over. If Chris Osborne had started out at West Ham, then he certainly hadn't set Upton Park alight. Billy returned to his notes and made sure they were legible. He wasn't interested in Chris bloody Osborne or his right foot. He wanted to know how the so-called Spear had managed to poke his way through the CPIB net.

 **eight**

CHRIS wiped his forehead again. His hair was that irritating mixture of dampness from the shower and perspiration. The humidity was inescapable. When he had warmed up earlier on the pitch, he was convinced the training session would go the same way as that shit interview.

Who was that bloke? Billy Addis. What a condescending prick. He had been a rising reporter at some of the local papers around London. So what? Chris had never heard of him. A couple of questions about his West Ham days, and then he waffled on about Asian food. What was Chris' favourite food? His favourite Singaporean dish? Could he handle the local spicy food? Who gave a shit? Chris was here to resuscitate his dying football career, not eat his way around the island.

After the shortest of interviews, Chris performed light stretches and was shocked to feel the sweat cascading from his temples. He lifted his head slightly to make sure no one else was looking and dragged his face across his training bib. It made no difference. His head leaked. The skinny Chinese guy beside him didn't appear to be perspiring and Danny Spearman wasn't either, which was extraordinary considering he was the most overweight midfielder Chris had ever trained with. Chris rubbed the palms of his clammy hands together and stood upright. He heard his father's voice screaming, "You're gonna miss, you're gonna miss, you're gonna miss." If he missed in the next hour, he was going home unemployed.

CHRIS took a piece of tissue paper off the rickety desk and wiped his forehead. The office was a joke. He remembered signing his first West Ham contract surrounded by oak-panelled walls and a massive framed photograph of Bobby Moore and Pele shaking hands after that legendary World Cup match between Brazil and England in Mexico. There they were, two of the finest gentlemen to grace the game—legends forever smiling down on the next Hammers hopeful putting pen to paper. Even the manager's office at West Ham inspired a giddy apprentice. The Raffles Rangers office had all the finesse of a foreman's portakabin on a building site—largely because it *was* a portakabin.

Chris sat on a plastic chair and stared across at two more white plastic chairs. All that was missing was a fourth chair, a plastic table and a tacky umbrella. At West Ham, Mick Peters, being the pretentious dickhead that he was, had paid for a handcrafted leather executive swivel chair with a pair of Hammers embossed on the headrest. Naturally, he spent the next fortnight telling anyone who would listen that the chair cost two grand. The Raffles Rangers coach sat on garden furniture.

"Don't be put off by the furniture. The real stuff is coming from Harrods. But that Fayed is so preoccupied with Fulham's relegation battle that he keeps forgetting my order."

Chris turned and smiled as the Raffles Rangers' coach dumped a bag full of footballs into the corner, moved some training cones out of the way and meandered through his tiny, cluttered office to his desk. Michael Nielsen was a broad-shouldered, muscular man with thick, frizzy, curly hair that betrayed his Scandinavian background. The giant Dane had impressed Chris in training.

Affable, easy-going and always positive, Michael appeared to be everything that Mick Peters and that prick Eddie McDonald were not. Raffles Rangers' players were mostly Malay and Indian, with a couple of Chinese and Western expats thrown in, and Michael communicated easily with all of them with that flawless, accent-less Scandinavian English that wasn't tainted by England's provincialism.

"We're not here to see if you can play," Michael had shouted to Chris during training. "We know you can play. West Ham do not usually take on shit players. We're here to help you fit in with our style of play and this sweaty climate."

From that moment, Chris wanted to play for Michael Nielsen and he did. His fears about the humidity were borne out. He was marginally slower on the turn and he struggled initially to pull away from his marker, but it didn't matter. Despite missing regular football and travelling from one hemisphere to the other and halfway back again, Chris was still fitter than just about every other player. In comparison, the mighty Spear looked like a fat bloke who had won a pub competition to train with an S-League club for a day. The training session was a breeze. Chris had stormed it and everyone knew it.

"Chris, we want you here, my friend," Michael said. "Both me and Adel are in complete agreement. We want you as our marquee player at Raffles Rangers Football Club."

The sudden surge of relief surprised Chris.

"That's wonderful, that's really great, really. Who's Adel?"

"Ah, Adel. Did you see that small bald man in a T-shirt and faded jeans at the beginning of the training session?"

"I might have."

"He's our team manager. He can't be here now. He's been called away to an important meeting."

"Are you signing more players?"

"No, he's got a consignment of rugs coming in. That's his full-time job. He sells Persian rugs. Apparently, they're the best in Singapore. I've bought two from him myself."

There were more jokes there than Chris could count, but he was too elated to bother. If a Persian rug-selling team manager believed Chris was the man to spearhead his forward line, then Chris was ready to jump on board and take a ride with Raffles Rangers. There were no clubs without a Persian rug-selling team manager willing to offer Chris a contract.

"That's great, it really is. So what do we have to do now?"

"I'll have a contract drawn up for you to sign tomorrow."

"Just like that?"

Michael laughed.

"I'm afraid you're not in the EPL now. I could've gotten it ready tonight, but Adel is buying his rugs."

"That's fine. I just want to play. That's all I want to do now."

Michael examined Chris' face. The unexpected frankness caught both of them off-guard. Chris wasn't being insincere; he really meant it.

"Well, don't get too excited, as I'm sure the famous Spearman has told you already, we've got a strict salary cap in the S-League."

"No, he hasn't, but that's OK."

"But fortunately, there's not a club in Singapore who bothers with it. So on paper, we'll pay you $8,000 a month, which is the maximum we are allowed under the cap. That means you'll be our marquee player. But I'm fairly confident Mr Teck will be willing to make up the difference to take you up to 10."

"Mr Teck?"

"He's the club's main sponsor. A super-rich *towkay*. That's what they call a wealthy businessman here. He's self-made, runs High Teck Construction. The name's crap, but they built half of the skyscrapers around Raffles Place, in Malaysia, Australia and even in your hometown. His company has built several sports stadiums around the world. He's been back and forth so many times to London, there's talk that he's going to be involved in the London 2012 Games. I think he will be. He's that kind of guy. He's worth millions, tens of millions, probably even more."

"Wow, sounds like he could buy an EPL club. What made him sponsor an S-League club?"

Michael smiled and picked up a brochure from his desk.

"National service. You see this? This is our fundraiser that's going to be held next week. We have one every year, and every year all our local MPs and ministers toast another S-League season and wish us all the best for another year, and they all raise a glass to Mr Teck's generosity. What a benevolent, civic-minded citizen he is, they all say. But the truth is, all of the big guys have been asked to back an S-League club. It's a national project so they must do their national service. They only need to put in around $750,000, maybe more at a bigger club like this one, which is a fair trade-off for the low taxes they pay. It's pocket change to them and it wouldn't pay Ronaldo's salary for a month, but it's enough. As long as the S-League continues to do a little bit better than the M-League in Malaysia, all the ministers are happy and we get enough money to survive."

"That's, er, interesting."

"No, it's actually great. Mr Teck never interferes, never questions our judgment, gives us what we need and really looks after the players. I've met most of the *towkays* at the other clubs and we're lucky to have Mr Teck. He really loves his football."

"And what are the fans like here?"

"The fans? Did you look around the stadium during training today? What fans?"

VINCE the Mincer craned his head around the cubicle and checked the toilet one more time. He heard the hand dryer from the women's toilet next door and instinctively froze. He knew he was taking a risk at such a VVIP event, but that was the point. Vince the Mincer was an Indian hip-hop artist who fused Bollywood with drum and bass. He laid down his own street lyrics over funky, hypnotic tunes like the themes from *Sesame Street*, *Knight Rider* and the *A-Team*, and achieved something uniquely Singaporean. Vince made a decent living in the local music industry without having to resort to crappy Cantopop ballads or cheesy Malay *mat* rock guitar riffs. Nor did he have to belt out "Stairway to Heaven" or "Hotel California" covers to Chinese *towkays* and corporate expats in hotel bars. He was Vince the Mincer, the heartland homie, and he didn't need to take shit from anyone.

Tonight was one of the exceptions. This was a favour to Danny Spearman. He owed The Spear—for lots of things. But most of all, he owed him for landing the Super Soccer gig. Danny spotted him at a roadshow on Orchard Road and invited him to appear on his programme. Vince did his thing and rocked the house. The producers gushed over him, a young Chinese intern on the show slept with him, and Danny endorsed him on air. Within weeks, the Super Soccer channel did for Vince in Asia what *The Ed Sullivan Show* did for The Beatles in America. His most popular hit in Singapore, "Yeah Lah"—a Singlish riff on OutKast's "Hey Ya!"—went to No.1 in Malaysia, Indonesia and even Hong Kong. Vince the Mincer was mixing it up with the kings of Cantopop. His management knew he had arrived when Malaysian bootleggers bothered to sell pirated copies of his CD. Ordinarily, they never bothered with local artistes because they never sold, and yet some wannabe gangster was arrested at the Johor Causeway trying to sneak 10,000 copies of *Yeah Lah* into

Singapore. Even the underworld knew about Vince the Mincer.

The Spear had asked Vince to perform at the Raffles Rangers fundraiser. Vince pictured the VVIP audience—starched white shirts tucked far too high into pressed black trousers and hair nailed down with a tub of Brylcreem. Faceless, humourless civil servants slurping on shark's fin soup and bowing and scraping to every white corporate face and politician were not Vince's audience. He was a boy from Bishan, a kid from the housing estates. His attire proved it—an extra large New York Yankees shirt that hung below his knees, baggy pants to show off the Calvin Kleins and plenty of bling. He was the bomb, the original Singapore bouncing bomb. True, the bling was gold-plated and the stones were pure CZ, but he looked the part and that's all that mattered. He would make his point. The heartland homies were his crowd, not suits and centre partings.

The hand dryer stopped, a door creaked and the footsteps faded away. Vince locked his cubicle door and moved quickly. He put down the toilet seat and poured the powder from a small packet, making a tiny pile in the middle of the seat. Vince chopped out two lines using a guitar pick. He knew an R&B singer, a well-known *Singapore Pop Idol* reject, who chopped up his lines using a small razor blade. Idiot, Vince had told him. Get stopped with a razor blade and you're finished. Get stopped with a guitar pick and nothing. You're a musician. Musicians carry guitar picks. Hip-hop cokeheads carry razor blades. No blur cop from Katong doing his National Service would ever spot the difference.

Vince rolled up a 50-dollar note. He always used 50-dollar notes. Jarvis Cocker had called cocaine the self-congratulatory drug of choice and he had been right. Use a five-dollar note for what?

Vince hovered over the first line and snorted. His eyes watered and reddened. He moved to the second line and smiled. Fuck the politicians and their shark's fin soup, he thought. Fuck their white shirts and high waistbands. Fuck their tubs of Brylcreem. Fuck their batik shirts. Fuck them all. He'd rock this place like it was Madison Square Garden. Overcome by euphoria, he snorted the second line and swept up any remaining powder with his fingertip. He grinned broadly and jumped to his feet.

"Yeah lah," he hummed. "Yeeah laaah, you're my rock-and-roll star."

He was flying. First class. It was the only way to travel. He was ready to rock the Royal William Farquhar Hall.

VINCE the Mincer grabbed the microphone and kicked its stand away. He jumped up and down like a pogo, and waved his left arm above his head.

"Everybody in the house, make some noise!" he screamed. "Everybody in the house shout, 'Yeah lah'!"

Vince stared down at the two round tables in front of the stage. A dozen crisp white shirts and eight bright batik shirts glared back at him.

"Everybody in the house wave your hands in the air, like you just don't care," he continued in a faux-American accent that was more Boston than Bishan. "Everybody wave those hands, yeah, wave those hands, yeah, wave those hands, yeah …"

Vince peered out at the crowd. There was not one hand being waved in the air like it just didn't care. Time to wrap it up.

"Ladies and gentlemen, you've been a great crowd. It's been an honour to play for Raffles Rangers Football Club tonight. They've got the S-League title and they're not going to give it back, baby. Give it up for the Raffles boys."

The white and batik shirts applauded for the first time. They loved their Raffles boys. Vince mistook the applause for validation and decided to continue.

"We've got our very own Happy Hammer. It's not every day we can say we've signed a player from the EPL, but there he is folks, the handsome Chris Osborne sitting at the back next to our very own Poh Wee Kin. Give it up for the deadliest strike force in Southeast Asia."

The shirts at the top two tables applauded again and nodded appreciatively. Vince was mincing it up now. He was on a roll.

"And then there's the Great Dane right beside them, ladies and gentlemen, Michael Nielson. An S-League title in his first season in Singapore and he's well on the way to making it two in two, right?"

Some of the Raffles Rangers players at the back of the hall shouted, "Yeah!" Danny walked over to his coach, patted him on the back and whispered into his ear. They both laughed.

"I know it's going to be two in two because I've spoken to some illegal bookies and they've said they'll make more money on Raffles' high-scoring games."

The applause petered out. Vince ignored the nervous whispering in the room and continued to swagger arrogantly across the stage, a cross between Liam Gallagher and Kobe Bryant.

"And then there's The Spear. Ah, man, I owe The Spear everything," Vince shouted. "If it wasn't for The Spear, I wouldn't be standing here now. Thanks, Spear."

Danny took his hands off his coach's shoulders and glowered at Vince.

"No, seriously, Spearman is great for the game. Look at his physique. The bookies are taking odds on The Spear to be the first player to score from outside the penalty box with his stomach."

For the first time, Vince picked up on the awkward silence in the room. The gear was wearing off. He sensed the turbulence. He was coming in for a bumpy landing. Economy class. He needed to return to his seat quickly. Vince bent over and picked up the mic stand, and struggled to snap in the microphone. He leaned forward and breathed heavily into the microphone.

"Well, ladies and gentlemen, it's time for the really important people to come on stage now so I've got to get off. But remember, we are the founders! We are the pioneers! We are the Raffles Rangers Football Club!"

CHRIS downed the last of his orange juice and watched the scrawny Indian rapper geezer strut off stage. Dressed in baggy clothes and a backwards baseball cap, the guy looked like an extra in an early Spike Lee film. Chris giggled as Vince the Mincer fist-pumped enthusiastically to a largely middle-aged crowd who rarely glanced up from their *ice kacang*. Chris was convinced the guy was buzzing, not regular buzzing, but Dagenham buzzing, Faces Nightclub buzzing. The signs were obvious from the moment the mad Indian had jumped on stage and screamed like a bad-ass American gangster. But that couldn't be here. Not in Singapore. Danny returned to the table with another tray of beers.

"Who the hell was that?" Chris asked, refusing the beer that Danny handed to him.

"Who was who?"

"Who do you think? Him up there on the stage. Bollywood's Eminem. He was a right dickhead."

"Oh, he's all right, really," Danny said. He took a long swig from his beer and wiped his mouth on his shirt cuff. "He's a top boy. I got him on my show and he's done really well. Gets really good ratings. Not as good as me though."

Chris raised an eyebrow.

"What do they see in him?"

"Can't you tell? He's street, mate. He's down with the hood. To you, he's a dickhead. But over here, he's hardcore, man. He's a

Singapore gangster."

They both laughed. Danny raised his glass.

"Anyway, let's toast Raffles Rangers before the really boring speeches start."

MR Teck's speech had impressed Chris. Mr Teck was unusually tall for a Chinese man. He dressed differently to the other big shots on the top table. His handmade shirt was actually silver silk to match Raffles Rangers' home strip. The man had a self-deprecating sense of humour. Judging by the speeches made by the other cardboard cut-outs at the top table, this was not an attribute shared by movers and shakers of Singapore. Mr Teck's hair was short, in a trendy brush cut not unlike Al Pacino's Scarface, and he was an attractive man. He also spoke softly. His money made the white shirts in the room listen. His smile and warm eye contact took care of their wives. He had mentioned Chris in his speech and wished him well at the club, and the name check pleased the Englishman far too much. Harry Redknapp had said Chris Osborne could play for England and he shrugged off the compliment with the brashness of youth. Mr Teck had said Chris Osborne could be the highlight of the S-League season and he blushed. Mr Teck was an enigmatic, captivating presence.

"I told you he was a good guy," Michael said, still applauding as Mr Teck posed on stage with some large, fake cheques.

Chris leaned across the round table.

"Yeah, he seems like a decent bloke."

"And the best part is, that's it now. He'll pop up for the odd game, but he'll leave us until the end of the season when, if we hang on to that title, he'll deliver the most expensive crate of champagne to our dressing room."

"Really? Is that what he did last year?"

"Yeah, it was fucking beautiful," said Danny as he stretched across the table to grab another beer. "We'd just got the call that Orchard FC had drawn at home and we'd won by two points when this crate of champers turned up in the dressing room, literally within minutes of the final whistle."

"That's fantastic."

"Yeah, and you know the best part is that we got just over 2,000 fans at that game. A title decider and we got fewer fans than a League Two game. And yet we've got Asia's answer to Roman Abramovich."

"It's great."

"Don't ever take it for granted," Danny continued. "There's only us and Orchard who know for certain that the wages go into the bank every month—win, lose or draw. The boys at the other clubs might only get paid if they get the right result."

"You mean if they win?"

Danny laughed. He lifted the glass to his lips.

"That depends," he muttered.

THE Minister for Home Improvement paused for dramatic effect. He turned his head from left to right, just as his party's public speaking instructor had taught him. Engage your audience with constant eye contact, she had told him, but try not to make it look mechanical. He took a sip of water. That was another old trick. Build the tension in the room before delivering the most important point of the speech.

"It is a work in progress, but we are immensely proud of the S-League," he said. "But we cannot rest on our laurels. Corruption continues to bedevil our national game. We had another tree corruption cases last season."

Damn, he thought. It's *three*, not *tree*—*three*. He had worked so hard on his "th" diphthongs with the instructor, too. The slip irritated him immensely. He was the runaway debating champion in college; no one could touch him; no one could counter him. But his damn pronunciation still needed work.

"That's three cases in the last three months of the season."

That was much better. Perhaps the audience missed the tiny mistake. Damn the Speak Good English Campaign. As Minister for Home Improvement, he had to be the figurehead of the ridiculous initiative, and every time he lapsed into Singlish, the foreign media had a field day.

"This is not a negative speech on such a positive occasion. On the contrary, Mr Teck's selfless generosity is indeed a cause for celebration and Raffles Rangers are in for another great season, but we must be on our guard at all times. Some call it match-fixing. Some call it *kelong*. It is corruption, pure and simple, and it has no place in the S-League. Besides, and I'm loath to admit it, Raffles Rangers doesn't need to be *kelong*; it's too good!"

The audience laughed loudly, eager for the speech to conclude on an upbeat note.

"As you all know, my Orchard constituency includes Orchard Football Club and to lose the title on the last day of the season still really, really hurts. But the best team won last year and that's all you can ask for this season."

The audience applauded loudly as the Minister for Home Improvement handed the microphone to the Minister for Sports (Land and Water).

"As Raffles Rangers happens to fall within my Raffles constituency," he said quickly, "all I can ask for is that the best team last year is also the best team this year."

The audience whooped and cheered. The Minister for Sports (Land and Water) glanced across at the Minister for Home Improvement. He nodded back.

"But seriously, I must echo the words of the Minister," the Minister for Sports (Land and Water) said. "We need to keep it clean. We need to build the reputation of the S-League. That's the only way to attract more players like Chris Osborne. That's the only way to attract more sponsors like Mr Teck. The only time I want to see the word '*kelong*' in a newspaper this season … is when I'm reading about an M-League match in Malaysia.

"Ladies and gentlemen, I do not have to be as politically correct as my fellow Minister here. Please raise your glasses and toast Raffles Rangers Football Club, the winners of this season's S-League title."

The audience rose and turned to face the players' tables at the back of the room and raised their glasses. Spread across three tables, the players and coaching staff nodded back in appreciation, but they were largely ignored. Hundreds of pairs of eyes were trained on just one player.

"They're all looking at you," Danny whispered to Chris. "You better be fucking good."

 nine

HE was better than good; he was exceptional. The S-League had not witnessed a player as technically accomplished as Chris Osborne since Michael Currie. Even then, Currie's game was all about wing play and speed in possession. Chris offered a complete package. Two-footed, he had an ability to turn defenders on both sides, and coaches rendered him almost unplayable. Even on the hard, dry, pockmarked pitches of the S-League, Chris ghosted past defenders and revelled in the kind of generous space he was never offered on West Ham's training ground. And he tackled, too. That was the difference. His father had been right. George Best was the greatest player of all time, according to Tony Osborne, because he tackled with the ferocity of a fullback. All strikers scored goals, but only the greatest players dropped back to regain possession because the greatest players were convinced they would determine the game's outcome every time they were on the ball. Like a loyal dog eager to please its master, they would go and fetch the ball first if necessary. Chris loved a full-blooded tackle. Most Singaporean players didn't. They shirked it.

Chris had an edge from the beginning. He conducted himself on the pitch not like a West Ham player, but a hungry West Ham player desperate for his first-team debut. Stamford Stadium quickly became his playground and he the classroom bully. On his debut, he lacked match fitness, struggled with the humidity and felt light-headed after his first run into the penalty box. It didn't matter. He scored twice in the first half and added a third in the second before fatigue got the better of him. It was easy, scandalously easy, a man against boys, and every S-League player could see it. Outsiders were bound to pay attention eventually.

YATI walked slowly towards Stamford Stadium. She had never been to the ground before, but then even her taxi driver wasn't sure where it was. He knew his football, loved the Malaysia Cup and adored Fandi Ahmad—Singapore's first son of football, he had called him—but he cared little for the S-League. *Kelong*, he said. Still, he had the occasional S-League bet. Other than Raffles Rangers and Orchard FC, he was unfamiliar with the other teams, but he took the odd punt nevertheless. He always played goals, high numbers of goals. That was the beauty of the S-League, he told Yati. There were always plenty of goals. Maybe the teams were lousy; maybe the teams were *kelong*. But there were always goals in the S-League. The standard was dreadful, but it was always good for a bet.

Yati had been surprised to learn that the taxi driver had heard of Chris Osborne.

"Oh, yah, the tall *ang moh* from West Ham," he had said quickly. "Ya lah, he very good player one. Always score goals. Very good. When his team play, I always buy five goals plus. Very good."

The conversation was excruciating. Yati had no interest in either football or gambling; the two were intrinsically linked in Singapore and made local men extraordinarily tedious. She had dated only three Singaporean men—two Chinese and one Malay—and they had driven her to distraction.

Her first boyfriend was a cute Chinese National Serviceman

with abs like Vincent Ng's, and whenever he returned from army camp, they had the most frenzied sex. It didn't last very long, but it was frenzied. They were both young and naïve. She loved his toned, tanned naked body. The trouble was once he put his shorts and singlet back on, he would slump back onto the couch, open a bag of peanuts, and waffle on about Giggs and Beckham. He once told her he was married to Manchester United. He thought he was being funny. She thought he was being a dick.

The second guy was Malay, which delighted Yati's parents, and looked a bit like the guy who won the first *Singapore Pop Idol*. Yati had met him on her journalism course. He was going to be a top music writer and eventually work for *Q* magazine or *Rolling Stone*. The last she heard, he was writing for one of the free nightlife guides left outside MRT stations and *ang moh* pubs around Clarke Quay. He obsessed over his family's Toyota Camry, which his father had taken a large bank loan to pay for, and spent every waking moment fretting over its upholstery and its customised headlamps and wheel trims. He often told her how fast it could go from nought to 60, and would show her glossy magazine photographs of the latest model cruising along an empty American highway. He only took the Camry to Marina South on weekends when his father let him use it. Yati always believed there was a direct correlation between how much time he devoted to the Toyota's body and how much attention he gave hers. The sex was just awful.

Yati really loved the third guy. He was the only one who made her fantasise about their future together. She wanted it all—the engagement, the down payment on a five-room apartment, the wedding at the Marina Mandarin Hotel, the baby, the maid, everything. He was Chinese, but he was a Raffles Institution old boy, English-educated, overseas arts degree graduate and a fan of alternative British comedy. He didn't speak a word of Chinese and constantly bitched about how the Singapore Government was alienating his generation with their Speak Mandarin campaigns. He listened to the right music, bought the right theatre tickets at the Esplanade and had copies of all the recent Booker Prize winners on his shelf. He was irreverent, edgy and highly critical of the Singapore Government. He was a young, upper middle-class Chinese Singaporean cliché.

Yati later realised he served as a bridge between the Asian man and the white man. He often mockingly called himself a banana. For many Chinese men, it was a condescending, derogatory remark, perhaps even racist, but he deliberately took it as a compliment, naturally. They had met on *The Newspaper*'s arts desk. He was a rising film critic and she was a lifestyle reporter. His reviews were liberally sprinkled with mentions of Fellini, Lean and Welles—directors whom Yati had never heard of, but felt that she should have. In one of his most memorable reviews, he had accused George Lucas of perpetuating outdated imperialistic stereotypes by giving the major villains in *The Phantom Menace* accents with a Japanese military-like flavour last heard in *The Bridge on the River Kwai*. *The Newspaper* received letters for weeks afterwards.

He had only one flaw. After a night out at the Penny Black pub in Boat Quay, they had all returned to a friend's house for some supper and the cards came out. He dropped a month's salary in an hour. At 1 a.m., the live match was switched on, and he called a bookie and put down a grand. Yati never understood the complicated details of the bet, but she never forgot his temper at the final whistle. Or his admission that he owed a loan shark called Tiger over $10,000. There was no way back after that.

White men didn't gamble. Or at least they didn't gamble to excess. It wasn't ingrained in their non-Asian DNA. They shared many of her last Chinese boyfriend's socio-economic beliefs, attended the same shows, and owned the same eclectic DVD collections of British and American comedies that she pretended to get. They were not preoccupied with the latest Toyota Camry, didn't listen to those childish Cantopop ballads on their Toyota sound systems and rarely spoke that ghastly Singlish. They could watch football without needing a "financial interest" in the game and they even played blackjack for fun. Commitment was the only issue. Relationships lasted as long as the employment passes. One or two did consider resettling in Singapore, but the religious conversion was always the final insurmountable hurdle. Yati knew she was good in bed, but no one was that good.

Yati loathed the Sarong Party Girl jibes. No one in the office called her an SPG to her face, but she wasn't stupid. She was an olive-skinned Malay girl who didn't speak Singlish and favoured Caucasian partners so she found herself labelled, thanks to that damn SPG book. Yati never considered herself an SPG. Those illiterate Filipinos and Indonesians working the crowd at the Four Floors of Whores—*they* were SPGs. They were in it for the money. They saw a white man's wallet. Yati saw a pleasant evening's company. Expat salary packages had nothing to do with her choices. She had even gone out with one white guy who didn't live in a condo.

Yati headed across the athletics track at Stamford Stadium. She peered at the Raffles Rangers players stretching on the pitch and failed to recognise any of them. No, wait, the fat *ang moh* with his thighs strapped up looked familiar. Yati had seen him on TV when she was in Muddy Murphy's one night waiting for the rugby to start.

There was a sudden cheer over her shoulder. She turned to see a small crowd of teenage girls, mostly Malay, jumping up and down on the concrete benches. Yati counted at least 20 of them. Two of them held up a banner that read, "Chris never miss". Yati laughed. Even the crappy banners were written in Singlish. The girls waved towards the players' tunnel. Yati noticed a tall, athletic *ang moh* jogging onto the pitch. He had neatly cropped blond hair and wore no shirt under his yellow training bib. He was tanned and his muscles were defined, but not unsightly—somewhere past Roger Federer but not quite Rafael Nadal.

Yati waved at him and he smiled back at her. She knew at that moment that the article was going to be a rambling, incoherent mess. Yati was supposed to interview Chris Osborne, the rising Raffles Rangers star who was doing for the S-League what The Beatles did for British pop music, and find out what the Londoner did away from the pitch in swinging Singapore. But all she really wanted to do right now was sleep with him.

CHRIS struggled to concentrate. She was stunning. He had never seen a girl like this before. She was dark-skinned with smooth, long legs that appeared to go on forever. Her long black hair was brushed back to accentuate her flawless face—not a scrap of make-up on it. Back at West Ham, when Chris had picked up girls at Faces, he was never quite sure if he was going home with an attractive girl or Max Factor. Back in the day, Ross and Chris had wandered around the shopping mall at Lakeside, deliberately hovering around the West Ham United Superstore on the off chance that someone might recognise Chris as a youth player at the club. No one ever did, but they still picked up. They were handsome boys, Chris in particular, and there were more than enough teenage girls to go around in Essex.

But this girl was a Bond girl. Even her name was distinct. Yati. In Dagenham, there had been a Tracy, a Joanne, a Clare and even a Kylie, but never a Yati.

"I know it's a boring question, but I've got to ask it like a good Singaporean journalist. How do you find the food in

Singapore?"

Yati grinned at Chris. Bloody hell, even her smile belonged in a toothpaste commercial.

"Well, the club has just put me up in a condo behind Orchard Road," Chris said. "So it's mostly food courts around that area. But I like all the usual, you know, chicken rice, noodles, and I love that … how do you say it … *how fan?*"

"*Hor fun.* The flat noodles."

"Yeah, that's great, and cheap, too. Four bucks. You can't buy a breadstick in London for four bucks."

Yati laughed. It wasn't that funny. Chris was on to something here.

"But I know I've got to try the more local food at the hawker centres. Wee Kin took me to one in a place called Toa Payoh the other day and the food was great."

"Wee Kin?"

"Wow, you really don't follow local football, do you? Poh Wee Kin. He plays up front with me. Good striker actually, low centre of gravity, turns defenders really quickly. He's played for Singapore loads of times apparently. You sure you've never heard of him?"

"I've got to be honest. I'm really not a football fan. This is more of a lifestyle piece, to get to know the man behind the jersey."

She glanced down at his perspiring chest.

"Well, you're not wearing a jersey."

"No, it's just too hot for me here. Don't get me wrong, it's fantastic when I'm sitting by the pool, but it's bloody murder when I'm trying to get past a defender late in the second half."

"You certainly look fit though."

"West Ham did that. I might have been in the reserves, but they still taught you good training and diet habits, which I've kept up."

"I'll have to look at some of these fit West Ham players then."

"I've got a DVD at my place. I could show you tonight if you want."

Yati flashed that smile again and nodded. Chris wrote his phone number and address down on her notepad. This was getting ridiculous. Even in England, he usually had to buy a few Bacardi Breezers first. He was acknowledged as a football talent in the clubs around Essex and East London, but only a rising one. He still had to work at his game. But in Singapore he was not just a rising talent, he was a foreign talent who was better than American Express. He was accepted everywhere. On and off the pitch, he was being offered too much space and being presented with one open goal after another. He couldn't miss. London was no longer calling. Chris was falling in love with Singapore.

 ten

DANNY nodded to the doorman, an obese, pockmarked middle-aged Chinese man, and headed into the KTV lounge. As Chris and Wee Kin followed, the doorman's chunky, clammy hand grabbed Chris' shoulder. Instinctively, Chris swung around, squared his shoulders and jutted out his chest. It was a reflex action. East London doormen didn't usually manhandle punters to exchange pleasantries.

"What do you want, mate?"

"You're Chris Osborne, right?" the doorman said quickly. "I guessed it when I saw The Spear go inside first. You're Chris Osborne, right?"

"Yeah, yeah, that's me."

"Wah, you damn *shiok*, man."

Chris turned to Wee Kin.

"*Shiok* means good," Wee Kin whispered.

"Ah, thanks, mate. That's really kind of you."

Chris meant it, too. After a few seasons in the West Ham stiffs, any compliments were welcome and he never took them for granted.

"No lah, thank you," the doorman said. He checked over both shoulders and then leaned towards Chris. His breath stank of Jack Daniel's. "Last week, you scored two goals, right?"

"Yeah, that's right, I did. It was a good game."

The doorman smiled and nodded towards Wee Kin.

"And your friend here scored one as well, right?"

"Yep, he certainly did," Chris said, putting his arm around Wee Kin. "That's why he's got the best name in football because he does it 'week in and week out'. Don't you, Wee Kin?"

Wee Kin blushed and stared down at his trainers.

"I don't score enough," Wee Kin muttered.

"Whatever lah, but he scored one and you scored two and The Spear was injured so your defence *jialat*, and you conceded two late goals and guess what?"

"What?" Chris sighed. He knew what was coming.

"I played five goals. Damn *shiok*. I played Singapore Pools and also played outside, so I collected double."

"That's great. Can we go inside now?"

"Yeah, yeah, can, can, no problem … Hey Chris? Let me know next time when you feel like a lot of goals coming, eh?"

"Yeah, all right, mate."

As Chris walked down the dimly-lit purple corridor, he stopped and faced Wee Kin.

"Is there anyone in this country who doesn't bet on the S-League?"

Wee Kin smiled.

"Yeah, me."

"What's your secret?"

"I'd get arrested by the CPIB if I did."

"Ah, that's all right. I prefer playing up front on my own."

"Balls to you, *ang moh*, OK."

The pair laughed.

The KTV lounge stank of stale bourbon and old fruit, a particularly pungent combination that turned Chris' stomach. There were individual rooms, separated by glass screens, where mostly middle-aged Chinese men sang weepy Mandarin ballads or cheesy soft rock by the likes of Glenn Medeiros, Peter Cetera and Michael Learns to Rock. Most of the rooms had at least one heavily made-up young Chinese girl in a tight *cheongsam*, pouring drinks and serving bowls of fruit. Chris noticed one girl sitting on a Chinese man's knee and feeding him slices of mango. The image was most incongruous because the man's white shirt was unbuttoned to the waist and he was belting out Tom Jones' "Delilah" in heavily accented English.

"Why the hell have you brought us here?" Chris shouted across the din as the trio passed a Malay guy with long curly hair singing Europe's "The Final Countdown".

"The owner is one of our sponsors and he loves his football," Danny bellowed.

"What the hell does he sponsor? Our half-time oranges? There's fruit everywhere in here."

"Yeah, that's how it works," Wee Kin said. "The women keep you company, supposedly for free, and bring you some fruit. But those fruit bowls can cost over a hundred bucks."

"What the hell does Raffles Rangers want with a shit hole like this?"

"I don't really know," Danny said. "I think the owner has something to do with the gaming machines in the clubhouses. Or he went to school with Mr Teck. Something like that. Who cares? Let's get U2 on and some women in here. I'll get us three girls."

"Spearmint, you know I'm a married man," Wee Kin said.

"And I'm with Yati now," Chris added.

Danny looked confused.

"Who said they were for you?"

Wee Kin watched Danny and Chris mangle The Clash's "Should I Stay Or Should I Go Now". Danny fist-pumped during the choruses and dominated the microphone. The *ang mohs* were standing in front of a dusty television and following the lyrics on a pirated DVD that kept jumping in the cheap player. Still Danny took centre stage. They shared a microphone but Chris never got close enough for his voice to be heard, which he probably preferred. Unlike the flamboyant Danny, Chris' self-conscious body language was a giveaway. He didn't want to be spending his night in a dilapidated KTV lounge in Balestier either.

But Wee Kin enjoyed Chris' company. The whole team did. He wasn't like the other *ang mohs*. He was self-effacing, modest and genuinely enthusiastic about settling into a new culture. Of course, an Orchard Road condo, a decent salary and an SPG girlfriend from *The Newspaper* certainly helped the acclimatisation process. But Chris often came to Wee Kin for advice on where to shop and eat, and was eager to explore the housing heartlands of Singapore—the real Singapore. No other foreign footballer had ever bothered. Certainly not Spearmint anyway. The fucking idiot was always telling everyone in the dressing room about the great dinner he'd had the night before at the Singapore Cricket Club, oblivious to the fact that half the team couldn't afford to eat at the Singapore Cricket Club. The Padang was Danny's second home. Whether it was some ridiculous soccer sevens exhibition for retired *ang mohs*, a charity auction, a corporate dinner or even a rugby event, Danny could always be found at the Padang with his pals. Wee Kin remembered reading at school that the Padang was a popular hangout for Sir Stamford Raffles and his *ang moh kakis*. Nearly 200 years later, it still was.

That never really bothered Wee Kin, though. The S-League was over 10 years old now, and foreign talent of all shapes and sizes had come and gone. Some were competent, one or two from the Middle East and Eastern Europe had been exceptional, and many had been a joke. Most of them got put up in condos, listened to jazz by the Singapore River and got pissed at the Padang. So what? Wee Kin still got paid to play for both club and country and quietly went about his business.

But Danny infuriated Wee Kin because he really couldn't play. Western footballers were always physically stronger than the majority of Singaporean players, Wee Kin included, and Danny was no different. He was built like a Russian tank, but that was it. Instead he talked a good game to anyone who'd listen, which, thanks to that shitty soccer show, was most of Asia. But Chris was the kind of striker that Wee Kin dreamt of being—quick, brave and strong. He was easily the best partner Wee Kin ever had up front. Wee Kin lined up alongside Fandi Ahmad once in a charity game at the National Stadium and technically the Singaporean was flawless, but he was in his late 30s by then and his legs had gone. In his prime, Fandi might have had a chance, but Chris stood alone now.

Most of all, Wee Kin needed Chris as his partner; he was more than just the perfect foil, he was the perfect distraction. Wee Kin wasn't pulling his weight, but neither the management nor the press had picked up on it yet because they were too busy being mesmerised by Chris' heroics. But Wee Kin was under no illusion. Chris was carrying him. It was only a matter of time.

Three Chinese women entered the room bearing their bowls of fruit. Their pancake make-up struggled to conceal the acne scars and too many late nights spent pouring Rémy Martin for *towkays*. They smiled at Chris and Danny and largely ignored Wee Kin. It was nothing personal, just a reflex action in their line of work. White was usually right.

"Hello, my name is Rosie and these are two of my girls," said the prettiest of the three. Rosie was also the oldest of the three. She addressed only Chris and Danny, never bothering to make eye contact with Wee Kin, who shifted uneasily on the sofa.

"Can I pour a drink for you?"

Rosie started pouring the Tiger Beer into three glasses, not waiting for a reply.

"Come on, Rosie, get yourself up here. We're gonna sing 'Kids' together. I'll be Robbie Williams," Danny said.

"You're certainly fat enough," Chris said.

"Piss off, you. Right, I'll be Robbie, and Rosie you can be Kylie Minogue. You've certainly got the arse for it."

Danny gently took Rosie by the hand and pulled her towards him, playfully slapping her backside as she stood beside him.

"Come on, then, Rosie, jump on board and take a ride with me."

Wee Kin turned away and downed the rest of his beer. He reached across the table to refill his glass.

"This is going to be a long night," he muttered.

The two other girls tried to squeeze between Wee Kin and Chris on the beer-stained sofa. Chris smiled at both of them and declined the offer of being fed some sliced mango. Every time he glimpsed at either of the girls, they tried to offer him something— fruit, another beer, a singing duet. Each time he politely refused, Chris saw the hurt in their eyes. The thought of sleeping with any of them suddenly repulsed him. He felt sorry for them. He wanted to hug them. To avoid embarrassment, he tried to watch Danny cavort with Rosie in front of the TV. Ever the professional, she played along with the appalling Patrick Swayze routine, but always manoeuvred herself subtly to keep him at arm's length.

"I'm just popping outside to get some air," Chris said.

"Are you all right?" Wee Kin asked.

"Yeah, yeah. I'm fine. Just wanna wake up a bit before I blow him away with my 'Wonderwall' ... Here, Spearmint, it's my turn next so get the Oasis disc ready."

Danny gave Chris the middle finger, never once taking his eyes off Rosie or his other hand off her arse.

CHRIS opened the door to the street and felt the warm air suck the perspiration from his pores. He checked his watch. It was 1 a.m. and still stifling. He stepped out onto Balestier Road and wiped his forehead. He liked this street because it was one of the streets that married with his original perception of what a Singaporean street should look like. There were crumbling two-storey shophouses, their cracks and peeling paint magnified by the multi-coloured neon shop signs, and late-night coffee shops on every corner selling *bak kut teh*, or pork rib soup, as Wee Kin had pointed out. The soup was peppery and delicious, and Chris often went there for a bowl after training.

Chris wandered by some overflowing dustbins outside the KTV lounge and heard the squealing sound of rats rummaging through the rubbish. That was a downside to living in a 24-hour city—there were rodents everywhere. Chris had been terrified of rodents since a mini-plague of field mice came down from Dagenham's cleared railway tracks and took refuge beneath the floorboards of every house in his street. The Singapore Tourism Board guide never said anything about rats the size of kittens running around his condo car park in the early hours.

He heard voices. He noticed the doorman outside the club talking quickly to a smaller, Chinese guy. The smaller man appeared to be pointing aggressively at the hulking doorman, who nodded apologetically. The smaller man was dressed quite smartly—black trousers and a white pressed shirt—and his hair was gelled down in that uniform Asian fashion, not a strand out of place. He remonstrated with the doorman, but it was not an argument because the doorman never retaliated. He kept nodding sheepishly, his massive, bloated head staring down at the floor. Chris headed back towards the KTV lounge. The argument had nothing to do with him.

"Hey, is that you? It's you, right? You that *ang moh f*ootballer?

The Raffles one?"

Chris stopped and peered across his shoulder. The smaller Chinese guy was looking at him and smiling. Chris glanced at the doorman, who smiled back in appreciation. Chris had presented a welcome distraction.

"Yeah, I am, yeah," Chris said, reaching for the door handle.

"Yeah, yeah. Chris something, right?"

The smaller Chinese guy grabbed Chris' arm just above the elbow. Chris resisted the temptation to shake it off. He hated being touched. You're not in Dagenham now, Chris, he reminded himself. He forced another smile.

"Yeah, Chris Osborne. I play up front for Raffles Rangers."

"Ya lah, I knew it, ah. I said to my friend, that *ang moh* over there is a footballer. And I say don't tell me his name, I can guess, right?"

"Yeah, yeah, he did," the doorman said nervously.

"Ya lah. I knew it. Seen you on TV highlights. Seen you in *The Newspaper*. You had that big, big story one, right? Big picture on cover of lifestyle, right?"

"Yeah, that was a few weeks ago now."

"Ya lah, but it was you, right? I'm a big, big fan. Love football, especially EPL and last time the Malaysia Cup. Wah, the Malaysia Cup damn *shiok*, but before your time. S-League, OK lah, but now quite good. Raffles good to watch. Like the Man U of Singapore, right? That's what they call your team on TV, right?"

"Well, I don't know about that."

"Don't be shy lah. It's good. You score so many goals, got Poh Wee Kin, also play for Singapore, and you got that TV guy also."

"Danny Spearman."

"Yah, yah, yah, The Spear. Ya lah, that's him. 'The Spear's Betting Tips'. Correct, right? Ha ha, I never miss that show. That's the best show in Singapore, Malaysia and some say Batam."

Both Chinese men laughed. Chris didn't get the joke.

"Ya, OK lah, The Spear. Maybe he never play so much, but he talk a lot of sense when he's on TV. Most of those guys talk cock, but he talk sense."

"Thanks, mate. I'll go up and tell him."

"He's here now? Inside the KTV? Right now? Really? Can meet him or not? I want to get a photograph with you both to show my son. Can?"

Chris sighed. He had really screwed this up. He stared at the doorman, hoping for a little support. None came.

"Well, you see, I think, the thing is … Well, that wouldn't be allowed, would it? We're not allowed to take people in, are we?" Chris said to the doorman.

"No, no, it's OK, if you're OK with it, sir. Tiger is a member, too."

"Tiger? Your name is Tiger?"

"No lah, it's a nickname, because I drink too much Tiger. So they call me Tiger. Lucky I don't drink Anchor, right?"

"So is he allowed up then?"

Chris gazed at the doorman, imploring him to say no.

"Yeah, yeah, sure, no problem. You're all members. If you are OK with it, no problem."

"OK, then, let's go. But we'll have to make it quick, mate, because we've got to be up early in the morning. You know, training and all that."

"Sure, sure, no problem," Tiger said quickly.

Chris ushered Tiger through the door and along the dark, purple corridor.

"So, Tiger, you're a big football fan then, eh?" he asked, unable to help himself. Chris' dad had always insisted on treating fans with dignity. Remember the butterflies the first time you met Carlos Tevez on the training ground, his father had said.

Remember that feeling every time a fan approaches you, whatever the circumstances.

"Ya, ya, all my life. Used to watch highlights show in the old black and white days last time, your old English First Division, before you were born, and I watch it ever since. I love football, man."

"That's great, mate. So, what do you do for a living, Tiger?"

"Me? I'm a taxi driver lah."

Chris heard Danny murdering The Kinks' "Lola" as he led Tiger past the other KTV rooms.

"Well, you can certainly hear him."

"*Wah lao*, his singing lousy, eh?" Tiger said.

"It's not good, no."

Chris opened the door to their KTV room. Rosie was pouring Wee Kin another drink, while Danny stood with the two other girls and belted out the last few "Lolas". Tiger tentatively followed Chris into the room and closed the door behind him.

"Who's this?" Wee Kin asked.

"It's Tiger," Danny said. He spoke softly, but into the microphone so his words echoed around the room.

"You two know each other? Chris asked.

"Not really lah," Tiger said quickly. "I'm just a big fan of Raffles. The Spear signed some jerseys for me last time for my kids. And I take my eldest boy to training sometimes."

"Yeah, yeah, that's right. Tiger's one of our oldest fans. He's been there since the S-League started. The man's a local legend. If we had more Singaporeans like this guy, we'd have 40,000 cramming into Stamford Stadium every week."

Danny hoped his characteristic bluff and bullshit covered his initial hesitation. He glanced around the room quickly. Wee Kin was so drunk he could barely get off the sofa and Chris was the new, oblivious kid on the block. He was fine.

"You wanna drink first, Tiger?" Danny continued. "We've got plenty of your namesake here, mate."

"No need, no need, thanks, man. I'm on the night shift tonight. I was hoping to get a photo with you and Chris and, hey, maybe even Wee Kin also, on my hand phone, so I can go back and show my boy."

"Sure, man, no problem, anything for Raffles Rangers' number one fan."

Chris had to admire Danny. He was the biggest bullshitter in the game, and that was some achievement in itself, but he was bloody good at it. Even Chris believed that Danny was genuinely thrilled to come across a loyal supporter in a KTV lounge at 1.30 in the morning.

Tiger pulled his camera phone out of his leather belt holster and handed it to Rosie.

"Please, take for me can?"

Rosie took the phone, but ignored Tiger. The sooner he was gone the better. He was bad for business. The footballers could not drink while they were posing for photographs. Tiger enthusiastically sat beside a barely-conscious Wee Kin on the sofa, and beckoned Danny and Chris to join him.

"My son is going to be very excited about this," he said.

"Hey, it's the least we can do, right Chris?"

"Yeah, sure, mate. No problem at all."

The four men all smiled for the camera. Even Wee Kin managed a half-smirk and a drunken thumbs-up.

"Everyone say 'tits'," Danny bellowed.

"Tits!"

Rosie pushed the button and Tiger immediately jumped up to examine the photograph. Even Wee Kin and Chris were curious.

"That's actually quite a good photo of us all," Chris admitted.

"No lah, it's fantastic. I'll make copies for you all and bring them to a training session."

"There's no need to do that, mate," Danny said.

"No, no, I insist, Spear. Just for you, can. No problem."

"OK, Tiger. Well it was lovely to meet you, but it's getting late," Chris said.

"Understand, understand. No problem," Tiger said. "Hey Spear, can I ask one last favour?"

Danny eyed the other people in the room nervously.

"Er, I suppose so, Tiger. If I can help."

"Oh, it's nothing lah. I've got a new football in my car boot for my youngest son. It's his birthday next week. 'The Spear Hits Out' is his favourite show. He never misses. *Aiyoh*, I must record it for him if he has extra tuition class. Can you come and sign it for me? It's just outside in my car."

"I don't know, mate. It's getting late and we've got to go soon."

"No, no, really, it's just outside. Two minutes to sign, I promise."

"Two minutes?"

"Two minutes. Then I got to go. Nightclubs closing soon, got to get down Orchard Road and get some fares, man."

"OK, Tiger, two minutes. Let's go and get this ball. I'll be back in a minute, boys. See if they've got 'Street Fighting Man'. Or anything by the Stones."

TIGER threw Danny up against a wall. Danny's head thudded against the brickwork. He winced as Tiger grabbed him by the throat. The smaller man had led Danny down an alley between two rows of shophouses in Balestier Road and pushed him into some damp sheets hanging over bamboo poles which clattered to the ground. The bulky footballer made more noise than a wild boar on Batam Island, but Danny was not unduly perturbed. Singaporeans never interfered in other people's business and rarely asked questions. They had been well trained.

"Shut that fucking mouth of yours, Spear," Tiger hissed into Danny's ear.

"I don't understand. What do you want? Everything's all right," Danny croaked. "You said five goals, right? You wanted five goals and it was five goals, 3-2, that's what you wanted. You didn't care who won, you just said five goals."

Tiger stared at Danny contemptuously. He was such a blithering idiot.

"I know lah. But you, bastard, you had to go on your show first like a big shot and predict a high-scoring game. Five or six goals, you said. On TV. On fucking TV."

"Hey, please, Tiger, it's my TV show. I'm just having a bit of fun. No one suspects anything. The press, CPIB, they haven't got a clue. It's just a TV show."

"Please lah, you've already been called up by CPIB. They're not that stupid. But I don't give a shit about them, I only care about outside bookies. They can smell *kelong* from KL. You get it right too many times. Your viewers must think you're damn solid, right? Get so many right on TV, steady lah, *ang moh*, they say, right? Fame gone to your head, is it? Because you're fucking it up for us. The outside bookies know lah. It's too obvious. You're like a psychic on TV. Even blur Singapore Pools dropped the odds on five goals after so many people buy."

"The score was 3-2. How could anyone predict that?"

Tiger pushed Danny's head back into the wall. The sudden ache made Danny grimace. He was terrified.

"I saw the highlights. Your mistakes were obvious. You think I never watch football before, is it? I tape the match and watch later. You spread open your legs like an *Ah Lian*. Anyone can see lah. You're lucky no one watches S-League. No one gives a shit. That's why S-League always pays so well. Other leagues too troublesome, too many fans, too many cameras, players paid too much money. But S-League always so easy. Players paid like shit. Or they play like shit, like you."

"You got what you wanted. You got five goals," Danny mumbled.

"But it paid shit. The odds dropped so much, it was a waste of time. I make more money on EPL than I make on S-League this week. You spoil the market. My boss is fucking pissed off because of you."

"So what do you want me to do?"

Tiger released his grip on Danny's throat. Danny lurched forward and grabbed his neck gingerly. Tiger smiled.

"Please lah. There'll be no mark there."

"What do you want me to do?"

"Easy. The big Danny Spearman is finished. That's it. Cannot play anymore this season. That ankle injury's too troublesome. Too sore every time you run, right?"

"But we have a physio who will check."

"And we have a very good doctor who can give a medical certificate."

"It's not that easy. Our club will still check."

"Check lah. Our doctor is very respected in Singapore, one of the best, got very nice clinic in Tanglin Road. He's just a lousy gambler. He bet on your friend's old team, West Ham, to win the FA Cup final. He bet outside. So now he's like you."

"There must be something else I can do."

"Like what?"

"I don't know, but we're going for the title again this year and with Chris in the team, we've got a good chance of retaining the title. We've never played football like this before and it's my last season anyway."

"Heck care lah. Suddenly you want to be a footballer now, is it? Last time, you wanted to be Singapore superstar, big TV man. Now you want to be a footballer again. You asked to get a loan for your football clinics, not me."

"I didn't know …"

"You think we are fucking Citibank, is it?"

"I don't know anything anymore."

"Fuck off, *ang moh*. You knew everything. You wanted Singapore lifestyle like all your *ang moh* friends, right or not? You wanted condo, Singapore Cricket Club, Raffles Hotel, nice lady from Orchard Towers, but your S-League salary shit. So you make a choice."

"Don't lecture me. You've already told me what to do."

"I haven't finished. That shitty betting show you do, get Chris Osborne to do it with you."

"What? Why? That's my show."

"Because everybody likes him and outside bookies in Malaysia don't know him. And he doesn't know about the S-League. Our S-League. You tell him what to say lah. If he says it, he won't fuck up our odds."

"But Chris is a good bloke. He's a decent guy."

"That's why people will trust what he says lah."

"He's a good footballer, too."

"Then he cannot stay in the S-League very long, right or not?"

Danny watched Tiger drive off towards Thomson Road, took a deep breath and walked towards the KTV lounge. He peered across the other side of Balestier Road. Half a dozen sleepy Bangladeshi workers sat around a table sharing a single bottle of Tiger Beer. The beer lady stood in a corner counting the dollars in her bum bag and the pork rib soup seller sat perched on a stool reading a Chinese newspaper. No one ever enquired or asked questions in Singapore. Danny nodded towards the doorman and forced a smile. He pretended to scratch at his neck to cover it up, just in case.

"Tiger gone already?" the doorman asked.

"Yeah, yeah, I signed his ball. And to thank me, he insisted on buying me a *teh tarik* first. Are the boys still inside?"

"Yeah, Spear, they're upstairs. I think they just did 'Jumping Jack Flash'."

"Hey, that's my song. I'd better get in there."

Danny dashed through the door. The doorman chuckled as he watched Danny jog down the long, purple corridor. He checked the street again. It was quiet and dull. It always was, even in Balestier. He took out a mobile phone from the inside pocket of his ill-fitting jacket. His chubby, chunky fingers dialled a number.

"Er, hello, ah, sorry to call so late," the doorman whispered. "Is that Billy Addis?"

 **eleven**

CHRIS stepped out of the lift and was confronted by a large framed print of David Beckham. It was signed "To the boys at Super Soccer, thanks for the interview, David Beckham". Chris was impressed. He glanced over at Danny and nodded towards the print.

"Yeah, I know. Looks good, right?" Danny said. "It was before my time. They interviewed him in Malaysia back in 2001 when he was there with Manchester United. The interview only lasted about two minutes and he wasn't that keen on signing the print, but it looks good in the foyer, doesn't it?"

"You certainly can't miss it as you walk in. It's almost life-sized, certainly impressed me."

That was indeed the first time he had been. When Danny first broached the subject of a guest slot on one of his shows, Chris had told him to piss off. He thought the shows were awful. Chris had never fully understood his father's admiration for Alan Hansen on *Match of the Day* back in England. He knew why he adored Trevor Brooking. That was obvious; he was his father's hero. But he never grasped the Hansen thing. Chris had seen enough footage of classic Liverpool matches to recognise Hansen's attributes as an unflappable defender, but he had always found him condescending and a touch smug as a TV pundit. He took it all back, however, once he arrived in Singapore. Compared to Danny and, even worse, Vince the Mincer, Hansen was Brian Glanville, Henry Winter, Stephen Fry and Ricky Gervais all rolled into one.

Danny just shouted. That was his only discernible gimmick. He was opinionated, dogmatic and clichéd. Chris once watched his show with the other Raffles Rangers boys after training and they mercilessly took the piss out of him. The Chinese boys had *makan* bets—dinner bets—on how often he repeated "at the end of the day" and "he wears his heart on his sleeve". They ridiculed Danny's ability to always conjure a relevant anecdote from his limited and patchy English football career. He always had a tale to tell about his days in the higher echelons of the EPL. Chris had stared at the coffee shop screen in disbelief. He had never heard of Danny and, more importantly, neither had his father. Tony Osborne took considerable pride in knowing most of the players and their basic attributes in the English Football League, let alone the Premier League, and he was embarrassed that one had slipped beneath his radar. He had asked all the lads in his Dagenham pub team and only one other player had heard of Danny Spearman, and that was because he had seen him on TV in a Bali beach bar.

In some ways, Chris had to admire Danny's capacity for bullshit. It was relentless. Through a story so convoluted it was difficult for even Chris to follow, Danny had claimed on air that through a friend of a friend at Sheffield Wednesday, he had suggested to Paolo Di Canio that a move to West Ham would almost certainly resurrect his career. Being just a skinny junior then, Chris had never really spoken to Di Canio at West Ham, but he was positive that Danny had spun a yarn on a TV show watched by millions of football nuts across Asia that simply wasn't true. But the big man not only got away with it, his popularity grew with every whopping story, and Danny obviously made more money from TV and his personal appearances in Malaysia, Thailand and Hong Kong than he did from Raffles Rangers. But if his Singaporean team-mates had not been taken in, why was the rest of Asia falling for the porky Pinocchio?

"I even had a beer with Becks," Danny said as they made their way down a corridor lined with signed framed prints of other famous football personalities.

"Really? How did that come about?"

"He was doing some promo thing in Tokyo, when he was at Real Madrid, and I was up there doing a piece for Super Soccer and we happened to be in the same bar and he'd seen my show while he was in Asia, so we got talking and had a couple of beers."

More bullshit. Come on now, Spear, Chris thought. Beckham seldom drinks, rarely hangs out in bars, if ever—particularly when his wife is with him, as she was during that promo trip in Tokyo—and he never invites washed-up footballers over to join him. Chris had actually met Beckham at some dodgy pre-season American tournament, when he flew over with the rest of the West Ham squad. Beckham played for the American All-Stars and had looked thoroughly bored and distracted. Chris never made it onto the pitch, but they shook hands when they posed for team photographs. Chris didn't have the heart to tell Danny. Danny wasn't merely a pathological liar, he appeared to be delusional. It wasn't just about sitting in front of a studio camera; he actually believed his own stories.

The studio itself was sparse and cheap. Chris noticed IKEA tags on the sofa and the cushions. There was a pair of sofas separated by a coffee table and an intricately-woven Persian rug. The rug was the only thing in the decorated studio of any discernible quality.

"Guess where we got the rug?" Danny asked, reading Chris' mind.

"I don't know, mate? IKEA? Like the rest of the furniture?"

"Nah. Adel."

Chris laughed.

"Adel? Our team manager Adel?"

"Yeah, he fitted all the studios out. There's an even bigger one on the floor of the *Sportsnight*'s studio. You can't even see the rug on camera, but Adel doesn't care. He gets his name on at the end of the credits."

"Isn't it embarrassing to have our S-League team manager selling his rugs at the end of every episode of *Sportsnight*?"

"We're bigger than the S-League, Chris. Who cares about the S-League in Hong Kong?"

Chris sat on a sofa opposite Danny as an attractive young Chinese girl attached a microphone to the collar of Chris' Raffles Rangers polo shirt. Another petite, pretty Malay girl dabbed his nose and forehead with powder. Chris smiled flirtatiously at both of them and wondered, not for the first time, if there were any unattractive women in Singapore.

"OK, as it's your first time, just follow my cues. It's easy. We've already gone through the weekend's tips together, right? So we'll say they're our tips, but I'll let you say them on air. The punters are sick of hearing my voice every week."

Chris glanced over at Danny.

"Yeah, sure, I don't mind. But I thought the tips were the highlight of your show?"

"They are, but I've also got to be honest, mate. No one is talking about me at the moment. They're only talking about you. It'll do well for our ratings in Singapore and you're almost as good-looking as me so we might start to pick up a few more in the rest of Asia.

"You want me to be on here regularly?"

"Depends how well you do tonight, doesn't it? … Hey, here's

the real star of the show."

Chris looked up and saw Vince the Mincer performing some complicated fist-bumping, twirling handshake right out of the Bronx with a bemused camera operator. He was wearing an XXL Canadian hockey shirt that reached past his knees.

"Hey, Spear, man. What's happening, bro?"

Vince's voice had tickled Chris at the Raffles Rangers fundraiser. This rapper sang in Singlish and spoke like an American, but he was a Singaporean-Indian who lived in a middle-class condo paid for by his doctor parents, and had never travelled further than Malaysia. Vince was an old friend of Danny's apparently, and had a habit of popping up after matches and training sessions. When he was in the mood, Chris found Vince's boy from the hood shtick entertaining.

"I'm all right, you old mincer," Danny shouted.

Chris giggled. *Ang mohs* always did when Danny called Vince an old mincer. Vince never understood the joke.

"Hey, if it ain't the greatest player Asian football has ever seen, man. How are you going, Chris?"

"Yeah, I'm fine, mate. You all right?"

Vince offered his hand to Chris and repeated his confusing, fist-pumping handshake. Chris held out his hand until Vince had finished molesting it, and then shook Vince's hand normally.

"With the three of us on air, together, bro, it's gonna be awesome, dude."

Chris cringed. No one said dude in Dagenham. No sane individual said dude in England. Vince jumped onto the sofa and edged towards Chris.

"I'm buzzing, mate, buzzing. Tonight's gonna be a good one," he muttered.

Chris examined Vince's hyperactive face. The rapper's eyes bulged.

"You've got some on your top lip," Chris whispered.

"What's that, bro?"

"You've still got some under your nose. You'd better wipe it off before you get your make-up done."

Vince quickly brushed his nose with his thumb and forefinger, and wiped his mouth and chin. Danny glanced up from his script.

"For fuck's sake, Vince, I told you about that," he hissed. "Don't do it before a show. You end up bouncing around the set like a fucking bag full of monkeys."

"No, man, it's OK. It'll be cool. It's gonna be a great show man."

THE Minister for Sports (Land and Water) stared at his 50-inch plasma screen in disbelief. He remembered that Indian idiot from the fundraiser, but even that farcical display didn't prepare him for this. Vince had said the unsaid word on air and on a betting tips show, for heaven's sake. The guy was clearly jittery from the outset, fidgeting on the sofa, distracting that Chris Osborne and annoying The Spear. When The Spear asked Vince for his thoughts on the Merseyside derby, Vince replied, "Don't care, man. I hate both teams." When The Spear made reference of Chris Osborne's early career at West Ham, Vince started waving his hands in the air singing "I'm Forever Blowing Bubbles". The show already made for excruciating viewing, but it reached its nadir when Vince broke the unwritten rule.

"How do you see our arch-rivals Orchard FC going this weekend, Vince?" Danny had asked.

"Hey, bro, that's a hard one to predict, man. I mean, the S-League's supposed to be *kelong*, right?"

Vince laughed. No one else in the studio did. In fact, the Minister for Sports (Land and Water) was certain he picked up a cameraman's nervous cough on his plasma speakers. Vince had crossed the line. There would have to be repercussions. Whether anyone actually believed the moron or not was irrelevant; too many people were watching. The Malaysians would have a field day, revelling in the welcome distraction away from their own failing national project. The M-League was hardly corruption-free. On the contrary, almost every major match-fixing scandal in English football over the last 15 years had a connection to a Malaysian syndicate somewhere along the line. When Bruce Grobbelaar allegedly took those bungs for a few soft goals, people north of the Causeway got rich. The Minister for Sports (Land and Water) had no doubts about it. But that was then, and right now this imbecile grinning goofily back at him from his plasma was going to cause him so many ministerial headaches.

The Minister's phone rang. He chuckled to himself. His oldest friend was as reliable as a Rolex. He sipped his cognac and picked up the phone.

"Hello."

"Did you see that idiot on TV?" the Minister for Home Improvement barked down the line.

"Yes, yes, I saw him. He's a moron. We both know that. You saw him at the Raffles fundraiser."

"But it's my team, isn't it?"

"What do you mean?"

"He said Orchard FC. I'm going to have to issue something to the constituents now."

"He never mentioned any team, lah. He was just talking cock about the S-League."

"That Spear was talking about Orchard's game this weekend, when that idiot made his *kelong* comments. It doesn't matter whether he was being specific, people will make the connection and it's guilt by association."

"Who are you playing this weekend anyway?"

"I don't know. That's not the point. The point is I've got to deal with the fallout for my club and you've got to deal with the fallout from the S-League. I'm only a damn patron of the club. I'd much rather be on the driving range than dealing with this nonsense."

The Minister for Sports (Land and Water) nodded. His old friend was right. He usually was. That's why he won all the school debates at Raffles Institution when they were kids. That's why he was Minister for Home Improvement and being fast-tracked. What sort of bloody portfolio was the Minister for Sports (Land and Water)? It was a few trips to the latest reservoir to watch some kayaking, the biennial junket to some godforsaken place for the Southeast Asian Games and the occasional trek to China to convince a few Chinese table tennis players on the fringes to swap flags at the next Olympics. Thanks to the foreign talent programme, the Minister for Sports (Land and Water) spent more time shaking foreign hands than he did Singaporean hands. At dinner parties, he still told the story of when he walked onto the Kallang pitch to greet the Singapore Lions before kick off and thought he was starring in a TV commercial for the United Colours of Benetton.

Foreign talent is the future. Foreign talent will preserve Singapore's future. If it were not for foreign talent, Singaporeans would still be selling homemade wooden animals from rickety old stalls. If it were not for foreign talent, the island would slowly choke—death by economic asphyxiation. There was no alternative. Foreign talent would be Singapore's salvation. It was the clarion call of the Cabinet. The Minister for Sports (Land and Water) had no issue with the reasoning when it came to his portfolio; half the table tennis players in sports-mad countries like Australia and New Zealand had Chinese names, but he had questioned the long-term benefits. At the end of their careers, would these foreign talents stay or quit? Of course, obese has-beens like The Spear would die on foreign soil. In Asia, he was a celebrity earning a respectable income. In England, he was a … well … no one was quite sure what The Spear was in England. But then, a player like Chris Osborne … what about Chris Osborne?

The Minister for Sports (Land and Water) smiled as the camera zoomed in on Chris' handsome face.

"Hey, are you still watching the show?"

"Of course. I've got to see what else the idiot says about my constituency's football club," the Minister for Home Improvement replied.

"He won't be allowed to say anything else now. You know that. Someone would've contacted the studio by now. But look at the TV."

"Yah, what? It's some *ang moh*."

"Yah, look at him. He's quite attractive, he's young, he's the top scorer in the S-League at the moment and Raffles Rangers' attendances have jumped by almost 2,000 just because of him."

"Are you serious? 2,000? Orchard don't even get 2,000 unless they play your boys."

"Yeah, I know. We averaged around 1,500 to 2,000, now we're getting well over 4,000. They had to put in extra plastic seats at Stamford Stadium. But that's not the most important thing. The most important thing is, he's got himself a nice, pretty local girlfriend."

"Someone famous? A Channel 8 actress?"

"No lah. I don't know who she is; it doesn't matter. The point is this guy seems to love it here. He's foreign, he's talented, he's got a local girlfriend, and Home Improvement are about to launch that new population drive … Do you need a diagram?"

"There could be something there, I suppose. A good-looking

ang moh poster boy. Maybe. I must admit something needs to be done quickly. Did you see that *TIME* magazine article? The *ang mohs* are staying, but no one is having any babies—local, foreign, no one. If I don't improve these birth rates, I might have to buy them myself from India."

"Hey, don't joke."

"But the timing's good. If he's keen, we might be able to use him. Hey, you're not just doing this because he plays for your team?"

"Are you serious? I was supposed to be having chilli crab at East Coast tonight. Now I've got to help draft another press release denying corruption in the S-League."

"Yeah, OK, OK. I'll fix something up."

"Do you need me to call up the club to get his contact details?"

"Please, lah. Don't insult me."

THE Scissor Sisters blared out through the speakers of Simon Jones' surround sound system. They didn't feel like dancing, but he did. It was Friday night and Simon really felt like dancing. The meeting with the Singapore Polo Club had been an unequivocal success. He had been a little apprehensive beforehand. With the economy tanking, not every expatriate was expected to ride out the recession in Singapore. Some would bail. Some would be kicked out. Either way, *X-Pat* was another Western expat's magazine in an already saturated media market and the core of its audience faced an uncertain financial future.

But *X-Pat* was unique. *X-Pat* was Simon Jones' magazine; it was his baby, the only baby he was ever likely to have, and he cherished his creation. Simon had made the rounds with *Fortune*, *The Peak* and *Prestige* in Singapore before coming to the sudden decision that if he interviewed one more CEO, spa owner, head chef, diamond merchant or British or Irish pub owner, he would kill someone. Five years in Singapore and he had interviewed only a handful of Singaporeans. He had money, but still wanted to discover the authentic Singapore. Surely there were other Western expats who shared his ambition?

X-Pat tested that theory—a media experiment to discover whether those wealthy American CEOs really did prefer hawker food to five-star restaurants, or were merely pandering to *The Newspaper*'s local readers. The experiment paid off handsomely. Within a year, *X-Pat* became the most popular expatriate magazine in Singapore. Within two years, it had branched into Southeast Asia, and eventually grew into the most well-read magazine among all PMEBs in Singapore—local and foreign—an achievement that exceeded even Simon's most optimistic expectations.

The magazine featured articles on the top 10 hawker centres in Singapore, the best local dish for less than five bucks and even a controversial article claiming local schools offered a better education than overpriced international schools. Dumbfounded Singaporean writers (particularly those working for rival publications experiencing a drop in sales) dismissed *X-Pat*'s attempts to cover all its bases by appealing to the lowest common denominator, but they were missing the point. Simon knew that his readers wanted a little taste of the street, nothing more—a frisson of Asian exotica on a Friday night before returning to the safety of their condos hidden behind palm trees and security posts. A three-dollar plate of chicken rice at one of the grottier hawker centres in Chinatown would give them something to tell the relatives and provide adventurous photographs for their Facebook pages, or something to Twitter about. *X-Pat* readers bought the magazine, followed its sanitised guide for a brief walk on the wild side and then laughed about their down and dirty experiences later around the condo swimming pool. It wasn't quite poverty tourism, as Singapore had few people left in genuine squalor (apart from construction workers from the subcontinent and they didn't really count), but it appealed to the same senses. And Simon cashed in.

In the juiciest of ironies, the blue-chip companies soon came knocking on Simon's door to advertise their latest timepieces and handbags alongside articles on the cheapest night markets in the Singaporean heartlands. Simon knew his lifestyle made him a hypocrite, so he overcompensated by revelling in the hypocrisy of others. The Singapore Polo Club had practically begged him for a four-page advertorial on the upcoming Rolex Cup. He agreed and immediately thought of placing such elitist nonsense alongside a piece he had commissioned on the tastiest pork rib soup in nearby Balestier Road.

Simon danced around his living room rug to the Scissor Sisters. The apartment was very Zen and minimalist—all-white walls and floors and open-planned, complete with an island bench in the kitchen. Simon loved his East Coast apartment and the expansive sea views. He loved it even more when his wife was out. She was having dinner with some friends at the Lucky Plaza food court. Simon had done his bit for society (and pacified his old mother living in a seaside bungalow in Brighton) by hooking up with a local woman, but marrying his Filipino maid made him such a tedious cliché. They did make each other laugh, and she loved him in a protective, maternal way and he sort of loved her in a brother-sister way. But it was more of a convenience and it was convenient for them to do their own thing on Friday nights. She spent her evenings gossiping in Tagalog at Lucky Plaza followed by a few drinks at a KTV lounge and supper at Newton Circus, while Simon had a night in with the chaps.

He picked up a couple of remote controls, turned down the CD player and switched his TV on. He fiddled with the cable TV remote control until he found the Super Soccer channel. Simon had a soft spot for Brighton and Hove Albion—because of his mother—but otherwise had little time for football. Still, some of the chaps might want the channel on later in the evening and Simon needed to call Vince once his tacky show had ended.

Simon poured himself a glass of red wine and glanced up at the TV. That ghastly fat footballer was ranting about a Singaporean referee's decision. Only in Singapore, Simon thought. He sipped the wine as Chris Osborne's head and shoulders suddenly filled most of the 42 inches of his TV screen. Simon sat up and stared at it.

"I don't think it's fair to blame Wee Kin. Strikers make the odd mistake, too. We're only human and Wee Kin will probably bang in a hat-trick this weekend," Simon heard the blond, tanned footballer say. He had no idea what he was going on about, but he couldn't take his eyes off the screen.

"So you think there's life in the partnership yet, then?" the fat one said.

"Of course there is. Wee Kin is one of the best strikers in the S-League with plenty of international experience. I mean, he's played for Singapore selection sides against Manchester United and Liverpool. I certainly can't say I've done that," the blond one replied.

"You must have played against those sides when you were at West Ham."

"Yeah, but only in the reserves. That's not the same. Wee Kin has scored against some of the world's top sides in front of 70,000 at Kallang, so I would never question his pedigree or his experience. He helped me settle when I first arrived and he's a top striker. You've got to remember, Spear, he's still the second highest goal-scorer in the S-League."

"Yeah, behind you."

"Well, I didn't want to say."

Simon gazed at the blond guy as he laughed with the fat bloke on screen. Still staring at the screen, he grabbed his mobile phone and started dialling.

"Hello Vince, it's Simon. I know you're probably still in the studio, although I didn't see you on the show tonight, but I've got to ask you a couple of things."

Simon sniggered at his own voice echoing down the phone line. He was talking so fast.

"First, I think we'll need twice as much as usual tonight. I know it's a bit short notice, but there's a few more people coming to my little party tonight. Don't worry about the money; the Rolex Cup is paying for this party. I'll tell you all about it later. But the other thing I wanted to ask is, who was that other *ang moh* footballer on your show? Not the fat host, the other one. He could be a possible cover for *X-Pat* magazine, maybe you could help me set that up. And Vince, you have got to invite him to one of my parties."

twelve

THE sports desk was almost deserted. The last page had been sent off an hour ago and Billy sat alone at his cubicle. His desk was covered in old newspaper clippings and printouts of online articles. He picked up the article on the top of the pile and stared at the headline. It read: LIGHTS GO OUT ON ENGLISH FOOTBALL. Billy smiled, dropped the article down and stretched his legs under the desk. He rubbed his face and rested his head on the palm of his hands and glanced at his laptop. The screen made him sleepy. He reached across the desk and grabbed another article. His byline was beside Danny Spearman's headshot. The headline read: SPEAR HAPPY TO HELP CPIB.

But Billy wasn't happy. He had painstakingly searched every article in *The Newspaper*'s database that contained CPIB, in both headlines and text, and every other story led to the same, inevitable conclusion—S-League footballers, whether they were local or foreign, always ended up in a courtroom if they had been called up to help the CPIB with their anti-corruption enquiries. Why was The Spear so lucky?

Billy rummaged through all the papers on his desk, until he found a scrap of paper with a number on it. He picked up the phone and looked up at the clock on the wall. 1.15 a.m. He'd still be working.

"Ah, hello, it's Billy Addis again. Are you still on the door? Can you still talk? Oh, great because I just wanted to check something," Billy said, reaching for his notepad. "I'll see you at the coffee shop at about 2.30 a.m. I'll buy you a *kopi*."

BILLY watched an old Malay guy sitting at a table across the coffee shop reading his article on Poh Wee Kin's dramatic loss of form. Billy was always pleased to see someone, anyone, reading his articles because it meant they were taking a token interest in the S-League. It gave him hope. The coffee shop had the usual post 2 a.m. crowd—some Indian cleaners having breakfast before going to work and a couple of KTV girls having supper with clients from the lounge across the road. The coffee shop wasn't packed. There was no English Premier League or Champions League match to watch.

Billy tried to avoid supper after work at coffee shops screening live matches. One or two of the punters always recognised him from his photo byline and usually expected him to get his crystal ball out and predict the score. When he first arrived, Billy had given a tip on a Man United-Chelsea game to a drunken Chinese guy with a tattoo on his neck. The tip was just his gut feel; it wasn't based on any research or team news, and Billy wasn't even close. After the game, the Chinese guy had called him a "fucking *gwai lo*". Even then, Billy was familiar with the derogatory Cantonese term for 'white ghost'. Billy never forgot the name because he liked it. He fancied himself as the investigative journalist lurking in the S-League's shadows, meeting seedy doormen at dimly-lit coffee shops and hunting down the secret members of the *kelong* clan. The "fucking *gwai lo*" will never be stopped so lock up your betting spreadsheets and hide your bookies' runners. The white ghost is coming.

The doorman from the Balestier KTV lounge took a seat

opposite Billy at the table and glanced over both shoulders.

"What can I get you to drink, mate?" Billy asked.

"*Kopi-o*," the doorman mumbled.

"Sure. Uncle, *kopi-o* and one more *teh tarik*, can? Thanks, ah."

"Your accent not bad, eh," the doorman said brightly, obviously impressed. "Quite Singlish already."

"When you speak to S-League footballers all day, if cannot speak a little Singlish, sure die one."

The doorman laughed.

"You'll be OK lah, *ang moh*. You married?"

"No."

"Got girlfriend?"

Billy shifted uneasily in his seat.

"Er, no."

"Wah, handsome *ang moh* like you. You should come and sing karaoke. The girls in my bar will definitely like you."

"It's OK, really."

The two men smiled at each other as a middle-aged Malay guy banged their drinks down and took the money that Billy had placed on the table. He counted out some coins from his bum bag, dropped them on the table and walked off. Billy watched him return to his counter and then leaned across the table.

"So you're absolutely sure Danny is involved with some loan shark," Billy whispered.

"Ya, Tiger lah. He's not really an *Ah Long* now, he makes too much from football."

"Why is he called Tiger?"

"Ha, depends who you talk to lah. Tiger always says it's because he drinks too much beer, but he hardly ever drinks. Some say it's because he's fierce like a Tiger, but that's childish. I heard it goes back to his gang days last time. When he was a young *Ah*

Beng, you know, like a local gangster, he would cut people several times on their arms if they owed money. Cut like tiger stripes. So Tiger lah. But who knows. In Singapore, everything's called Tiger—beer, airline, cream for piles—so might as well call the top gangster Tiger, right?"

"And he's involved with match-fixing?"

"Not always. In Singapore, can make enough just from outside betting. Fix for what? But Tiger must be *kelong* sometimes, lah."

"How do you know?"

"He never loses."

Billy sipped his *teh tarik* and stared at the darkened KTV lounge across the road.

"And you saw him push Danny around over there?" Billy said, pointing his mug towards the KTV lounge.

"I didn't have to see. Danny had some bullshit story about signing Tiger's football for his son and came back sweaty with his shirt all messy. Tiger doesn't even have a son. He's got a daughter at uni. She's studying to become a lawyer. Unbelievable, right? Her fees are paid by illegal gamblers."

"Bloody hell, he must have a lot of guys working for him."

"I only see him with one other guy. Skinny Chinese called Ah Lian."

"*Ah Lian*? Isn't that a girl? Like a female chav?"

"A what?"

"You know, er, like a loudmouth, hangs out on street corners."

"Ya lah, Ah Lian. But Tiger calls him that because he's small and skinny and looks like a girl. No, Tiger works for one of the big gangs, probably from Malaysia."

"Like a betting syndicate?"

"I don't know what that is, but ya lah, one of the *kelong* gangs."

"What's *kelong*? What are they fixing?"

"Everything, man. I told you. Did you read up on the floodlight thing?"

"Well, there were a few. They reckon there was a floodlight failure at Upton Park back in 1997, I remember that one. Another one at Wimbledon when they played Arsenal in the same year. But the most famous case was in 1999, that Malaysian betting syndicate. They planned to sabotage the floodlights at Charlton's match against Liverpool. It was pretty elaborate. They supposedly had remote control units to control the floodlights and a Charlton security guard said in court that Malaysians had tried to bribe him. It was mad. Even the Asian Football Confederation said that Malaysian gambling syndicates were targeting British football. It was unbelievable. I never knew they got so far, that they penetrated so deep. It's crazy. Malaysians screwing up floodlights at an English football match."

The doorman smiled as he peered into his cup.

"They were not all Malaysian," he muttered.

Billy laughed.

"Nah, I'm not having it. That Tiger guy was involved in fixing an English Premier League match with Liverpool? A guy who loiters around Balestier KTV lounges and threatens washed-up footballers. You said so yourself, he's got just one guy with him. Some skinny kid who looks like a little girl. Now you're telling me he has the power to fix the floodlights at an EPL game?"

"Not him, but the people he works for, his boss maybe, I don't know. But his gang was definitely involved in that floodlight thing lah."

"How do you know?"

"He told me about it before it happened."

Billy glanced at the doorman. His forehead was damp and his thick neck was perspiring, but then he was wearing a monkey suit at 2.30 a.m. in Singapore. He was clearly agitated, but that didn't necessarily mean he was lying.

"You've known Tiger since 1999 then?" Billy asked, examining the doorman's face.

"Longer, man. When you work on the door, you always meet these people. Taxi drivers who act like pimps, loan sharks, *Ah Beng* gangsters, pissed karaoke singers. I have to work with all these people and so does Tiger."

"Why?"

"Because they all fucking gamble lah."

The doorman's face briefly flushed with anger and the sides of his neck reddened. Billy saw an opportunity.

"Why would he tell you about the floodlights thing? It's a bit risky, right?"

"He didn't tell me exactly lah. He was really drunk in a massage parlour I used to work in at Joo Chiat last time. He was upset that some Liverpool match had lost him money and was shouting about how Liverpool would be fixed at Charlton. He was piss drunk and showing off in front of some girl, trying to get a free hand job. I heard him tell her, lah. And then when I saw it on TV, I was damn shocked, man."

Billy stared at the doorman.

"Why are you telling me all this?"

"Because this fucking asshole has got to be stopped."

"I'm only a journalist. I'm not a policeman."

"Ya lah, but if you write the story about Danny, everything will go public and Tiger will have to be questioned by the CPIB."

"Why do you care?"

"Why do you think? Because I gamble lah. It's always about fucking gambling."

THE Minister for Home Improvement had good reason to feel very pleased with himself. His office had tracked down Chris Osborne's mobile phone number in a matter of seconds and, according to one of his minions, the brief conversation had gone better than expected. Chris had expressed some surprise that the Ministry had managed to contact him directly so quickly—he had grown up in England after all—but soon understood that this was the Singapore way. If the Ministry needs a phone number, it gets it. He was flattered that the Ministry was taking an interest in his fledgling S-League career before the season had even ended and he would be honoured to meet the Minister for Home Improvement for lunch. He damn well should be, the Minister thought. His time was precious and lunch appointments were usually reserved for his family, superior ministers or racing certainties. Chris Osborne had the makings of a racing certainty. That was the only reason for the invitation. No lunch was free in Singapore.

The restaurant was busy, but not packed, just the way the Minister for Home Improvement preferred it. Five-star elitist establishments had too many fawning waiters and not enough customers, and the lack of ambience always made the conversation stilted and uneasy. The latest, trendy restaurants were definitely out of the question because they usually had too many noisy sheep queuing outside to get in and sample the latest culinary fad. Staff ushered patrons out of the door as soon as they had gobbled down their last mouthful and the image was unsightly.

That's why the Minister always asked his staff to book a table at Melt. The Mandarin Oriental hotel crowd usually consisted of high-end tourists—which meant they were manageable—and local businessmen entertaining clients so their corporate talk was hushed and discreet. Best of all, Melt was a world café so even the fussiest of *ang moh* eaters could be catered for with kebabs or a curry, and the Minister simply adored the chocolate fountain.

Chris smiled when the waiter told him he was a big fan as he ushered Chris towards the Minister's table. The waiter had probably never watched an S-League match or a game involving Singapore players since the Malaysia Cup days, but he was an avid viewer of *The Spear's Betting Tips* show. They always were.

The Minister stood and shook Chris' hand firmly. He always sat facing the restaurant's entrance so he could monitor patrons as they came and went—force of habit—and he had followed the footballer across the room. Chris Osborne walked with an upright, but slightly casual swagger typical of many Westerners in this part of the world. The fancy footballer was confident. That was good. That would come through on the posters and the ad campaigns. But arrogance could not work. Arrogant *ang mohs* antagonised the masses in the heartlands. The foreign talent debate was always a contentious and potentially divisive issue, particularly during times of economic downturn. Singaporeans did not take kindly to highly-paid white faces beaming down at them from bus stop posters in government campaigns when there was talk of job cuts and rising unemployment. Confidence was necessary, but arrogance was inflammatory. The Minister had to determine if this kid from London was willing to walk the line.

"Come, Chris, sit down," the Minister boomed. "I'm surprised there wasn't a line of fans following you into the restaurant."

Chris smiled, but failed to hide his embarrassment.

"No, it's nothing like that, really."

"No need to be so modest, Chris. You have almost single-handedly revitalised a struggling league. Raffles Rangers' attendances are going through the roof and the whole of Asia is watching you on the Super Soccer channel."

"No, it's not like that. I'm just desperate to get my career back on track, you know. Things didn't work out for me at West Ham, or even in Melbourne, and I'm just grateful to the S-League for giving me the chance."

The Home Improvement Ministry could really do something with this guy. Permanent residency status and then the chance to play international football with Singapore were both a given, but the Minister realised that Chris Osborne had so much more to offer. The Minister had sat through every tedious Cabinet meeting about declining birth rates and the ageing population. He had also heard the faint thud of distant alarm bells during the confidential meetings about GDP and unemployment projections for the next couple of years. There was no room left for belts to be tightened—to borrow one of the Cabinet's favourite phrases— and some voters were going to be suffocated. But the economy depended on increased foreign labour, both skilled and unskilled, for its survival.

He had also read the most controversial paper of all. If Singaporeans were not willing to have enough babies to cover the shortfall, then too bad, foreigners could inflate the numbers. What happened then if foreigners outweighed Singaporeans? The impact upon the social fabric might be devastating. Not to mention the potential for political upheaval. Foreigners who appreciated Singapore's security, low taxes and education system didn't always have the vote. Singaporeans who had no more notches left on their belts did. Everyone in the Cabinet knew the reality, but no one in the Cabinet had a solution and that irritated the Minister. He had a deserved reputation for being the government's problem solver, but he had struggled on this issue. What was needed was a unifying distraction, something that could serve as an emollient during the recession. The Minister for Home Improvement thought the answer might be eating a kebab in front of him.

"Where do you see yourself three years from now, Chris?" he asked.

"Wow, I don't know, really. Footballers tend to live pretty much day to day, or from match to match. Most people use a calendar. I use a fixture list. I get one at the start of every season and write all my family and friends' birthdays on it. I think the last real calendar I had was a Spice Girls one when I was a kid."

The Minister chuckled. This boy was almost too good to be true. He was self-effacing, self-deprecating and, most importantly for face-saving Singaporeans, he was humble.

"I only ask because I think even you must have noticed that no footballer since Fandi Ahmad has captured the public's imagination quite like you have."

"Well, I don't know about that."

"No, I really don't think you do. The coverage the S-League gets now isn't the norm. It's always been a single column story or a brief in the newspapers. Or just a score line at the end of the TV news. Singaporeans love football. It's the national game. They just don't really love Singapore football and you'll find it's mostly the same across Southeast Asia. Ask anyone about football in this part of the world, and they'll tell you about Liverpool or Manchester United. Go to Liverpool or Manchester and ask anyone there about Southeast Asian football and they'll tell you it's all corrupt. But you are helping to change that perception. We've got kids watching local football again, thanks to you."

"Yeah, that's great."

"It certainly is."

The Minister for Home Improvement sipped his tea and gazed at Chris.

"And I'm sure you know by now Chris that we have a vibrant foreign talent sports scheme. We are a small country so we try to attract sportsmen and sportswomen to settle in Singapore and take advantage of opportunities they may not get elsewhere."

"Yeah, I know about that. We've had one or two African lads come down for trials at Raffles, but they didn't work out."

"Er, yes, exactly. Whether it's business, finance, education, health or sports, Singapore's success is built on integrating local knowledge with foreign experience and skills. And we'd love you to be a part of it."

Chris was careful to pause. He had guessed that the politician would get round to this eventually—he hadn't been invited to lunch because the guy was a West Ham fan—and he needed to choose his words carefully. Chris had not been lying when he expressed his gratitude towards the S-League. He lived like a king in Singapore and although he wasn't sure if he loved Yati yet, he certainly loved the sex. But he didn't fancy being the next Danny Spearman 10 years from now either, sitting in a TV studio and bullshitting about a West Ham career he never really had.

"I suppose I'd like to help you guys if I can," he said slowly. "I feel I owe the S-League something, definitely."

"Do you feel like you owe Singapore anything?"

"How do you mean?"

"Well, you said you owe the S-League. Do you feel you owe Singapore something? Is Singapore a country where you might want to set up home with your Singaporean girlfriend? I've heard she's beautiful. Imagine the children you might have one day."

Chris pushed his kebab around the plate. He had never told this guy about Yati.

"I certainly like Singapore. It's a wonderful country to live and work in."

Perfect, just perfect, The Minister for Home Improvement thought. The kid's even trained in sound bites.

"Yes it is. To live, work, raise a family. Everything really."

"Yeah, I'm sure it is. No doubt about it."

"So if you do believe this is a country worth staying in, how would you feel about playing for Singapore one day?"

Chris looked up and laughed. He couldn't help himself.

"Just like that?"

"Just like that."

"But don't I need to be, like, a citizen or something?"

"You do, Chris, you most certainly do."

"And how would that happen?"

"Well, you'd have to apply to the Home Improvement Ministry first."

"And they could make it happen?"

"I could make it happen."

 **thirteen**

YATI despised S-League matches. Quite frankly, they were beneath her. She spent her working life interviewing theatre directors, movie icons and genuine rock-and-rollers. On Friday morning, she had listened to Noel Gallagher berate those rock stars who thought that their albums and gigs made a real contribution to saving the planet. Yati only had a 10-minute phoner, yet Gallagher still found the time to work his way through the perilous state of the current music scene, *American Idol*, North Korea and the correlation between his brother Liam's hairline and the band's success. Yati was flying when she got off the phone, genuinely buzzing. She had dreamt of interviewing bands like Oasis when she ploughed through those dull media textbooks night after night. Days like this reminded her why she became a journalist. And then Chris called and invited her to an S-League match at the weekend. Even on the phone, Yati struggled to contain her indifference. She liked Chris and loved showing him off at parties and magazine launches. But he was still only an S-League footballer.

Yati shuffled past a row of sweaty legs in the VIP box of Stamford Stadium. Some VIP box. It was nothing more than a few rows of pale blue plastic bucket seats shoved in the middle of a grey, featureless concrete stand. Most of the so-called VIPs came dressed in shorts, singlets and flip-flops, examined betting slips and, in that awful, awful Singlish, rambled on about how many goals were expected. Yati found her seat beside Billy Addis and as she sat down she heard a voice from behind mutter, "Hey, that Chris Osborne a lucky boy, eh."

Yati turned quickly.

"Fuck off," she said to no one in particular.

"Hey, you can't say that," Billy whispered, gently holding her shoulders and turning her round. "If they know you work for *The Newspaper*, they'll definitely write in to the editor."

"I fucking hate it here," she hissed.

"Well, that's what your boyfriend does. He's an S-League footballer. At least he's a good one."

"That doesn't mean much to me."

"It could be worse you know."

"How?"

"Your boyfriend could be an S-League reporter instead."

Yati laughed. She enjoyed Billy's company and not just because he was white, even if that was the reason why she had initially sought him out during a reporter's induction course at the office. He was smart, funny and well-travelled; he was all of the things that she would've been had she been born in the West.

"If he was a reporter at least I might see him once in a while for dinner or a drink. Chris is obsessed with his career, always training. Even in the evenings, he's stretched out on the living room floor doing push-ups."

"But that's why he has a fancy condo near Orchard Road and I have a small HDB flat in Toa Payoh."

Yati's beautiful brown eyes stared at Billy.

"I suppose so, but size isn't always everything."

She was flirting on auto-pilot. She couldn't help herself.

"Come on now, behave yourself. If anyone here heard you

talking like that, they'd hang me from the floodlights."

Yati laughed and took a sip from her Polar water bottle. Billy watched her. The idiot sitting behind was right. Chris Osborne really was a lucky bastard.

"Excuse me, are you Billy Addis?"

Billy looked up to see a slim Caucasian guy in his early 40s grinning back at him. He was not particularly handsome, but he was neat and his clothes were clearly not bought in a Toa Payoh night market.

"Yeah, I am, mate, yeah."

"Great, thought you were, recognised you from your photo byline. My name's Simon Jones. I'm the editor of *X-Pat* magazine. You might have seen it in the shops."

"Ah yeah, yeah, I've read it. It's really popular. Where to buy the best *roti prata* and all that sort of thing, right?"

"That's the one."

"Great, well, do you want to come and join us?"

"If you wouldn't mind."

Simon nodded to Yati as he passed her slender legs and sat on the other side of Billy.

"I've actually been meaning to speak to you for a few weeks now."

"Oh, really. What's up?"

"I noticed in the paper that you're the regular S-League correspondent."

Billy looked at Yati and laughed.

"I'm probably the only S-League correspondent. Or at least I was until Chris Osborne came along. Now we've got everyone from *Her World* to *Men's Health* magazine coming down to do interviews with him."

Simon blushed and fiddled with the cord on his khaki Ralph Lauren shorts.

"This is rather embarrassing," he muttered.

"Ha, you want to interview him, too?"

"Cover story actually. He's a young, good-looking expat who appeals to locals and foreigners, men and women. It's a no-brainer really."

"Yeah, I suppose so."

"So I was kind of hoping you'd introduce us after the game."

"Yeah, that's no problem, mate. Although she's the best person to speak to."

Billy gestured towards Yati. Simon leaned forward and smiled at Yati.

"Ah, are you a journalist too?" Simon asked.

"She's more than that, Simon. She's Chris' missus."

Yati glared at Billy.

"Are you really? That's just wonderful," Simon gushed, unable to hide his excitement. "We could do a great story on the pair of you."

"No, I think you'd better just focus on Chris," Yati said. "I don't think *The Newspaper* would like it very much if I was splashed all over *X-Pat* magazine."

"Sure, sure, I completely understand. My lips are sealed," Simon said, theatrically waving his hand in the air before bringing it over his mouth. "But I'd really love to have a one-on-one with Chris though."

Yeah, I bet you would, Billy thought.

"OK, then, I'll set you two up after the game," Billy said. "Sadly, I'm actually here to do some work so I'd better shut up and concentrate because the players are coming out now."

"No, I completely understand," Simon replied. "I'm eager to watch the game, too. It'll give me an idea of what kind of player Chris Osborne is."

"A bloody good one," Billy whispered.

The Raffles Rangers players ran out onto the pitch and the roar from the capacity crowd impressed even the cynical Billy.

"He really has transformed this place," Billy muttered, glancing over both shoulders.

Chris looked up at the VIP box, spotted Yati and enthusiastically waved at her. She half-heartedly waved back. There were enough dirty old men leering at her in this wretched alpha-male fortress. She was not overly keen on drawing any further attention to herself. Both Billy and Simon noticed her reluctance to wave back at Chris and they both smiled. They were going to enjoy this game.

MICHAEL Nielsen still laughed about his brief, ill-advised stint as coach of the Singapore Under-23 side for the Southeast Asian Games, where he was forced to hold training sessions in a car park. He would never forget his time in the M-League, where a rival Malaysian coach politely asked him to go easy in a fixture so he could pay off a persistent loan shark. Michael reported the coach, but his players still lost the game. Michael later realised he made the mistake of telling his players about the bribery attempt before the game. M-League players were not paid particularly well. When he moved back south to the S-League, he struggled with the empty stadiums, the general apathy towards the local game and the gambling obsession that permeated every level of his beloved sport. But he got on with the task of turning Raffles Rangers into one of the most competent, attractive football sides in the region. The banter, the training sessions, the youth clinics and the productive supper nights with his senior players at Newton Circus all helped to keep him focused on his task, and allowed him to ignore the fact that his team manager was a Persian rug salesman. When your team manager left suddenly in the middle of a half-time team talk to meet a banking CEO to discuss rug colour schemes for a Nassim Road property, then you could be fairly sure that you'd seen everything that the game had to offer. Nothing could faze Michael now. Nothing could surprise him.

Until the humblest, quietest footballer in his squad got sent off for breaking a defender's jaw.

Poh Wee Kin walked slowly towards the dugout and burst into tears. He stopped in front of Michael and wiped his eyes.

"I'm so sorry, boss," he whimpered.

Michael felt the glare of 5,000 pairs of eyes boring into his back. He heard the booing echo around the stadium and glanced up at the VIP box. The coach picked out Billy Addis beside Chris' journo girlfriend, but he was the least of his worries. The Minister for Sports (Land and Water) was sitting beside Mr Teck. They looked horrified. The S-League was going to make the front pages now. Michael leaned towards Wee Kin's ear.

"Can you hear that? We've got a full house here and you do that? What the hell is wrong with you?"

"I'm sorry, boss. I'm just so, so sorry," Wee Kin sobbed.

Press photographers crowded around the front of the dugout to provide their picture desk editors with the kind of shots they could only dream about. Singapore's leading goal-scorer—the only Singaporean to score against an English Premier league side in an exhibition match—crying like a baby in front of 5,000 screaming fans. Half-empty water bottles bounced off the roof of the dugout and onto the touchline. A curry puff hit the distraught Wee Kin in the chest. Michael picked up the curry puff and hurled it into the dugout, before glaring towards the general direction of the culprit to register his disgust. The referee blew his whistle and stopped the game to again order Wee Kin down the tunnel to prevent a riot.

"Look, stop crying like a little girl and fuck off into the

dressing room," Michael barked.

"I'm sorry, boss. I'm really, really sorry."

"Yeah, me too. What the hell happened to you?"

Poh Wee Kin had never wanted to play the game in the first place. His erratic form had been a concern for some time and it was no longer being attributed to the electric form of Chris Osborne. The *ang moh*'s explosive arrival had papered over the cracks temporarily, but even The Spear was having difficulty sidestepping the issue on his TV show now. There was an upcoming Asian World Cup qualifier for Singapore and there was some speculation that Wee Kin, the most experienced striker in the squad, might be forced to start on the bench. For possibly the first time this season, journalists were up in the press box with an angle on the deteriorating form of a Singaporean, rather than an Englishman's latest goal spree.

There had been dips in form before. All strikers experienced peaks and troughs; it was as cyclical as it was fickle. Wee Kin had gone 10 games without a goal, but Chris had scored in most of those games thanks to assists from Wee Kin. That was what Michael Nielson told the media anyway, but both player and coach knew that something was awry. In a private chat in his cluttered office, Michael had attributed the goal drought to the overwhelming presence of a former West Ham United strike partner. To stop Michael from digging any further, Wee Kin nodded in agreement, but was extremely insulted by the half-baked, patronising psychology. Wee Kin had taken on, and beaten, defenders from Japan, South Korea and every major footballing nation in the Middle East in Asian Cup and World Cup qualifiers. Chris was a genuine guy and a terrific footballer in the S-League, but he was hardly Fernando Torres. The crisis had nothing to do with Chris.

Ironically, there had been whispers that Wee Kin had been

approached. The CPIB had issued a standard "no comment" when asked by Billy Addis if officers were concerned by Wee Kin's sudden loss of form. Ordinarily, Wee Kin would have laughed. He could count on one hand the players he knew who were categorically straight and he was one of them. He never gambled. There was no heartrending story about an abusive, gambling father or a childhood home wrecked by loan sharks. Wee Kin just didn't gamble.

He liked to always be in control and gambling just never appealed to his sensibilities. That was why his current predicament really grated. Wee Kin was a self-confessed control freak, but that woman pulled his every string. She had called him earlier in the morning, insisting on $5,000 or she would make the call. Wee Kin had said he was past caring. She chuckled down the line and calmly told Wee Kin to remember that she had male friends—many male friends—from all walks of Singapore life who were always willing to do her a favour. Wee Kin could expect a warning during the game itself, on the pitch, to prove that she was not bluffing about her threat to go public. He had laughed and slammed the phone down.

Shortly after half-time, the threat was delivered. A young defender from China, whom Wee Kin vaguely recognised, chopped him down from behind and happily accepted the yellow card from the referee. He helped Wee Kin to his feet and, in Mandarin, whispered, "Tell me something, Singapore superstar. Do you think about your wife when you fuck the KTV hostess on video?"

Without thinking, Wee Kin swung around and shattered the defender's jaw with a right hook.

"Oh my god! Did you see that? Oh my god!" Simon exclaimed, grabbing Billy's arm. "Did you see that?"

"I saw it, mate. I saw it. I'm already making space on the front page for it," Billy replied, dialling his mobile phone.

"It's just terrible," Yati whispered. "Look at the guy's face. It's covered with blood. He doesn't even know where he is."

"Look, they're getting a stretcher for him now," Simon shouted over the booing and jeering. "I wonder what will happen to the chap who got sent off."

"He's finished," Billy whispered.

The spectators in the VIP box mostly stood, craning their heads to find a less restricted view of the fallout. S-League officials, always easy to spot in their formal trousers and long-sleeved shirts, stood silently with their hands on their hips watching the nightmare unfold on the pitch. A couple of guys in shorts and singlets jeered a weeping Wee Kin as Danny Spearman, dressed in a club tracksuit, guided him towards the tunnel. At the back of the VIP box, a scrawny Chinese guy in his mid-twenties stood on top of a plastic seat and screamed abuse in a mixture of English, Chinese and Hokkien at Wee Kin. His skimpy white singlet showed off a tattoo of a dragon on his left shoulder and a number of prominent scars on both arms. Several spectators in the VIP box had moved away from him. There was only one other guy left in his row of seats, but he was obscured by the standing spectators.

"You're finished Wee Kin," the skinny man shouted. "Your career is over, man."

The guy sitting beside him tugged at the top of his shorts and pointed towards the seat.

"Hey, you forget where you are, is it? Sit down lah," he shouted over the din of the heckling crowd.

"Come on ah, Tiger, did you see or not? That Wee Kin is crazy, man."

"Sit down now."

The skinny man smirked, but he did as he was told. Tiger

grabbed his arm tightly.

"You see. You behave like an *Ah Lian*, and I will call you Ah Lian. Remember where you are, idiot. He just fucked everything up and now I got to fix it. And you're jumping around like an *ang moh* hooligan."

"Hey, relax, lah. It's OK, what."

"Balls to you, OK. This is serious. Now get your phone."

TIGER zigzagged his way carefully through Thomson Road. The traffic was congested at the best of times, being so close to the PIE and the CTE, the two major highways that linked the four corners of the island. But a Saturday evening brought out families heading for the latest trendy eating spots and shoppers returning home in the opposite direction. Tiger was an accomplished driver. Most Singaporean drivers had to be to deal with the incessant traffic, the constant lane-changing and aggressive overtaking. Tiger was one of the few drivers who bothered to signal before changing lanes. He always indicated, even if no one else did, and stayed within the speed limit. His occupation made him the most courteous of drivers. Loan sharks and bookies' runners would never want to be pulled over or involved in an accident. They never knew what they might be carrying in their cars at the time.

Tiger turned into Balestier Road and cursed. This area used to be his old stomping ground. When he was a young *Ah Beng* gangster, he ruled the estates from Toa Payoh to Orchard and everywhere in between. Balestier, Serangoon, Potong Pasir, Novena and even into the newer condos of Newton, he controlled them all. His best business came from the top-end condos around Newton and Orchard. Every new development brought another 100 construction workers from the subcontinent. Their foremen paid them peanuts, and yet the monkeys couldn't keep either their wallets or their dicks in their trousers. Singapore was one of the Tiger economies in the mid-1990s and Tiger cleaned up on the back of the construction boom. When the Asian currency crisis hit in 1997, almost every major industry, including construction, hit the skids. Except money-lending. Unemployed construction workers needed Tiger's money more than ever before. In less than two years, Tiger had taken care of his mortgage, bought a small two-bedroom house in Perth which he rented out only to Singaporean-Chinese university students (they rarely got drunk and always paid the rent on time) and put aside enough money to pay for his daughter's education all the way through to her master's degree.

Since then, he outsourced the manual labour and focused only on lucrative, long-term projects. He was a business leader, working closely with like-minded successful business leaders in other Asian cities. This shit was beneath him. Tiger left the mundane, day-to-day stuff behind years ago. Ordinarily, he would have delegated this nonsense to Ah Lian, but he was still breaking him in and besides, this particular house visit was personal.

Tiger pulled up beside the Balestier KTV lounge and jumped out of the car, leaving the engine running. He nodded towards the doorman outside the club.

"Oi, go park this round the back," Tiger shouted across the Balestier Road traffic.

"Hey, cannot lah," the doorman replied. "Saturday night our busy time. The boss said I must watch who comes in."

Tiger glared at the doorman.

"You want me to speak to the real boss, is it?" he asked, in a low, calm voice.

"No, it's OK."

"Good. Now go park the fucking car lah."

The doorman glanced over his shoulder and then jogged over

to the car. Tiger walked briskly down the ugly, purple corridor. He strolled past a couple of empty KTV rooms—it was still relatively early in the evening—and headed for a private staff room at the end of the corridor. He opened the door without knocking. Inside were three young Chinese hostesses in their underwear, standing in front of a mirror and applying heavy foundation to their weary skin. They saw Tiger over their shoulders in the mirror and smiled nervously. They never bothered to cover themselves. Tiger never bothered to look away.

"Oh, hi Tiger," one of them said slowly. "You come for special service?"

On almost any other occasion, Tiger would've laughed at the absurdity of the request. His special service days, and there had been plenty of them, were sadly long gone. These days he struggled to raise a smile in the mornings.

"No need, had one already," he said, always keeping up appearances. "I'm looking for your boss."

"I'm here lah," said Rosie, entering the staff room behind Tiger. "Hey, girls, go check that the rooms and the DVDs are ready. Tonight's going to be busy. I'll come outside when clients are here."

Tiger watched the girls dress quickly and held the door open for them. He smiled at each of them as they went out. The last girl stopped and glanced over at Rosie. She nodded reassuringly and gestured for her to leave. Tiger closed the door behind them quietly and turned the key in the lock.

"OK, Rosie," he said slowly. "What the hell have you been doing?"

"Nothing lah," Rosie replied uneasily, fiddling with a vanity case on a cluttered dressing table.

"Rosie, I'm supposed to be taking my daughter for *makan* now. She's waiting for me at Beach Road. We're having steamboat.

I promised her I wouldn't be late and I'm late already so don't piss me off, ah."

Tiger took a step towards Rosie and she winced. She tried to cover up with a playful smile, but it was forced and they both knew it.

"Remember, your boss is my boss, ah," she said quickly. "I've got many customers, you know."

"Please lah, Rosie, you think I'm going to hurt you, is it? You know how many years I've been doing this already. In 30 years I never touch a woman. Hurt you for what? It's bad for business. Have KTV hostesses with black eyes and see how much money you make."

Rosie relaxed a little and sat down on a stool in front of a mirror.

"I'm getting old," she said, straightening the crow's feet around her eyes. "Cannot do this for much longer."

"Rosie, come on ah."

"In five years, I need to retire."

"You're paid well, what. No other KTV lounge in Singapore pays you this much."

"Ha, no other KTV lounge in Singapore is *kelong*."

Tiger laughed in spite of himself. He had always found Rosie's feistiness attractive. That's what made her such a prized asset.

"Why did you blackmail him?"

Rosie looked up at Tiger standing behind her in the mirror.

"Who said I blackmailed him?"

"Please lah, Rosie, you think you're the only one to have contacts in the China S-League team, is it? They're the most *kelong* team in Singapore. Everybody has deep throats in that team. You pick the most obvious team to upset Wee Kin."

"I did what I was told."

"You were supposed to fuck him only. Nobody told you

to blackmail him, not before we had the chance. Now, you've spoiled the market."

Rosie stared at herself in the mirror. She still looked good, even at her age. She sighed.

"No choice," she whispered.

"Who says? We were paying you extra. If you needed more money, you could've come to me what."

"No lah, had to try to scare him off because the idiot said he had fallen in love."

"With you?" Tiger laughed. "Are you serious?"

"Of course I'm serious. Told me he was going to leave his wife and children and come with me. I told him cannot lah, but he was serious. Can you imagine? I'd be in all the papers, then this place would be in all the papers and then maybe you also."

"Don't bluff me, lah."

"Hey, screw you, OK. I tried everything. I flirt with his friends, I dance with that fat Spearman, I give little play lap dance to the new *ang moh*, I kiss other men when he comes here, all to piss him off. But he never listens. Told me he wants to marry me. Always happens with these idiots. We give them better sex than they get at home so they think it's real."

"Why you never come to me?"

"And you do what? Break his legs, is it? He's nice. I like him. I just don't want to marry him."

"So how?"

"I try to leave him; he says no. I ignore him when he sings karaoke with his friends, so he sits in the corner and gets drunk. I say I'm busy with clients and give him young, pretty girls, but he just goes home. So I blackmail him. I say give me $5,000 or I'll tell his wife."

"What did he say?"

"He said 'do it lah'. He was going to tell her anyway. So I

got desperate. One night I set up a camera and recorded us in bed. The next day I told him about the video and asked him for $5,000 or I would send it to his wife, the Super Soccer channel and *The Newspaper*. He never believed me so I told him to expect a warning at the match. Now he believes me."

"Yeah, he believed you and now everything is messed up. We were going to use him soon. How can we use him now, you used him already and for what? Because the idiot fell in love with you? Because you try and blackmail him for a lousy $5,000? Here, take this."

Tiger took out an envelope from his back pocket and dropped it onto the dressing table.

"That's $10,000," Tiger said. "No more blackmail, no more threats, no more nothing. You leave now."

"But I need the money here. Cannot afford to leave the club."

"Heck care lah."

"This is my business."

"No, it's our business. Cannot have Wee Kin here crying for you every night. We already got some *ang moh* reporter following Spearman around. Cannot have any more attention around this place. Got a big project coming up, cannot fuck it up."

"I thought I was helping you," Rosie said, wiping her eyes.

"You were, but you fucked it up. Cannot use Wee Kin now. No chance, too many people watching him. Never mind. We make a bit already. His form so screwed up in past few months, we manage to make a bit betting outside, but cannot use him anymore. We needed you and him. You fucking him would help us later, but now no more. No more Spearman. No more Wee Kin."

"I'm sorry, please let me stay," Rosie whispered, as tears rolled down her cheeks.

Tiger leaned forward and gently wiped away Rosie's tears.

"*Aiyoh*, Rosie, why you so good at your job?" he said softly. "You were only supposed to fuck him, make him tired and stressed, and then we take over later. But you, ah, you had to make him fall in love with you."

"It's not my fault."

"No, but we cannot go back. Must look forward now. You've got to leave tonight. We find someone else to run this place."

Tiger headed for the door, but suddenly checked himself. He turned and faced Rosie.

"Hey, where's the video, ah?"

Rosie wiped her eyes with a piece of tissue paper and blew her nose.

"I, er, deleted it already. It's gone."

Tiger smiled. That's why Rosie had been so reliable over the years.

"Where's the video, Rosie?" Tiger asked firmly.

Rosie sighed. She leaned across the dressing table, grabbed a handbag and unzipped it. She rummaged around inside before pulling out a DVD in a blank case. She handed it to Tiger, avoiding eye contact.

"Thanks, Rosie," he said, smiling. "Now, I know there may be extra copies also, but you've been paid $10,000 for them. And you're too clever to give them away, right?"

Rosie nodded as Tiger checked his watch.

"Are you OK or not?" he asked.

"What do you care?"

Tiger stroked her hair. He would miss Rosie. They were kindred spirits, devoted to money and nothing else. And he really, really liked the video idea.

 **fourteen**

CHRIS was in no mood to see the manager. His father had already been on the phone, demanding to know why his son's partner—the baby-faced Chinese assassin, the Singapore striker who had never been previously sent off for either club or country—had hospitalised an opponent. Tony Osborne followed every S-League match live from his Dagenham living room, thanks to the league's official website. Like many web reporters tasked with providing live updates, the S-League's website editor was a staunch supporter of hyperbole in every sound bite. Tony Osborne nearly fell off his dining room chair when he read: "46TH MINUTE: POH WEE KIN SNAPS. PUNCHES OPPONENT. KNOCKS HIM OUT. BLOOD EVERYWHERE. CHRIS OSBORNE CLOSE BY. RIOT ON PITCH. POH WEE KIN CRYING."

In reality, Chris Osborne had no role in his team-mate's red card, but the S-League website editor had been ordered to mention the English striker as often as possible to capture all those Google searches for the former West Ham man. It was all about search engine optimisation and it worked. The S-League website had never experienced as many hits before Chris Osborne arrived, so he had to be involved in everything on the website.

By the time Chris had convinced his horrified father that he had nothing to do with the red card and had, in fact, scored the game's winning goal, he was ready for a beer—not a debrief. But his coach wanted a one-off, post-match discussion to address the unexpected broken jaw.

Chris moved some muddy red cones to one side and knocked on the door. A sheet of A4 paper was stuck to the door with Scotch tape. On the paper, the words "Michael Nielson, Raffles Rangers team coach" had been scrawled with a marker pen.

"Come in, please come in," Michael's voice said, surprisingly polite and officious. Chris guessed that his coach was not alone.

He opened the door and saw a freshly-showered Michael sitting opposite Mr Teck and the Minister for Sports (Land and Water). Only Mr Teck stood up to shake Chris' hand. The Minister nodded. Michael eyed the two men on the other side of his desk nervously.

"Great game, great game, as always," Mr Teck said, still holding Chris' hand tightly. "It's at times like this when the best players really deliver, right? If nothing else, you will help us to get some positive headlines tomorrow. That keeps us clear of Orchard and you're racing away with the top goal-scorer's trophy."

"Ah, thanks, thanks," replied Chris, grabbing a red plastic stool to sit at the side of the coach's desk. He glanced at all three men, waiting for one of them to say something else. Eventually, Michael cleared his throat.

"Er, Chris, well, er, Mr Teck and the Minister asked to see you today, just for a couple of minutes, just to get your side of the story."

"How do you mean?"

"Well, you know, our longest-serving striker has never done anything like that before and he's your team-mate and …"

"I honestly don't have a clue," Chris interjected. He meant it, too.

"We understand that you guys are a tight unit and I'm proud

of that," the Minister for Sports (Land and Water) said slowly. "But as a patron of this club, and a proud fan I might add, it's important that we get to the bottom of this before the media does."

"I agree. It wasn't like Wee Kin to do that. He's a quiet bloke, but I get on really well with him. I tried to speak to him just now, but he'd gone. It's so out of character. I was as shocked as you were when it happened. He just exploded."

Mr Teck glanced across at Michael, who shrugged his shoulders. Mr Teck smiled at Chris.

"I know you're his friend and I know that you've been out with him a few times," Mr Teck said. "But we've heard rumours involving a KTV lounge."

Chris stared back at Mr Teck.

"Yeah, we've been to a KTV lounge a few times. Wee Kin usually comes with us. It's in Balestier. I don't know too much about the place. Karaoke is not really my thing and I haven't gone there much since I've been with Yati. Spearman's the one to speak to. He took me there first. It's almost his second home."

"The club has heard that Wee Kin might have been close to one of the hostesses there," Mr Teck said.

Chris laughed incredulously.

"Wee Kin? Old 'week in and week out' with a KTV hostess? No chance. He barely speaks to them whenever we're there. He just has a few drinks, sings a couple of songs and goes back to his wife."

Mr Teck and the Minister for Sports (Land and Water) smiled at each other.

"Quite right, too," Mr Teck said. "We thought as much, too. We just wanted to clear that rumour up once and for all. So if you happen to hear anything, or if your partner hears anything at *The Newspaper*, you can dismiss it on the club's behalf."

"Sure. Do you know what will happen to him now?"

"He'll be dealt with by me," Michael said. "Whatever the S-League imposes, I will make damn sure that …"

"The club will settle the matter internally," Mr Teck said.

"I know you played football for West Ham and you had to deal with all that media intrusion," the Minister for Sports (Land and Water) said.

"Well, there wasn't that much really. I never made the first team," Chris said sheepishly.

"No, but still, I think it gave you a good grounding in dealing with the media. Our players don't have that here. They're just not used to speaking freely. And we want to help them communicate appropriately, so we do it for them. We help them to decide what they want to say. That way, we're always on message, as a club. Wee Kin must be punished, obviously, and it may go beyond the S-League and into the courts. It's not for me to say at this stage. But bodily harm was inflicted in front of over 5,000 witnesses. We have to take a dim view of such behaviour in Singapore. I hope you understand."

"I do, but there must be something else, something on Wee Kin's mind. He just wouldn't do that."

"Absolutely, I agree with you completely," Mr Teck said, smiling. "I've known Wee Kin and his family for years, and believe me, no one in that stadium was more shocked than me. We will get to the bottom of this. But we will keep it all in-house. That's what everybody wants here. If we maintain a calm exterior, then Singapore football will survive."

"Sure, OK. I understand," Chris said.

He didn't.

"OK, then," the Minister for Sports (Land and Water) said. "It's been a pleasure to have a chat with you again, Chris. Keep up the good work. I've heard about your meeting with the Minister for Home Improvement and the ministry's tentative plans. It all sounds very exciting, so just keep doing what you're doing."

"Yes, thanks again, Chris," Mr Teck said, shaking Chris' hand again. "If you need anything, anything at all, just come to me, OK?"

"As long as I'm still a Raffles Rangers player, right?"

Everyone in the room laughed. Chris was adept at breaking the ice in uncomfortable situations.

"Well, ideally, yes," Mr Teck laughed. "But you never know … Good to see you again. Michael, keep up the good work. And keep Orchard FC away from the title."

They all shook hands as Michael led Mr Teck and the Minister for Sports (Land and Water) out of his room, closing the door behind them.

"What was all that about?" Chris said.

"You still haven't been in Singapore long enough," Michael said. "This sort of thing just doesn't happen here. You should've seen them when they first came in here. They were furious."

"I can imagine."

"At least you'll get the weekend off for the first time this season."

"What do you mean?"

"Well, you won't be on the back pages now, will you?"

TIGER was pissed off for three reasons. First, the fallout from the Rosie-Wee Kin affair had ruined dinner with his daughter and caused a long sleepless night of phone calls back and forth to Kuala Lumpur. Second, it would not stop raining and Tiger had just had his car polished in the Bishan Junction 8 car park. And third, Ah Lian would not stop talking. The skinny gangster sat in the passenger seat of Tiger's parked car as the pair of them tried to peer through the teeming rain to watch an East Coast apartment. Ah Lian leaned forward and bent over his seat, his fingers fumbling around under the seat until he found what he was looking for.

"What the hell are they?" Tiger asked.

"Binoculars lah," Ah Lian replied, adjusting the focus.

"I know that, idiot. Why have you brought them?"

"So I can see inside the condo, wha'."

"It's raining. What do you think you can see?"

"Vince the Mincer."

"But why watch him? We're not spying on him. He knows we're meeting him."

"Must practise lah."

"You're an idiot."

Ah Lian squinted as he tried to make out a condo unit through the rain. The sea breeze blew the rain sideways across the windscreen. There was little visibility.

"What will happen to Wee Kin now, ah?" Ah Lian asked excitedly.

"Don't know. Not my problem."

"But he punched that *kelong* China player!"

"Then he'll be punished."

"Can go to prison or not?"

"You think I'm a judge, is it?"

"You think Raffles Rangers can win the league title or not?"

"You ever stop talking or not?"

Ah Lian smiled and continued to play with the focus on his binoculars.

"Eh, put that away lah," Tiger said.

"Put away what?"

"Your cock. What do you think? Your binoculars lah. There are families over there at East Coast Park. You look like a pervert."

"Must see if Vince is coming, right or not?"

"Use your eyes, lah. *Chee bye.*"

Ah Lian reluctantly put the binoculars back under his seat and took out a white mobile phone from the hip pocket on his tight black jeans. He fiddled with the buttons as Tiger reached for a copy of *FourFourTwo* on the back seat.

"What's that ah?" Ah Lian asked.

"It's a football magazine."

"In Singapore?"

Tiger sighed. He had spent much of his adult life around the fringes of a game he genuinely loved, working with people who knew so little about it.

"No, it's from England. Very good magazine. Can also check the fixtures."

"*Aiyoh*, buy *ang moh* magazine for what? Can check fixtures on my hand phone already."

"It's got good stories about the EPL."

"Ah, heck care lah. Just need to read prediction, enough already."

In the round-up section of the British leagues, Tiger noticed a tiny article on the League Two clash between Dagenham & Redbridge and Brentford being postponed because of floodlight failure. Tiger didn't really know either team, but he knew that Chris Osborne came from Dagenham. The syndicates had nothing to do with this one, Tiger was certain of that, because there was no money to be made from League Two football. The real high rollers, the Asian whales, had no time for leagues they didn't know. The standard of League Two football might even be higher than that of the S-League, but that was not the point. It never had been. Gamblers had to be in the know. Asians knew the English Premier League and the Champions League and the M-League and the S-League because they were local. They had some knowledge of the odds and what was at stake. They felt that gave them an edge. It didn't, of course, but it always made them feel better. The only edge came from knowing which matches were fixed and which weren't. Tiger did. They didn't. That's life.

And the Dagenham match wasn't *kelong,* but Tiger still saw it as a positive sign, a distinct connection—a light went on as others went off. He read on and discovered that an electrical fault caused the floodlights to fail. Tiger laughed. They always attributed floodlight failure to electrical faults even when the blackouts really were fixed.

"What so funny ah?" Ah Lian asked.

"Nothing lah, play with your hand phone."

"I change my ring tone already. Do you think I should have 'The Final Countdown', 'Brother Louie' or 'Forever Young'?"

"I don't care."

"I also like Michael Learns to Rock."

"Stop talking now."

VINCE the Mincer struggled to make out Tiger's car through the incessant rain. It wasn't so much the monsoonal conditions as it was the aviator sunglasses he insisted on wearing whatever the weather. The rapper believed the sunglasses complimented the LA Lakers jersey and the cubic zirconia bling. He wiped his sunglasses again and spotted Tiger's car. He noticed that Tiger was with that Ah Lian gangster again. Vince hated Ah Lian. Vince liked to play the gangster at TV and radio studios, concerts and exclusive private parties at Bukit Timah condos. But he had to drop the act around Ah Lian. Vince knew he was a ferocious boy from the heartlands, a street kid who censored neither thought nor deed. Vince saw it in Ah Lian's eyes; it was something that Vince would never have—anarchy. Ah Lian didn't appear to give a shit about anything or anyone. Law and order, social conventions, crime and punishment—nothing bothered Ah Lian. The little Chinese pit bull would be a rare breed in any country, Vince thought. In Singapore, Ah Lian was practically unique. He was the real deal. Vince was playacting. When the pair occasionally stood side by side, it was easy to spot who was wearing the CZ bling.

Vince took a deep breath and tapped the window on Tiger's side of the car. Tiger glanced up from his magazine, saw Vince standing in the rain and frowned.

"Come on lah, leave him in the rain," Ah Lian giggled.

"Shut up. Don't talk, OK. You always irritate him," Tiger whispered.

"OK lah," Ah Lian mumbled.

Tiger gestured towards the back seat. Vince glanced across at a smirking Ah Lian.

"No, it's OK," he shouted through the closed window. "I'm late already."

Tiger opened his window a couple of centimetres and glared at Vince.

"This is the East Coast. There are families in all those rain shelters," he said slowly. "So get in the car. Now."

Reluctantly, Vince did as he was told. Tiger cringed as Vince's T-shirt and shorts soaked his upholstery.

"I've just had this car cleaned," he scowled.

"Sorry, man, dude," Vince said, slipping effortlessly into rapper mode. "What's happening, bro?"

"Steady, lah, brother. It's the best gangster in Singapore, JB and some say Batam," Ah Lian mocked.

"Shut up lah," Tiger hissed. "Ignore him."

Tiger didn't like Vince either, but experience brought indifference. When he was Ah Lian's age, he might have behaved in a similar fashion. Vince the Mincer was a phoney. That much was obvious. But he was hardly original. Tiger had seen them all in his line of work. Buffed TV stars playing cops on crappy crime dramas, kung fu actors in cheap Jackie Chan knockoffs and now rappers singing about the hood; they all fancied themselves as hard men, particularly after a few white lines. But then they always had the cash for the powder and that's all that mattered. Tiger was willing to overlook their egotistical foibles. Besides, in a country as safe and sterile as Singapore, every drunken banker who bared his bum at Boat Quay thought himself a gangster.

"It's OK, bro," Vince jived, keeping up appearances. "It's cool, man. It's cool."

"How much do you want?" Tiger asked.

He had no time for small talk.

"Ah, the usual is cool, man, bro," Vince said. "Our *ang moh* editor wants a little boost before his interview. He always likes to be fired up when he's overseeing a big interview."

"Really," Tiger said, looking at his watch. "Well, it's $3,000 this time."

"Serious? Last time it was only $2,500."

Ah Lian stared at Vince through the rear-view mirror.

"We got credit crunch also," he said. "You want to bring it into Singapore, is it? Big shot gangster man."

"Hey, come on, I expected it to be $2,500, that's all."

"When economy down, customs get tough, looking for more illegal immigrants," Tiger reasoned. "Risks much higher now. No one wants to get hanged for $2,500."

"No need to talk like that, bro," Vince said quickly. "It's OK, it's OK. I go upstairs to Simon's place and ask him for extra $500, no problem."

"Wah, you good ah, gangster," Ah Lian mocked. "You going upstairs and ask him for money when he does big celebrity interview, is it?"

Tiger backslapped Ah Lian across his right arm.

"I told you already," Tiger said. "Never mind, Vince, you can give us the rest next time. You're a good customer. No problem."

"No, really, I'm also in the interview," Vince said. "You see, Simon wants me to do this celebrity interviewing another celebrity, like some *Observer* magazine style in the UK. It's a cover story, man. I interview Chris Osborne about his season because we're both on The Spear's TV show."

Tiger turned around and faced Vince. He thought that karma and fate were all bullshit. He made his own luck. That was why he never gambled on a game that wasn't fixed. That was why he usually won. But the Dagenham floodlights really had been an ironic sign.

"You're going upstairs now to interview Chris Osborne?" he asked.

"Yeah, we're doing the interview and the photo shoot at Simon's place," Vince replied excitedly. "It's good, right?"

"Yeah, it is good," Tiger said quietly. "It's very good."

VINCE slammed the back door of Tiger's car. He dashed along the road as the rain dribbled down his face. He stopped between two parked cars and waited for a gap in traffic. He noticed a middle-aged Chinese uncle, wearing a white singlet and a pair of scruffy shorts, dozing in the driver's seat of one of the cars. Vince smiled. That's the best place to be right now, he thought. He craned his head, saw that the road was clear and splashed his way across the road and headed past the security post of Simon Jones' condo.

The sleeping uncle opened his eyes, took his mobile phone off the dashboard and dialled a number.

"Hello, yah, it's Senior Officer Tan," he said. "He's just gone into the suspect's condo."

 **fifteen**

JIMMY Tan was a proud Singaporean who loved his country and, therefore, his job. Drug dealers were scum. No, drug dealers were worse than scum. They were a cancer. Scum could be cleaned up, but cancer could only be treated. It went into remission, a temporary withdrawal, but malignant cancer usually returned. And drug dealers never went away. Jimmy had seen what the parasites had done to Thailand, Cambodia, Vietnam and parts of Malaysia, and he loathed their presence in Singapore. There were not too many, of course. The death penalty, stringent security and constant vigilance made sure of that, but there were still a few rodents scurrying around the back lanes and alleyways of the city.

In his 10 years as a narcotics officer with the Central Narcotics Bureau—the last five as a Senior Narcotics Officer—Jimmy had tracked them all, hiding in the shadows and waiting for another opportunity to add a notch to his truncheon. The hunt wasn't about his crime stats or any desire to climb the CNB ladder, and it certainly wasn't about the money. Jimmy Tan was deeply proud of his country—the only country in the world to rise from Third World to First World in a single generation. The socio-economic miracle was the only example of its kind in human history, a fact that Jimmy always enjoyed sharing with his regional counterparts when they worked on undercover operations together.

Jimmy wanted to keep his country clean—no more, no less. When Western detectives visited from overseas bureaus and narcotics agencies, CNB bosses always earmarked Jimmy for tour guide duties. He banged the government drum every time, not because he was paid to, but because he really believed it. Singapore was one of the safest countries in the world to raise a family. He didn't need to fabricate or embellish. That was a fact. And one of the most loyal and dedicated officers in the CNB helped to make that possible.

That was why decent, hardworking Singaporean men like Jimmy Tan made it their mission in life to bring down pampered, whiny Western men like Simon Jones. Jimmy grew up in a one-room apartment in Woodlands, which he shared with three other siblings. Woodlands was the major northern public housing estate in Singapore's working class heartlands. Jimmy's parents reminded their children constantly that they lived in privileged luxury after their previous home—a dilapidated wooden hut in Sembawang built on stilts to keep out the rats and snakes.

On the other hand, according to Simon Jones' file, the Englishman lived in a five-room East Coast apartment with a market value of almost $1 million. His patronising *X-Pat* magazine was published independently, by Simon, who hoarded most of the profits like an old miser. And he married a beautiful Filipino woman, presumably to keep up appearances, and the pair wined and dined their friends at any expensive restaurant of their choosing.

And still Simon Jones needed to take drugs. Like all Western men, the world was not enough. They craved something extra, something beyond the norm, something over the edge. Wealth, privilege and regular networking functions and dinners opened the kinds of doors that would be locked to the average Singaporean.

Why, then, would men like Simon Jones always open the door to lowlifes like Vince the Mincer?

Because they could, Jimmy reasoned. A decade in the CNB had left him with no other worthier or more profound explanation. Most Asian men were satisfied with a loyal, loving family, a decent home and a car, a golf club membership and the occasional gamble. Most Western expats were not.

Jimmy's early career had been spent monitoring the heroin-trafficking coming across the Causeway, and those couriers, dealers and addicts were nothing like Simon Jones. They were weak, desperate and pathetic. Their crazed, muddled reactions during raids over the years had been pitiful. Jimmy had found heroin stuffed in vacuum cleaners, under cooker hoods and in air-con vents. The culprits were rarely logical or rational. He had arrested dazed and confused young Singaporeans who had been duped by West African syndicates; some of the women had willingly shoved heroin balloons up their rectum for Nigerian men they had fallen in love with. They were nearly always poor, uneducated broken people. Jimmy never agreed with their actions, but he understood them.

When Jimmy moved on to the cocaine syndicates, however, everything changed. The number of raids went down, but the suspects' IQ scores went up. These people didn't squat together in the gutter to share a needle; they gathered on their knees around polished glass tables in East Coast condos to celebrate their success. In recent months, Jimmy had seen them all come and go. The bone-thin actresses who played the wholesome, angelic girls-next-door in the drama serials; the Asian correspondents working for prestigious international news networks; the Southeast Asian Games gold medallists who had cried on the podium during the national anthem; and that damn rapper who served as courier, dealer and pimp for the party guests.

They all came to Simon Jones' apartment on Friday nights. Jimmy had been watching the house of cards for months. He was going to blow the house down and he was going to enjoy the moment.

Jimmy sat in his car opposite the condo and stared at the rain as it hypnotically trickled down his windscreen. He reached over to the passenger's seat and opened up a white, polystyrene box. The Hainanese chicken rice was cold, but that's why he always asked for an extra pack of chilli. He pulled the lid off the chilli and hummed to himself as he poured the chilli over the boiled chicken. He glanced up at the condo and almost dropped the chilli pack. He saw that famous S-League footballer, Chris Osborne, getting directions from the condo security guard.

CHRIS thought the interview had been a disaster. What was it with the media in this country? Did they ever ask a question that didn't involve local, spicy food or favourite Singaporean hangouts?

"How did you find the interview?" Simon asked.

"Oh, great, great, yeah. Vince over here asked some decent questions," Chris lied.

"That's good. I'm sure it's going to make a fabulous cover story," Simon gushed, patting Chris on the thigh.

"Er, yeah, I hope so. Yati said *X-Pat* is a decent magazine."

"That's good to hear. She's a gorgeous girl, Yati. You two really do make a very attractive couple."

Chris suddenly felt the humidity. He looked up at the air-conditioning unit in Simon's living room. He saw the green light. It was certainly on, but he was sweating. He heard the toilet flush and then saw Vince bounce into the room, wiping his nostrils before flopping onto the sofa. Despite Vince's usual lack of tact and subtlety, Chris was surprisingly pleased to have him back in the room.

"All right, Vince," Chris said.

"I'm buzzing, man, I'm buzzing. That was a great interview, bro. Your sales are gonna go through the roof next month, Simon. No problem."

"I'll certainly drink to that," Simon enthused. "Come, Chris, let me pour you another glass of wine. This is none of that cheap South Australian muck from FairPrice; this is from a specialist in Tanglin Road."

"No, I'm fine, really."

"Come on now, Chris, we've got some friends arriving later and it should be a great night. I know they'd all love to meet you, maybe get some photos taken with you and a few autographs. Would be a great networking session."

Simon held the wine bottle over Chris' glass and smiled at Vince, who shifted uneasily on the sofa. Chris leaned forward to cover his glass.

"No, I'm fine really, thanks, mate. I've got a game tomorrow and it's the live game on TV. And I'll be playing up front on my own now that Wee Kin is suspended, so I need to stay sharp."

"That was such a shock what that man did," Simon said. "I was in the stand watching with Yati and her friend Billy Addis and …"

"He's her colleague," Chris interjected. "Billy is not really a friend; he's more of a colleague."

"Oh, I see. Right, sorry, I didn't realise," Simon added quickly, but he noted the flash of irritation. It pleased him enormously.

"So Chris, are you up for Simon's party tonight, dude?" Vince said.

"No, I'd better not. I really want to be right for tomorrow's game. We're getting near the end of the season and Orchard are bloody chasing us."

"Come on, man. My friends would love to get some tips from you, Chris. These guys bet big money. Not just on the S-League, but on the EPL, too. Champions League, Spanish, anything, man."

"Vincent, no talk of gambling, please," Simon said. "You know how I have no time for gambling, such a wasteful pastime in Singapore. It really does make for the most tedious of conversations here, don't you think, Chris?"

"It's not really my thing. Well, it's not my thing. S-League footballers are not allowed to gamble on their own league, but I'm not into it anyway. Never have been. But each to their own, I suppose. Live and let live and all that."

"My sentiments exactly," Simon gushed. "Well, maybe next week, then. I'm having a much bigger gathering next Friday. My wife is heading back to Manila to spend some time with her family, so while the wife is away, the expat can play."

Chris smiled and noticed that Vince laughed nervously.

"I do have a Friday game next week, so if we win, it might be a nice way to celebrate with a few drinks," Chris said.

"Exactly, exactly, it'll be a great night," Simon bellowed. "I'll have friends from the media here, maybe a couple of the models that we use in our magazines, some boring businessmen, which I promise to keep out of your way, and Vince, and perhaps even The Spear. I know The Spear is always a popular chap with the gambling guests."

"Sounds good, mate," Chris admitted.

"Hey, man, Simon's parties are the best in Singapore," Vince said. "Plus I always rap a few tracks on his Bang & Olufsen sound system, man."

"Shit, I'm definitely not coming then."

Simon laughed theatrically and poured himself another glass of red wine.

"No, it'll be a fabulous night, Chris," he cried. "A chance to celebrate your first cover on my magazine."

"OK, I'll do you a deal," Chris said. "If we win on Friday night, I'll come. How's that?"

"It's a deal," Simon said, clearly delighted "I have every confidence in Chris Osborne and Raffles Rangers Football Club. Cheers."

The trio leaned across the glass table and chinked their glasses together. Chris looked over at Simon.

"Oh, it's OK if I bring Yati to the party, too, right?"

"Of course, it is, Chris, of course it is. You both make such a lovely couple."

Simon downed the red wine and quickly poured himself another glass.

BILLY Addis stepped out of the taxi and stood at the edge of the field. So this was the mighty Farrer Park, he thought. The spiritual home of Singapore football, a traditional breeding ground for Malaysia Cup winners, a place for kids who came to escape the wooden huts for a few hours and dream of playing for Manchester United or Liverpool. Billy had been told often enough about the mythical Farrer Park by older sports journalists. Boys walked onto the pitches at Farrer Park and men stepped off. The hallowed turf swallowed up the *ikan bilis* kids. (*Ikan bilis* was Malay for anchovies, Billy had been told, and any scrawny village boy with legs like anchovies was called *ikan bilis*.) On weekends and after school, every blade of glass was once covered with a muddy boot. Kids of all ages chased balls in all directions. Fandi Ahmad, V Sundramoorthy, Dollah Kassim, the Quah football dynasty—they had all worked on their kind of magic at Farrer Park. They worked in the business of making magic, Billy was always told by the old-timers at his office, before football became a results business.

Billy glanced across Farrer Park. High-rise housing estates, both public and private, bordered the pitches, seemingly closing in on the ever-decreasing green space. A group of no more than a dozen kids, mostly Malay, worked on their one-touch passing and dribbled around miniature cones. Apart from an old Chinese uncle sitting on a bench and reading a newspaper, the park was deserted. The magical Farrer Park was no longer making magic.

The same could be said for Danny Spearman. Billy spotted the fallen Spear standing among the boys. He had a whistle around his neck. The retro 1970 Brazil shirt was ill-fitting and the tight green shorts were ill-advised. Billy hadn't seen Danny for a couple of weeks, but the weight gain was noticeable even from across the pitch.

"Danny," Billy shouted. "Have you got a minute, mate?"

"Oh, fuck," Danny muttered under his breath. "All right, lads, just carry on with the drills. I've just got to have a word with this sports writer. His name is Billy Addis. You might have seen his photograph in *The Newspaper*."

"Does he write about the English Premier League?" a young Malay boy asked excitedly.

"No, he writes about the S-League."

"Ah, the S-League lousy one. Except Chris Osborne lah. Everybody else is lousy."

Well, you'll never be good enough to play for the S-League, you little fucker, Danny thought.

Billy watched Danny walk towards him. He still had that cocky swagger. He certainly had balls. The man had been called up by the CPIB after Raffles Rangers had conceded some bizarre late goals, and he had been seen with a reputed loan shark outside a KTV lounge used by the players and where a former hostess shagged Poh Wee Kin. Everyone in the office knew the story about the hostess and Wee Kin. Most of the journalists had slept with one of the hostesses there at some point. The Balestier KTV lounge had always been seedy. That's why it was so popular.

Danny had been ruled out for the rest of the season with the reliable ankle injury just at the right time. The S-League title run-in always generated the most public interest and only the tiniest percentage of it was legal. But he still had his TV shows and he still had his Mickey Mouse clinics. So what did the wily Danny do? He combined the two. He convinced his Super Soccer channel guests to make a fleeting appearance at one of his clinics and informed the kids' parents that his clinics were the only clinics in Asia that offered coaching from some of Britain's finest former players. They had beer bellies, hangovers, left their wives in the UK and chased after *sarongs* at expat bars, but the kids' parents always loved having their photographs taken with retired, fat football legends.

"How are the football clinics going, all right?" Billy asked.

"Ah, great, mate, yeah, terrific," Danny said. "I've still got room for a few more participants if you want to join up. You never really played football, did you? Not at a decent level anyway."

Billy smiled. Danny really was on edge. He might as well have gotten his cock out and compared sizes.

"Yeah, that's true, Danny, I must admit. Although some would say, I wasn't much of a writer either."

Billy stared straight at Danny. That's checkmate, he thought. What stick will you try to beat me with now, dickhead?

"Nah, nah, it's good, mate," Danny fumbled. "You're making a bit of a name for yourself."

"I've noticed the size of your clinic is quite small."

"Yeah, yeah. We did that deliberately, more one-to-one coaching, smaller group sizes, more precise coaching, tailor-made for the individual."

"Why did you pick Farrer Park? Why not Stamford Stadium? Or the Padang in front of the Singapore Cricket Club? Or even the Singapore Sports School?"

"This is our grassroots programme so we thought we'd bring it back to the grassroots. Everyone knows about Farrer Park and its long football history. This is a special place. It's produced so many Singapore internationals here, so we're hoping it might produce one or two for us, too."

"And Farrer Park is free."

Danny glared at Billy and clenched his fists. He wanted to punch him.

"But it's not just about where you coach young players, it's also about who does the coaching," Danny said.

"Yes, I heard you've got Trevor Bonds coming down," Billy said excitedly, his mask temporarily slipping. Trevor Bonds had played for Newcastle, Tottenham and Liverpool when Billy was in secondary school. He was a left-back—quite an accomplished one, Billy recalled—who was capped by England, but was never really able to dislodge Stuart Pearce. But then, Stuart Pearce now worked with the England squad. Trevor Bonds was on his way to a bone-hard, near-empty pitch at Farrer Park.

"Yeah, we've got Trevor helping us out," Danny said. "He's in Singapore for three weeks as a guest of the Super Soccer channel, of course. They fly him over and put him up at Raffles Hotel, but he's happy to give something back to local football while he's here."

"That sounds great. How does it benefit your clinics?"

"The kids all love it and we give the clinics a little plug on my TV shows."

Of course you do, Billy thought.

"It's win-win all round then, really."

"It doesn't do any harm. And we're hoping that Trevor Bonds

will be the first of many."

"That's great. That's really great."

Danny eyed Billy nervously and Billy smiled back awkwardly. Both men knew that Billy wasn't at Farrer Park to cover a private football clinic. They watched the kids stumble around the cones for a few moments.

"Look, Danny, I know I'm beginning to sound like a broken record, but you know I've got to ask," Billy said slowly. "Raffles Rangers are top of the table, thanks mostly to Chris Osborne, and are an absolute certainty to retain the title. And yet the rumours surrounding that club are everywhere. If you go into any Singapore Pools outlet, you'll see that the odds are too high for a team who look like they've only got to turn up for the last couple of games to win the title. And yet, still, the punters are not so confident. And I've heard that outside betting, the illegal betting, is throwing up even stranger odds. It's almost as if the market knows something we don't. That somehow Orchard FC are going to snatch it when you guys meet on the last day of the season."

"I don't know anything about that, I'm out injured at the moment," Danny muttered.

"Yeah, I know, but you're around the club. You're practically the voice of the club with all those TV shows."

"Not anymore," Danny whispered.

"But you must be hearing the whispers. Someone, somewhere must be telling the market that Raffles Rangers are *kelong*; that something is going to happen to deny them the title. The odds for Orchard FC are closing all the time, and based on the form of both sides, there's no reason for that to happen."

"Don't pay too much attention to the S-League odds, mate. They go up and down more times than a tart's knickers."

"I was there, mate. I saw what Poh Wee Kin did. That wasn't just out of character. That was Jekyll and Hyde. The man is the

Gary Lineker of Asian football—squeaky clean, always smiling, always scoring and all that. And suddenly, he's throwing his fists around like it's rugby league, and Raffles Rangers have lost their most experienced striker for the rest of the season."

"I think you've been listening to too many taxi drivers, mate. Not every Singapore football match is fixed, you know. Wee Kin just snapped. It's happened to the best of us in our careers. You've never played professional football, so you don't know the pressure."

"Ah, come on, Danny, you're not going to give me that old chestnut, are you? Really? You've been called up by CPIB, your best striker is out, and there is a link to a KTV lounge that you all use and the odds are all over place …"

"Trevor, how are you mate?"

Danny shouted across the field as Trevor Bonds tiptoed his way across the pockmarked pitches. He was plump, sunburnt, and wearing an Australian surfing T-shirt, Bermuda shorts and flip-flops. Billy was stunned by Trevor's appearance. He had been a stocky, nifty fullback in the Paul Parker or Gary Neville mould. Now he looked like a perspiring publican.

"I'm fucked, mate," Trevor replied. "I'm still knackered from last night. I'm sweating Singapore Slings here. It's a nightmare. They should make this whole country one big air-conditioned bubble."

"Keep it down a bit, mate, I've got the kids running some drills over there."

"Oh, sorry, mate," Trevor said, wiping his forehead before offering Danny a clammy hand to shake. "Good night last night, eh?"

"Yeah, it was."

"That place we went after CHIJMES. On one of those Floors of Whores, where was it?"

"Orchard Towers."

"Yeah, that's it. It was a blinder, wasn't it? That bird you got me, I couldn't believe it. We got back to the hotel, right. And you know those little vodka bottles, the ones you get in the hotel mini-bar? Well, she's took one of them and she's only gone and put it …"

"This is Billy Addis, Trevor. He's a journalist."

"Ah, hello, Trevor, it's great to meet you," Billy said. "You, er, used to be one of my football heroes growing up."

"What do you mean, 'used to be'? I still am, right?"

Trevor and Danny both laughed as Billy blushed.

"Nah, you're all right, mate. I'm only messing about," Trevor continued. "There are only two types of journalists—the Sky Sports journalists and the rest. And I only like the Sky Sports blokes because they pay my wages."

"And the Super Soccer channel, Trevor," Danny interjected.

Trevor laughed and looked at Billy.

"Listen to him. He thinks he's a big star now. I'm only here for the charity golf event, mate. Got some great courses at Sentosa and Tanah Merah. Play a few rounds every time I come here. Speaking of which, I've got a tee-off time in two hours, so what do you want me to do?"

"Er, well, just a few coaching tips, maybe a bit of passing practice with them or something," Danny mumbled.

"Ah, fuck that. I've got a raging headache. Where do you think we are? The David Beckham academy? I'll go and tell them about the time I sent Beckham into the front row at Old Trafford. That'll do."

Trevor headed towards the children in the middle of the pitch.

"Right, you boys," he bellowed. "Gather round near the centre circle and listen to a real footballer."

Billy watched one of his childhood heroes—bleary-eyed and overweight—struggle to keep a small group of distracted kids entertained. At that moment, he understood why Danny would never leave Singapore. Here, he was The Spear. In England, he would be just another Trevor Bonds, wearing a monkey suit and a headset and sitting in a Sky Sports studio staring at a monitor.

"So, er, he's still a bit of a character then," Billy said.

"Yeah, he's a legend all right. Great TV pundit and a pretty good golfer, too."

"That's important."

Danny's phone rang. He grabbed it quickly, desperate for any distraction.

"Hello? Ah, hello, Chris, mate, how's it going? … What sort of party? … Yeah, I know Simon Jones, been to a few of his parties, top bloke, living in denial and all that, but a top bloke. Yeah, I'd be right up for that … Of course, we'll win. And it'll be a good piss up after we win … Yeah, I'll be there. Simon's flat, East Coast. Yeah, no problem … Are you bringing Yati? … Trust me, mate, you might wanna bring her … OK, fair enough. I'll leave it with you. So if I don't make it down to the game on Friday, I'll see you after at Simon's then, mate."

And you'll see me there, too, Billy thought.

 sixteen

YATI knew that sleeping with another white man hardly helped her reputation in the newsroom. She also knew that she didn't have to explain herself to anyone. She was a feminist and a well-read one. She wrote columns about her feminism for *The Newspaper*. She was a prominent member of AWARE and often reminded readers of that fact. She simply preferred white men. It wasn't a race thing, and heaven knows it certainly wasn't a size thing. There was a myth that Asian men had smaller genitalia. Sadly, Yati knew better. She discovered the very English word 'chipolata' while sleeping with a yachtsman from Essex, who was briefly in town for the Straits Regatta. He didn't dock for long at the Changi Sailing Club, and wasn't that the truth. He would always be her little chipolata.

No, it was a cultural thing. Yati had made that clear to her oh-so-Singaporean colleagues and if they didn't like it, they could go fuck themselves. She had the long legs, the olive skin and the flawless complexion, which was a rarity on this sweaty island, and they had their issues and insecurities. They spent their weekends writing columns about being young, single and career-oriented or blogging about foreign talent saturating the meagre job market. She spent her weekends having sex with erudite, well-travelled Caucasian men. Globalisation had made both Singapore and Yati an attractive proposition to educated Westerners. No, she slept well at night, when her partners gave her the chance to sleep.

But recent developments had complicated her current relationship. The incident with that footballer getting sent off for breaking another player's jaw had kept Raffles Rangers in the news forever. Ordinarily, she ignored the publicity, but her boyfriend's face seemed to be staring back at her every morning at the breakfast table. Normally, it was just the sports section and she always threw that section straight down the rubbish chute, unless she was going out with someone who obsessed over the sports pages. But since the punch-up, he had been popping up on the front and back pages. He was unavoidable. And so were the gossipy questions in the newsroom. She had to nip it in the bud.

Yati got out of bed and wrapped a *sarong* around the bottom half of her naked body. She never bothered to cover the top half. She always made a point of keeping her breasts out when she had to tackle a thorny issue with a partner. They usually made it difficult for a boyfriend to concentrate, and reduced the likelihood of any unpleasantness.

On all fours, she slowly crawled across the bed. Her breasts gently touched his back and shoulders as she leaned over his ear.

"It's time to wake up," she whispered. "It's just gone 3 p.m., you've got to get to the match."

"Give me five more minutes," Billy mumbled.

"No, you've got to get up now, darling. I've got to tidy up the apartment before he gets home."

Yati was under no illusions about her predicament. She loved Caucasian men. But she had never shagged two at the same time before. As a rising journalist and lifestyle columnist, she accepted that sleeping with the most famous footballer in Singapore was a risk. She also acknowledged that sleeping with the journalist who was assigned to follow the career of the most famous footballer in Singapore was, potentially, career suicide. But Yati was a pragmatist, not an idealist. She always played the odds.

Billy was better-looking and he read books other than sports autobiographies. Chris was fitter and athletic, but Billy had a more mature sex drive. Yati had met Chris first, and he was able to get her in to parties and events that were beyond even her media pass, but Billy was educated. He made the other female writers in the office laugh whenever he poked fun at an American president or discussed current affairs. They would envy Yati had they known about Billy. They would be jealous. They knew about Chris. He was a typical Yati-type of *ang moh* boyfriend. That bothered Yati, but she could wait. She would have the last laugh when the office eventually heard about Billy. The petty sniggering in the newsroom and the snide Facebook comments would stop then.

She was desperate to go public with Billy. No matter how famous Chris might become in Singapore, he was only ever going to be a big fish in a puddle. Uneducated, monolingual Singaporean Sarong Party Girls pined for S-League footballers, according to Yati, not almost-famous journalists. It was obvious what needed to be done, but Billy was reluctant. He had stressed the importance of establishing their careers first. He hadn't been in Singapore that long and was still on a temporary 'green card', so there was an even greater risk for him.

The Newspaper was a traditional, conservative Asian business, despite its cutting-edge media and marketing tools. Office romances were frowned upon and actively discouraged. Even Billy's sports editor, Peter Chan, had mentioned the company's policy of keeping working and personal relationships distinctly separate. Ironically, the ruling had little to do with Asian values and everything to do with married, respected editors failing to keep their dicks in their trousers.

For the longest time at *The Newspaper*, one of the unwritten perks of becoming a section head or an editor was a salary hike, a secretary and a young, nubile, impressionable female rookie reporter. Editors needed an added incentive to justify those long hours and the rookie reporters held aspirations of becoming editors. The affairs became so prevalent and blatant that if secretaries couldn't find their editors, they would call the rookie reporters instead. The editor-in-chief was then left with no choice but to convene an emergency meeting and put an end to this long-standing managerial perk. He was not a happy man. He had taken advantage of the rookie reporter perk for years.

Billy had a plan, and it was logical and plausible. Chris Osborne was too good for the S-League. Everyone could see that. One season and he'd be on his way back to Europe and probably an English Championship club. Billy was also closing in on Danny, Tiger, Ah Lian, the KTV fiasco with Poh Wee Kin and the *kelong* rumours that always swirled around Raffles Rangers. His editor was happy to indulge Billy's Mickey Spillane pretensions as long as they didn't interfere with his day-to-day sports reporting.

Billy had most of the dots in place, but he had nothing to link them all together. But if he could find that connection, he was golden. Raffles Rangers would be blown apart, a major betting syndicate would be smashed by the CPIB and Billy's special report would make international headlines. And Chris Osborne? Who'd give a shit about Chris Osborne when Billy Addis was Journalist of the Year and being courted by everyone from the BBC to the *Guardian*? And no one at the *Guardian* had a girlfriend as sexy as Yati.

Billy had enjoyed his share of girlfriends, even the odd one-night stand after a piss up somewhere in Hackney or Stratford (he did work in East London after all). But no one came close to the exotic qualities of Yati. There was that Indian girl from Mile End with long, silky black hair, who had inspired Billy briefly during his Monica Ali-*Brick Lane* phase. It was around that period when Billy entertained the prospect of travelling and working his way across Asia. They had spent long nights together putting the world to right and her multicultural viewpoint had impressed heavily upon Billy, who came from the monolingual, predominately white (and therefore racist) world of Essex. For a while, he was convinced that he had found his Asian muse. He hadn't, but he still smiled whenever he heard Oasis' "Talk Tonight". The song brought back all those late-night conversations, and he was grateful for them.

But the Indian girl couldn't match Yati's physical beauty. Few women could. Billy always prided himself on not being a typical Essex boy. He was educated and wanted intellectual stimulation from a woman, rather than just a pretty face. And then he spotted Yati for the first time at a basic reporting course and wanted to have sex with her right there on one of the desks. Billy had a First-Class Honours degree from a top British university, a promising career in journalism and had travelled the world. But his penis was still made in Essex.

Billy rolled over and almost got a nipple in the eye. Yati's breasts were hanging over his face. She was smiling down at him.

"All right, mate," he said. "God, you really are stunning, aren't you."

Billy reached up to grab Yati's breasts, but she stopped him. Perfect, she thought. She had him.

"No, not yet, darling. I've got to ask you something first," she said.

"Anything for you, you know that."

"When do you think all this Raffles Rangers stuff will blow over?"

"What do you mean?"

"You're in the paper almost every day. Your photo byline is always there. You've been on the TV talking about it. You've been in the news almost as much as he has. It's too risky."

"It's easing off now. We're almost at the end of the season. And once that's over, it will calm down. Anyway, he'll probably be off to the UK by then."

Yati looked away. She stared at a photograph on the dressing table beside the bed. It showed her and Chris standing in front of the Merlion Tower at Sentosa. They were both smiling, but Yati stood slightly apart from Chris.

"I don't think he's going back," she muttered.

"What?"

"I don't think he's going back. He wants to stay here. He's loving it here. He sees the kind of lifestyle that Danny has and he wants it."

"But that's crazy. He's ten times the footballer Danny ever was. Danny's stuck here because he has no choice. He has a choice."

"He's been having talks with the government. They want to make him an honorary resident. Give him permanent residency and make him ambassador for a million different things and he's loving all the attention."

"Bloody hell."

"Worse than that, they wanna make us some sort of pin-up couple, a shining example of foreign talent and local talent working together."

"Fuck."

"You don't know the government like I do. That'll just be the start. Soon it'll be baby-making campaigns, reading programmes for kids, sports-for-all talks, shaking hands with MPs at housing estates, turning up at boring dinners and functions. I don't want any of that. I want to travel the world with you. And I could be stuck with him at some crappy, half-empty stadium every week."

"What are we going to do?"

Yati sighed and got off the bed. She picked up her bra and clipped it on. She had no time for sex games now.

"I'm going to have to tell him," she said, bending down to grab a T-shirt.

"You can't tell him yet," Billy said quickly, sitting up in bed.

"Why not? If I don't tell him soon, we'll be having tea with the Prime Minister before you know it."

"You know how close I am with this *kelong* story."

"Oh, Billy, please. I've told you before. No one gives a shit about Asian football here except gamblers and loan sharks."

"That's my point. I'm almost there. I know who these people are and who they are connected to in football."

"It's just one exclusive. You've had loads since you've been here."

"Yeah, but they were only little ones. Players out injured, players being released and all that. This is the big one. Some of these people have got links going right back to some of the match-fixing attempts in England years ago. Floodlight failures involving top clubs like Liverpool, Charlton and West Ham."

"Don't be ridiculous."

"I'm telling you. These betting syndicates are everywhere, all over the world. And they start here. Here and in Malaysia, I know they do. I just need to go to that party tomorrow night and get one more chance to speak to Danny when he's had a few beers."

"Do you really have to go? Don't you think it's going to be awkward?"

"Why would it be awkward? I'm there as Simon Jones' guest. He invited me to thank me for setting up the interview with Chris and Vince the Mincer. There'll be other journos there, loads of people. I'll just be there in the background. I won't even speak to you."

"You'll have to speak to me, for god's sake. We work in the same office."

"All right, I'll speak to you then. You know what I mean. I just won't take you into the bathroom and take all your clothes off."

Billy smiled at Yati and she giggled.

"We're not going to the Long Bar again, are we?"

"No, I reckon the men's toilets will be safe this time."

Yati pulled her T-shirt down and over her breasts. It was almost two sizes too small—just how she liked it.

"If you look like that tomorrow, maybe we'll have to use the bathroom."

"Stop it."

"Do you think there'll be any gear at this party?"

"I hope so. There usually is. I'm going to need it if you two are going to be in the same room."

"It'll be fine. I'll get what I need from Danny this time and everything will be settled by the end of the season."

THE security guard smiled confidently at Ah Lian and waved across the street. He was not usually so pleased to see Ah Lian, but he had an ace up his sleeve this time. He had spoken to Chris Osborne this morning and the *ang moh* was talking goals—lots of goals. Even if Raffles Rangers failed to win, lots of goals paid well, particularly outside.

"What's up?" Ah Lian asked distractedly. "Very busy today ah, Friday always busy day. You got something about Chris Osborne, is it?"

"Ya, ya, got something really big. Chris Osborne stays here, right?"

"I know that lah."

"Ya, I speak to him every morning. Always talk to him a bit when he walks past. Always ask if he can score today or not, and score how many? Always joke a bit, and he always says same thing—ball is round, cannot predict, cannot say, will try his best. But today he was different, today he said something different."

Ah Lian took off his sunglasses and glanced up at the security guard.

"What he say ah?"

The security guard smiled knowingly at Ah Lian.

"He said today he feels especially confident. Today he knows he will score. Today he goes for a hat-trick."

Ah Lian stared at the security guard.

"And that's it? That's what he say?"

"Ya."

"He never say anything else about the match?"

"No lah."

"He just say he feels confident he can score, is it?"

"Ya."

"Never say anything else about the match, the players, the other team, injuries, nothing?"

"No lah."

"He just wants to score?"

"Ya."

"You're a fucking idiot."

"What? What? That's good, right? You ask me to call you if he ever says anything about the match."

"You're a waste of time. Lucky you don't owe Tiger so much, ah."

"But I did help you, right? Can I play this weekend or not? I wanna buy goals, at least five goals. I want five goals for 50 bucks."

"You're joking, right? I drive all the way from Geylang to Orchard for 50 bucks. The ERP and the parking cost me nearly 10 bucks already."

"OK, OK, I give you 100. Hundred can? Five goals. This week you should play big goals."

"Please lah, don't tell me how to play. I know how to play. I work for Tiger. You're an idiot."

"No, this week will be a big game. I know. Even that *ang moh* writer is here to speak to him before the big game."

"What *ang moh* writer?"

"That one who writes in *The Newspaper* every day about the football. I saw him go up there earlier."

Ah Lian looked up at the condo.

"Who else is up there?"

"Don't know. The girlfriend maybe, I don't know. I think I saw her come this morning, but she may have left already."

"OK, I'm going up to speak to the *ang moh* about the match tonight," Ah Lian said quickly. "If you see him or the girlfriend come down, let me know ah. Don't speak to them, just let me know when I come back if you see them or not."

"Ya, OK."

The security guard looked puzzled as Ah Lian ran off towards the lift lobby of Chris Osborne's condo. As he ran, Ah Lian pulled out his mobile phone and checked the storage space left in its gallery.

seventeen

SIMON Jones had surpassed himself. He had promised his guests the Singapore party of the year and he had not disappointed. His wife's friends had dutifully provided the food, without their employers knowing, of course. The maids had sneaked over to Simon's apartment and prepared the dishes. They only worked for a few hours, but Simon paid them more than a week's salary. In a foolish moment of exuberance, he had even invited them to stay for the party, but they had sensibly declined. They all had to be up early on Saturday morning to mop Madam's floors and wash Sir's cars.

The wine for the connoisseurs and the beer for the footballers and gamblers had come courtesy of several of *X-Pat* magazine's major advertisers. One high-end advertiser, knowing the kind of celebrity clientele expected to attend, had even offered to sponsor the entire party in return for a photo spread in the next issue. Simon had politely declined the offer. He took great pride in guaranteeing privacy for his guests to be themselves at his parties, and they loved him for it. And Simon loved to be loved.

The menu was outsourced and Vince the Mincer always supplied the dessert. Simon was most uncomfortable with Vince's presence at his gatherings. He was uncouth and largely uneducated, and he wasn't even particularly good-looking. Simon made every effort to fill his apartment with Singapore's most beautiful people and Vince was quite often the only exception. He insisted on singing that woeful rap, too. The expatriates laughed at Vince's lyrics about life on the Singapore streets and the locals found him humiliating. And those hideous clothes. When Vince turned up at Simon's first party in an LA Lakers singlet, baggy pants and a pair of white Nikes with no laces, one or two American expatriates actually sniggered in Vince's face, but the imbecile had failed to notice. The kid from the Singapore housing estate was preoccupied trying to talk jive to an African-American lawyer from Boston.

But Vince's dessert separated Simon's parties from the rest. It was always of the highest quality. Everyone usually joined in with Simon's party games wholeheartedly, free of all inhibitions, after dessert. The dessert was becoming increasingly expensive, but it would never be cost-prohibitive—not for Simon's guests. When they played his party games, the dessert was worth every cent.

As for the night's theme, no one ventured an opinion or decorated the apartment. Simon was the only event planner. His preparations were meticulous, and he spent weeks fretting over themes, tones, costumes and decorations. This time round the choice had been surprisingly simple. It was topical, specific and satisfied Simon's soft spot for double entendres—it was all about balls. He had covered every wall in the apartment with green, velvet sheets and decorated them with life-sized cut-outs of famous footballers, past and present. (He got the idea from The Beatles' *Sgt. Pepper's Lonely Hearts Club Band* album cover.) He'd even managed to find photographs of Raffles Rangers players and blow them up, pasting them alongside the likes of David Beckham, Cristiano Ronaldo, Fernando Torres and a young George Best. All the pretty boys.

As a tribute to his guest of honour, he had also made a life-sized cut-out of Bobby Moore, Geoff Hurst and Martin Peters holding aloft the 1966 World Cup. Like Chris Osborne, they had been former West Ham players. But Simon wisely avoided using any current West Ham players.

The fancy dress was obvious enough, but there was genius in its simplicity. Every guest, male or female, had to wear a football kit of his or her choice. There were only two rules. Shirts, shorts and socks were a must; football boots were not required as his tiled floor was too expensive. And secondly, no two people could wear the same kit. The kits could be home or away, present or past, classic or retro, long-sleeved or short-sleeved, but there just couldn't be two of each. Every guest had to call Simon in advance to check there was no kit clash. Simon knew his Brighton and Hove Albion strip would pose no problems, but he could think of nothing more tedious than half a dozen Chinese men and women wearing identical Manchester United and Liverpool kits. Chris had called to say he would wear West Ham's definitive long-sleeved, round-collared shirt worn in the 1975 FA Cup Final. Simon had to admit it—the Essex boy had class.

Simon danced effeminately around the rug with one of his party guests. They were locked arm in arm, singing along to Kylie Minogue's "Can't Get You out of My Head". Simon slurred the words and stumbled. His dance partner, a short, handsome Chinese man dressed in a tight mid-1980s Liverpool kit, complete with Crown Paints sponsor, grabbed Simon around the chest and held him up. Simon threw his arms in the air.

"Is everyone having a good time?" he asked.

There were a few muted cries of "yeah" in his apartment. Simon pulled a face.

"I said, is everyone having a good time?" he shouted.

A few guests cried "yeah" a little louder.

"Then let your faces know, you miserable bastards!"

Simon looked around his apartment and laughed. His home looked like a colourful, pre-season TV commercial for the Super Soccer channel. He was surrounded by attractive men and women in football kits. The surreal image brought back long-forgotten memories of his childhood. His right-wing, Thatcherite parents would buy *The Sun* newspaper, and when they were pottering about in their garden Simon would take the paper and sneak a peek of the day's Page Three glamour model or the muscular Page Seven fella. Back then, he never discriminated. He accepted beauty in all forms and still did in many ways. He admired the women's figures and the men's physiques in his apartment, all complimented by their tight-fitting football kits (tight-fitting kits were not a requirement, but they were most certainly encouraged). Simon laughed loudly as his young dance partner twirled him around the rug. His fancy dress idea had been a masterstroke. After all, no matter how drunk, it didn't take much effort to remove a football kit.

"Are you enjoying yourself, young soccer star?" Simon bellowed.

He waved at Chris, who sat on a beanbag in the corner of the room with Yati. Chris waved back, but Yati never responded. She looked nervously towards the front door of the apartment.

"Yeah, I'm having a blinding time, mate. You really know how to throw a party," Chris shouted back, raising his can of Tiger Beer to Simon.

He wasn't being polite. He had never seen so many Singapore celebrities in one room before. Chris wasn't familiar with all the names, but he knew their faces. Newscasters, weather girls, sports presenters, actors and actresses, reality TV show contestants and magazine models had all been introduced to Chris during the evening. Singapore wasn't overwhelmed with celebrities to begin with, but most of them appeared to be at Simon's party. Simon had led Chris by the hand to meet different people in the crowded room. Chris already knew some of the guests, but he never let on. Simon was clearly having too much fun.

The only people who appeared to be genuine football fans were the rowdy group—mostly Chinese and mostly young—who sang football chants and spent the night sending text messages. When Chris met them, the group were not interested in either his profession or his celebrity. They just wanted his opinion on the weekend's fixtures. They talked odds, number of goals and team news. Their statistical knowledge of both the S-League and the English Premier League had astonished Chris, but they didn't seem to particularly like the game much. Their presence at the party was jarring. They were neither famous nor noticeably affluent, and they drank heavily and swore loudly in Chinese dialects. Yet Simon not only tolerated their unruly behaviour, he indulged them, topping up their drinks and joining in the football chants.

"That's good to hear, Chris," Simon shouted. "Chris, can you hear me? That's good to hear. If you need anything, well, go and get it your bloody self, because I'm not going anywhere while Kylie's playing."

"All right, mate," Chris said.

"And that goes for you, too, Yati. Hope you're enjoying yourself."

"Yeah, I'm fine," Yati said.

Chris glared at Yati.

"You could make more of an effort to show it then. You've sat there with a face like a smacked arse all night."

"Don't start, Chris."

"Who's starting?"

"You are."

"I'm not starting. But you've hardly spoken to anyone all

night, including me. You've not really eaten or drunk anything, and you jump every time the doorbell goes."

"I told you. I didn't really want to come here."

"No, that's not true. You did want to come here, and then right at the last minute you said you didn't, and by then it was too rude to let Simon know."

"I'm here, aren't I?"

"Ah, thanks for that. You've really put yourself out. I might as well talk to the beanbag. We're supposed to be celebrating."

"Celebrating what?"

Chris gritted his teeth.

"You know what," he hissed. "We won 4-1 and I scored twice. We beat Orchard next week and the title's ours."

"Yeah, I know. You'll win the S-League title."

"Don't fucking … Yati … don't, don't do that … don't fuck me off. You know how much this means to me. I've never won anything in my professional career. It means everything to me."

"Yes, you have said that, once or twice already."

"Did I? Sorry if I'm boring you."

Yati craned her head and looked around the room.

"Where's Vince?" she asked.

Chris sighed.

"Where do you think he is? He's hanging around outside the bathroom probably, where he always fucking is."

"I need to see him."

"Do you, really?" Chris whispered. "You don't think you've had enough of that shit already."

Yati faced Chris.

"Not enough. I can still hear you," she said.

"Oh, just go. Go on. Fuck off."

Chris watched as Yati got up and navigated her way through the packed apartment. She found Vince outside the bathroom door, whispered in his ear and the rapper led her into the bathroom.

"Excuse me, Chris, this is going to sound really rude of me, but I don't think she's treating you respectfully."

Chris turned around and saw a sexy Chinese girl sidle up beside him. She was older than Chris, probably in her late 20s, and had long, straight hair. Her pencil-thin figure was accentuated by the skin-tight football kit. That was the second thing he had noticed, after her inviting smile. It was a Queens Park Rangers kit.

"I'm sorry?" Chris said.

"I was sitting on the beanbag just over there and I heard what she said and it sounds like she's treating you like shit," she replied.

"Look, I don't think …"

"It's any of my business and I'm an interfering bitch and you should tell me to go away."

Chris laughed.

"No, I was going to say I don't think anyone should wear a QPR kit."

Now they both laughed.

"I studied in West London," she said. "And an *ang moh* friend took me to see a game there once and bought me this kit. Was it called Loftus Road?"

"Very good, very good indeed … I've seen you before, right? You're the woman who reads the news every night, right?"

"That's me, I'm afraid. Hope my English was good enough."

"No, it was perfect. You look really good on TV."

"Thanks, thanks."

They smiled at each other.

"Look, again, I know this is none of my business, but your girlfriend has a reputation in media circles for only dating white men," she said.

"Again, I'm not sure if that's …"

"And we both know why she's gone into the bathroom. He's not an *ang moh* and he can't make a living selling 500 of his shitty CDs a year."

"Yeah, I know," Chris muttered.

"So they're going to be in there for at least 15 minutes and this party is really crowded."

"So?"

"So, how about we go into one of the bedrooms and I give you the best blow job of your life?"

Chris smiled. Singapore and Essex had quite a bit in common really. He started to get up and the girl followed.

"No, no, I'm going to get another drink," he said quickly. "I appreciate the, er, I really do. But she's my girlfriend. I know about all the rumours. I know what people think and, yes, I know what a Sarong Party Girl is and I've been told all about the Pinkerton Syndrome, but it's not that with her."

"OK, if that's what you think, fine," the girl replied, visibly hurt.

"Besides, people could say the same about you, right?"

The girl pulled herself up from the beanbag and straightened her QPR shirt.

"Please, there are at least 10 other *ang mohs* in this room."

"So why did you pick me, then?"

"Because I don't think you're like them," she said, regaining her composure. "I think you're one of the good guys."

She stood on tip-toes to kiss Chris gently on the cheek and then wandered off to speak to one of the Caucasian investment bankers Chris had been introduced to earlier.

JIMMY Tan sat in his car and calmly read a newspaper. A young Indian guy sat in the passenger seat with his binoculars fixed on

Simon's apartment. He was smartly-dressed in a white shirt and black trousers, and clearly impatient. Siva was a narcotics officer and he was Singaporean. So he wanted to be a Senior Narcotics Officer like Jimmy as soon as possible.

"Do you think we should go in yet, sir?" he said quickly.

"No, I don't," Jimmy replied, not bothering to look up from his newspaper.

"But some people are starting to leave already, sir."

"But we're not worried about some people, are we?"

"No, sir."

"We want ringleaders. That's what we want—ringleaders and scapegoats. And we still have plenty of both up there. We want Vince the Mincer and I want Simon Jones. And we also want a few footballers, too. Why do we want footballers?"

"Because we want scapegoats."

"Simon Jones is our scapegoat."

"Because they're famous?"

"Because they're role models lah. They're sporting role models. We have the Youth Olympics coming to Singapore. We have the Sports Hub coming to Kallang. We cannot have sporting role models taking drugs. And some more they're foreign talent. Foreign talent is already a sticky issue, right or not?"

"Yes, sir."

"We are already struggling to maintain that balance between foreign and local talent, correct?"

"Yes, sir."

"We need a calm exterior to keep everybody happy. We cannot have *ang moh* footballers earning good salaries taking cocaine, right or not?"

"Yes, sir."

"We're not like other Asian countries. We make no exceptions in Singapore. We don't care if you're an Australian backpacker, an American CEO or an English footballer. We treat them all the same, correct?"

"Er, yes, sir, suppose so."

"Right. And Danny Spearman and Chris Osborne are still up there?"

"I think so, sir."

"Then we can wait. Do you know why, Siva?"

"No, sir."

"Because while we wait, they get more drunk and stoned. And when they get more drunk and stoned, they heck care already. I've seen it so many times before. They start off nice and careful, always go to the bathroom. Then they use the kitchen because they get impatient, and then people like Simon Jones think they can do anything and they chop up lines on the coffee table."

"How do you know, sir?"

"Because I've been involved with syndicates in Singapore and Malaysia for over 10 years. They always sell to people like Simon Jones, because in Asia, people like Simon Jones think they are above the law. At home and in the office, they get treated like kings, so they think they are kings. But not here. Not in Singapore."

Siva nodded as he refocused his binoculars on the lift lobby.

"Sir, more people are leaving the party, sir," he said nervously. "They look pretty drunk, sir. I recognise some of them. That one is the famous news presenter and that one is an actor from …"

"I know, let them go. We don't need them this time. The Youth Olympics are coming, I told you, right? We need sports stars now."

Jimmy picked up a walkie-talkie from the dashboard and smiled. It was almost time. He felt a surge of adrenaline as he pushed the button on the side. He was ready to blow the house of cards down.

"OK, this is Senior Officer Tan," he said firmly. "Remember this is a crime scene so do try not to disturb too much, ah. There will be substances in the bathroom, the kitchen and maybe the living room, and I want it all photographed first. They should not struggle, but do not give them any chance to clean up. OK? Right, all units stand by. We go in only on my orders."

DANNY Spearman enjoyed being in Trevor Bonds' company. His stories reminded Danny of his glory days. They had been brief, very brief, and Danny secretly conceded that he lacked Trevor's overall game, even without the debilitating injuries and the weight struggles, but he had at least made it. The same could not be said for Chris bloody Osborne. The Cockney was a top bloke, but the euphoria surrounding the boy still pissed Danny off. No other footballer in Southeast Asia had come close to generating the kind of publicity the kid had generated, not even Tony Cottee or David Rocastle in Malaysia, even though Chris had never played a single senior game at professional level in England.

Danny had. That's why he revelled in swapping stories—real English Football League stories with Trevor at parties. He never had anything like the number of tales that Trevor had to share, but that wasn't the point. He had stories. Chris had fuck all. The one-season wonder had no choice, but to sit quietly and listen to Danny and Trevor.

"So I said to Beckham, you might be good-looking, son, but you'll never have the pace to get past me, mate," Trevor said.

He sat on the corner of the living room rug with Danny, Chris, Yati and Simon's young football friends. Red-faced and perspiring, Trevor swigged from a can of Tiger Beer.

"And the little bastard said, 'I don't need to' and he swerved a cross with his right foot right around me and it spun around to the near post and right on to Andy Cole's head. I looked a right twat.

Mind you, he'd have trouble bending it round this belly now."

Danny laughed and took another swig from his drink.

"Come on, Trev. I'll get you another one," he said.

"Yeah, go on then. I'm supposed to be playing golf in the morning."

"Do you want one, Chris?" Danny asked.

"Nah, you're all right, mate. I've had a skin-full already."

Danny glanced at Trevor and nodded towards Chris.

"Look at this, one season in the S-League and he thinks he's a model pro," he smirked.

"Nah, it's good," Trevor said. "I used to be like that at his age."

Danny trudged off to the kitchen. Trevor watched him go and leaned over towards Chris.

"He's a right dickhead, isn't he?" Trevor whispered.

"Nah, he's all right. He's a good bloke really."

"He's a twat and he's got his own show. I couldn't believe it. I've played for England and over there we've got Sky Sports, BBC, ITV, talk sport radio and now we've got this bloody Setanta and I'm struggling to get regular pundit work. And over here, they're treating this bloke like Gary Lineker."

"His show is really popular."

"I'm sure it is, mate. But back home, we've got European Cup winners fighting for a guest spot on the radio."

"Yeah, I suppose. But back home, I couldn't make the West Ham first team."

Trevor looked thoughtfully at Chris and smiled.

"You're all right, you are, Chris," Trevor said. "I saw you play and you've definitely got something. That second goal was quality. I'm not a scout or anything, but I've got some mates down at Leyton Orient and I know they'd be up for a striker like you."

"Yeah?"

"Yeah, definitely. I know it's not the Premier League, but it's the Football League and it's an East London club for a Cockney like you."

"Yeah, yeah, that's great. I'll have a chat with my Dad about it."

"Nice one … Oh look, here he comes now."

Danny strolled across the rug holding three beers.

"There you go lads," he said.

"I said I didn't want one," Chris muttered.

"Oh, I'll drink yours then."

"Nah, don't waste it. I'll have it, Spear," Billy said.

Danny turned to see Billy standing behind him on the rug. Billy grinned and offered him a hand, which Danny reluctantly shook.

"Oh, I didn't know you were coming," Danny hissed.

"Yeah, yeah, Simon invited me, his little thank you for setting him up with an interview with the S-League superstar there," Billy replied, pointing at Chris.

"How you going, Chris, all right?" Billy continued. "Two great goals again, mate. I reckon that's the title sewn up now."

"There's still another game to go," Chris said.

Billy turned towards Yati, who was staring down at her drink.

"Hello, Yati, didn't expect to see you here," Billy said, wiping his nose. "How are you doing? You having a good time?"

"Yeah, I'm fine," Yati replied, looking up only fleetingly at Billy. "You seem like you're having a good time."

"Yeah, yeah, I saw that Vince on the way in and he sorted me out. So we're sharing stories then, are we? You got any for me, Spear, about you and the CPIB? I've been waiting to hear that one for months."

"What's the CPIB?" Trevor asked.

"Oh, hello, Trevor. How are you enjoying your trip with the

Super Soccer channel? Are you having a good time, mate? Didn't he tell you the CPIB story then?"

Trevor glared suspiciously at Danny.

"What's he going on about, Danny?" Trevor asked.

"Nothing, nothing. You know what these bloody journalists are like. Come on, Billy, we'll have a quick chat in the kitchen."

Danny took his mobile phone off the coffee table and led Billy into the kitchen.

Simon sauntered into the living room, arm-in-arm with Vince. The *X-Pat* editor was glassy-eyed and unsteady on his feet. Vince bit his lip and eyed the remaining guests in the apartment. He had spent most of the night either outside the bathroom or in the kitchen. It had been a highly profitable evening, so much so that he hadn't realised most of the guests had left.

Vince noticed that the footballers were still there, along with Simon's collection of football fans, and Yati. He had watched her earlier in the night in the bathroom. He had given her a couple of lines for free on Simon's orders. The *ang moh* had ordered Vince to give Chris Osborne and Yati whatever they asked for, gratis. Vince had no issue with that. Simon always dutifully picked up the bill. But Vince was astonished by his reaction when he had stared at Yati as she bent over the toilet seat. He wanted to lick every inch of her. He would never be so lucky of course. No matter how many white lines he served up on a toilet seat, Vince knew he would never be white enough.

"Hello, my lovely ladies and gentlemen," Simon slurred. "Or should I say, lady and gentlemen, sorry Yati. It has been a memorable night and it's time for the finale for my dearest friends. It's time for the party games."

The young Chinese guys sitting together quietly stood up suddenly, and cheered and clapped theatrically. Simon raised a glass of wine back at them.

"That's the spirit, boys. Singapura *boleh*! Are we all up for some party games?" Simon said, smiling drunkenly at Chris and Trevor.

Simon flopped like a rag doll in front of a coffee table and, with the help of Vince, dragged it to the centre of the rug.

"OK, everybody, if you could just gather round this delightful see-through coffee table," Simon shouted.

The young men gleefully took a space around the table. Yati and Chris reluctantly shuffled across the living room. Trevor didn't move.

"How about you, Mr Bonds?" Simon shouted.

"No, I'm all right over here, mate, with the beer. Each to his own, you carry on mate."

Simon leaned across the table conspiratorially.

"I see. He's one of those who likes to watch," he whispered.

The young men all giggled.

"We're going to play a game with this coffee table. If you notice, it's see-through, so you can lie underneath and see everything that goes on above it," Simon continued. "That's the fun part. But before we do that, Vince, can you bring out the dessert?"

Vince sighed and took out a small packet from his back pocket and prepared to pour the cocaine in the middle of the coffee table. Simon leaned over suddenly and put his hand under the packet.

"No, no, wait. That coffee table cost me a fortune," he said quickly. "We'll put something over the top of it."

Simon staggered over to a wall in the hallway. He stopped in front of a framed photograph of the Pet Shop Boys and smiled.

"This is what we need," he shouted.

Simon unhooked the framed photograph and meandered back into the living room before ceremoniously placing it carefully on top of the coffee table.

"We've certainly got some West End guys in here tonight,"

Simon said, gazing across the room before stopping to stare at Chris. Simon smiled as Chris shifted uneasily on the beanbag. "We've got some East End boys in here, too."

Vince emptied the packet slowly onto the Pet Shop Boys' photograph, making a small pile over Neil Tennant's head. He took out a credit card and chopped up the powder.

"Right, that's me, I'm afraid," Trevor said suddenly, standing up. "I've got to get up early for golf in the morning. And if I have a little toot now, I've got no chance of getting up. Simon, lovely to meet you. Chris, I'll give you a bell about Leyton Orient when I get back and tell Danny I'll see him at Tanah Merah in the morning. I'll see myself out."

"You're not staying, Trevor?" Simon asked.

"No, no, mate, you carry on. This isn't my thing, but you carry on and have a good time."

Trevor walked briskly across the living room, slipped his flip-flops on quickly and slammed the door behind him. Chris stared at the door long after Trevor had closed it. He wanted to go with him. He then peered at the people around the coffee table. Simon was barely coherent, Vince was the snake in the grass, the Chinese lads couldn't wait to get stuck in, and even Yati—his partner, his so-called career-minded, feminist lover—was obviously keen on snorting a couple of free lines. And Danny had disappeared to the kitchen to be interrogated about match-fixing by that reporter again, that fucking reporter who liked to sniff around Yati when he wasn't sniffing around suspect footballers. Chris thought about that nameless newsreader who had called him a good guy. As he watched Vince roll up a 50-dollar note and hand it to a gleeful Simon, Chris suddenly didn't feel so good.

JIMMY lifted the walkie-talkie to his lips and then stopped. He leaned forward and squinted at a figure staggering along the pavement. He cursed under his breath.

"Give me the binoculars," he hissed at Siva.

Jimmy grabbed the binoculars and focused on the distant figure.

"I knew it," he muttered. "It's that *ang moh* idiot on TV yesterday. It's Trevor Bonds."

Siva sat up excitedly.

"Trevor Bonds, really ah? He used to play for my team Newcastle last time," he said.

Jimmy lowered the binoculars and glared at Siva.

"Really ah? You want to go and ask for his autograph, is it?" Jimmy said. "This guy might fuck up the entire operation."

Siva looked away. He knew his boss was angry. Senior Narcotics Officer Tan never swore during a stakeout.

"What do you want to do, sir?" Siva asked softly.

"I don't know. But we can't go charging past him, can we? We need to get rid of him."

The pair watched Trevor stumble along the street. Occasionally, he would stop, lean over the kerb and look both ways before continuing. The two police officers smiled at each other. Jimmy picked up his walkie-talkie.

"This is Senior Officer Tan here. As you can see, that's Trevor Bonds, an ex-footballer and party guest. We cannot go in until he's out of the way. He's obviously waiting for a taxi and we can't risk a taxi stopping here now. So can the nearest unmarked car go over and take him back to his hotel."

"Er, that's me, sir. You want me to arrest him?" a voice crackled down the walkie-talkie.

Jimmy gritted his teeth. At times, he believed he was the only officer in the Central Narcotics Bureau to demonstrate any initiative.

"Arrest him for what? Being a lousy football pundit? Go and

pretend you are, what is it, a Newcastle fan, just passing, say you're a big fan, and offer to give him a lift. He's so drunk he won't think about the coincidence until morning. Now go."

Jimmy bit the tip of the aerial on the walkie-talkie and waited anxiously. He checked his watch. It was late. They were running out of time. The party would still be going, but there would be no drugs left. He peered through the passenger window as an unmarked CNB car stopped abruptly beside Trevor Bonds about a hundred metres further down the street. For heaven's sake, Jimmy sighed to himself, why didn't the driver just turn on the siren and wave his handcuffs at Trevor.

Jimmy flicked the walkie-talkie aerial up and down against his teeth as Trevor edged towards the car. The ex-footballer stopped, rested his forearm on the passenger door and glanced inside the open window. Jimmy watched nervously as Trevor chatted with one of his plain-clothes officers. Get this right, Jimmy thought, and the *makan* is on me tomorrow. Get it wrong, you *sotong*, and you'll be on desk duties at a neighbourhood police post tomorrow. Trevor stepped back from the car. Jimmy pushed the button on the side of his walkie-talkie.

"If Bonds walks away," Jimmy said, "we have no choice. We go in and scoop him up with the rest of them upstairs. It's his decision now. Stand by."

Jimmy watched Trevor as he stood about a metre from the car and asked the driver something. Trevor listened to the reply and hesitated.

"All units stand by," Jimmy whispered.

Trevor pulled a small, rectangular object out of his pocket and stared at it.

"What's that? What's in his hand?" Jimmy said, dropping the walkie-talkie and picking up the binoculars. He focused on the object and laughed.

"He's getting in the car. The idiot can't remember where he's staying so he's checking the address on his hotel room card key."

Trevor put the card back in his pocket, opened the door and stumbled into the car. Jimmy watched the car slowly and quietly pull away. He picked up the walkie-talkie again.

"Right, I'll take Simon Jones and I want every other person in that apartment arrested. No one gets away, no one," Jimmy shouted. "All units, go, go, go!"

 eighteen

SIMON Jones savoured the sensation as he wiped his eyes and cleaned his upper lip. He grinned at the young Chinese men crowded around the table. The night was almost over, but the party had only just started. He heard a faint noise. He always found it hard to distill all the background noise and focus on a person's voice after a fine dessert, but this sound was distinct. Was that his doorbell ringing? It sounded more like someone hammering aggressively on his door. That couldn't be right. Simon never suffered from paranoia, no matter what the drug. He glanced down and saw Neil Tennant's powdery face singing to him through the snow. That wasn't right. He wasn't there. Simon concentrated hard and mustered the strength to lift his head up from his cherished see-through coffee table. He stared at the other faces around the table. They had heard it, too. They were all a mixture of surprise and uncertainty.

"Isn't that someone banging on your door?" Chris muttered.

"Certainly sounds like it," Vince the Mincer replied.

"It's, er, it's, er, I wonder if it's … er …" Simon mumbled.

Danny and Billy wandered into the living room from the kitchen.

"You know who that is?" Danny slurred. "That's Trevor coming back for a nightcap. I knew he wouldn't be able to resist.

I told him he wouldn't get a cab. I knew it."

"Ah, great, good, another ... er ... friendly face for our, er, party games," Simon shouted. "Spearman, go let him in and let's get on with dessert ... Yati, I notice you haven't had your's yet."

Simon handed Yati the rolled-up 50-dollar note and gestured towards the lines on the table. She stared at Chris and then glanced quickly at Billy, who was squeezing between two of the young Chinese guys in Manchester United shirts on the other side of the table. She leaned over the table and snorted as Danny headed towards the front door.

Danny was surprised that the door was closed and locked from the inside. Singapore homeowners rarely closed their front doors, particularly when guests visited.

"Here, Simon, why have you locked this door? This is Singapore, mate, not Afghanistan. What do you think is going to happen?" Danny grumbled as he drunkenly fumbled with the lock.

A fist pummelled the other side of the door.

"All right, Trevor, you grumpy old bastard, I'm opening it. Simon's a bit paranoid about security."

Danny turned the lock and opened the door.

"Oh look, it's The Spear," said Tiger.

Tiger and Ah Lian, who had a camcorder pointed at Danny's face, pushed past Danny and strolled casually into Simon Jones' apartment. Tiger quietly closed the door behind him.

SENIOR Narcotics Officer Jimmy Tan and Narcotics Officer Siva ran across the lobby of Simon Jones' condo and through the complex's landscaped garden. They were quickly joined by six other plain-clothes officers and the group sprinted towards their cars parked in the street. As he ran past the dozing security guard, Jimmy reached for his walkie-talkie.

"What the fuck just happened?" he screamed breathlessly. "What the fuck just happened?"

"HELLO, sorry to interrupt your party," Tiger said. "But I've just come to talk a bit and then I will go, OK?"

Tiger sat down on an armchair as Ah Lian worked his way around Simon's living room, recording everything on his camcorder. The *ang moh* host, the footballer, the two journalists, the pop star, the fat TV pundit and the pretty boys all sitting together around a table covered in cocaine—Tiger's cocaine. Tiger smiled. He never expected it to be this easy.

"Who the fuck are you?" Yati screamed, her upper lip still covered in Tiger's product. "What's he doing with the video camera? Get the fuck out of the apartment. Chris, kick these fuckers out of the apartment."

Chris stood up quickly and grabbed Tiger by the starched, hard collars of his white shirt and pulled him out of the chair.

"I'll kick your fucking head in," Chris shouted into Tiger's face as their noses almost touched.

Tiger never flinched.

"Look at everyone else in the room. They know who I am," Tiger said softly.

"I know who you are. That fucker from the KTV lounge. The idiot fan," Chris snarled.

"He's not, bro," Vince muttered. "He's the one who gets me this."

Vince pointed at the cocaine on the table. Simon jumped up and emitted a high-pitched, effeminate scream.

"He's the ... er ... dealer. You've brought the dealer into my house," Simon cried deliriously, hopping around the room. "I didn't know you had a dealer."

"Come on, Simon. Where did you think I got it from? You

think I go to Colombia every two weeks just for your parties? I get it from him," Vince said.

Chris glared at both Simon and Vince, thoroughly confused. He turned and faced Tiger again and grabbed him by the throat.

"Well, I don't give a fuck if you are a dealer, mate. If he doesn't turn that camera off, we'll rip his arms off and throw you both out."

"Look at everyone else in the room," Tiger said slowly. "Look how many people are in the room. Why are you the only one so angry, huh? You and your girlfriend. Apart from that expat *chee bye* jumping around, everyone else knows who I am."

Chris threw Tiger down into the armchair and surveyed the room. Tiger was right. Vince stared at the floor. Simon was sitting on his sofa crying and his Chinese guests sat silently around the table. Billy and Danny eyed Tiger nervously, never breaking eye contact.

"Are you blokes going to sit there and let this guy film you like this?" Chris asked the young Chinese men sitting around the table.

Tiger stood up suddenly.

"You can go now," he said firmly.

He gestured towards the door and the Chinese men got up slowly and smiled at Chris. One of the men, the youngest and best-looking one, blew a kiss at Chris.

"Enough already," Tiger said. "Get out."

Within moments, the men all slipped silently out into the night.

"You see, our *ang moh* host likes some company at all his parties. So he calls his famous friend Vince and Vince calls me. Your rent boys, Mr Jones, belong to me, not you," Tiger said. "But they very handsome on camera, right or not?"

Simon sobbed on the sofa, too scared to look up at Tiger. Ah

Lian stood over the weeping *X-Pat* editor with his camcorder and zoomed in.

"Hey, *ang moh*. Can put this on your next cover or not? I write the headline for you. 'ANG MOH EDITOR FUCKED'," Ah Lian giggled.

"Enough lah," Tiger said. "No more games. I'm here for business and then I'll go."

Chris edged towards Tiger again.

"Look, mate. I don't care if you're a scumbag dealer and a pimp. I could still break your fucking jaw right now," Chris said.

"That's true lah. I've watched you play. You're strong, quite physical, you like to tackle. Not many strikers in Asia like to tackle. I like watching you play. You're good."

"These guys might be shit scared of you. They've been in Singapore too long, but if he doesn't turn that camera off I will …"

"You will what? What you going to do ah, S-League superstar? Call the police, is it? Good lah, call them. Let them see your SPG girlfriend with the cocaine on her nose. Good lah, let them see the cocaine all over the apartment. Good lah, let them speak to my boys and find out what really happens at these *ang moh* parties. Good lah. You fuckers look down on people like me. You call me pimp and scumbag. But I spend my weekends having seafood with my family. What do you do in here? This *ang moh* over here interviews all the big shots for his magazine, has dinner with prime minister, takes movie stars and singers around Singapore. Look at him now. Crying like a little girl. But fuck him lah. I don't care about him."

"What do you want, Tiger?" Billy said slowly.

Chris glanced across at Billy. It was the first time the journalist had spoken.

"You know this prick?" Chris asked incredulously.

"I think I know what he wants," Billy muttered.

"Wah, you so clever, been asking all the questions, right," Tiger said. "You think I don't know, is it? You think I don't know that you speak to The Spear, you speak to the girls at the KTV lounge, you speak to the doorman, you tell your editor you got a big story about me. Billy Addis. The voice of the S-League got a big, big story on the king of *kelong*, right?"

Billy blushed and turned away.

"Wah, turn red is it, *ang moh*? Never know I know so much, right? You know how many of your big shot journalists like to gamble? You know how many big shot writers at *The Newspaper* cannot pay their mortgage? You know how many people call me every week? You think you got deep throats? Ha, all my deep throats work inside your office."

Tiger and Ah Lian laughed.

"OK, turn the camera off. I want to talk business now with these journalists and Chris," Tiger said.

"I've got nothing to say to you," Yati hissed. "You're a fucking asshole."

"Ya lah, maybe. But that stuff in your nose came from a fucking asshole."

"Fuck you," Yati shouted.

"Perfect," Ah Lian giggled, as he finished his recording with a close-up of Yati's swearing, cocaine-stained face. Tiger checked that Ah Lian had switched off the camcorder.

"As you know, next week is the final game of the season and the S-League has made sure that the top two teams face each other. This is the S-League that will stop corruption," Tiger said, smiling across at Ah Lian.

"Some things must happen in the match and they might seem obvious lah, to some people, like Mr Voice of the S-League here, so we need some things to happen and we need some people to be quiet."

Chris laughed.

"Look, mate, if you think I'm going to fix a match, then you can fuck right off," Chris said. "Sorry, mate, grew up in the wrong culture. I know you all laugh at our food, say we can't cook and our weather's shit, but we don't gamble on everything from the EPL to two cockroaches in the street, and English players don't fix matches."

Tiger looked at Danny and Billy, and smiled.

"He doesn't know English football, right?" Tiger said. "But it's OK. I knew you were going to say that. Like I say, you're a good footballer. You're a good guy, Chris. I needed some help and lucky for me, your girlfriend helped me."

Tiger held out his hand and Ah Lian passed him a mobile phone.

"Luckily, we managed to get some photographs of these two fucking."

Tiger pointed at Yati and Billy.

"What?" Chris said.

"The photos are not very good, but the video on the hand phone's better, thanks to you Chris. Most *ang mohs* like air-con, 'cos Singapore's very hot, right? *Ang mohs* cannot take the heat and because you live on a high floor, you keep your doors and windows open, nice and breezy. No one to disturb you up there, so high. I don't have a condo on the 20th floor, but I think there's more privacy, right? Nobody walks past. So you can shag and no one will see."

Tiger lifted the mobile phone up to Chris' face.

"On this phone, got a good video. Got quite a big screen though you cannot see much. But can hear, right? If you look here, you can just see Billy's backside through the door, can see or not? And can you hear that screaming? That's your girlfriend. *Wah lao*, listen to all that noise. Wait first, keep watching. When they finish, you can just see her through the door to the bathroom in only her *sarong*, very pretty. Can I ask one question, Chris? Does she make that much noise when you fuck her?"

"Cunt," Chris screamed.

Chris stepped forward and punched Tiger in the face. The punch lacked direction and caught Tiger across the right cheek and nose. Tiger flopped backwards onto the armchair and dropped the phone onto the floor. Chris stamped on it.

"Fuck you, SPG, fucking, lying, two-faced SPG bitch!" Chris shouted. "There. It's gone. Your phone's fucked now."

Tiger smiled and touched his right cheek softly.

"I'll give you that one *ang moh*, for now. I shouldn't have mentioned the noise. I'm sure she screamed for you also lah. SPGs like to scream. And thanks for doing that to the phone, Chris. That was, how you say, incriminating evidence. But we've already made several DVD copies ready to send to *The Newspaper*, the S-League, Raffles Rangers, West Ham, maybe even that Australian team. Those boys will find it damn funny and, of course, your father. Must also send him a copy of this new party video. I think he'll find it damn funny."

"Fuck you, you don't know anything about my father."

"Come on ah, I'm a diehard Raffles Rangers fan. My son goes to every game. I have to go to every game with him and find out all the facts and figures on his favourite players, right or not?"

Tiger picked up a piece of tissue paper from a box on the cocaine-covered coffee table and wiped away a tiny trickle of blood from under his nose. He leaned towards Chris' ear.

"So of course I know where your father lives in Dagenham," he whispered.

Chris took a step backwards and stared at Tiger.

"It's, er, true, if what I know about him is true," Billy mumbled. "He could know where your father lives."

Chris turned quickly and glared at Billy.

"I'm not fucking interested in anything you've got to say. I'll sort you out in a minute," Chris shouted.

"Exactly, let's get the business out of the way and you three can do whatever lah," Tiger said quickly. "OK, then. Next Saturday, Raffles Rangers takes on Orchard FC in the last game of the season, correct? Raffles are three points clear with a better goal difference and are playing at Stamford Stadium, right? Everyone expects them to win and the odds are shitty, very shitty, waste of time. So we spread rumours that the game is *kelong*, that Raffles are going to throw it away and we can take Orchard. But that's too obvious and also, I know you, Chris Osborne, you are a good guy. We cannot make you miss. I know that. So we make you score. We tell everybody the game is *kelong*, correct, and so the odds on Raffles too high now. That's right, ah, Mr S-League reporter? So everyone buys lots of goals. Everybody buys Orchard FC because they think it's fixed. They think sure a lot of goals because it's fixed. It *is* fixed, but the other way round. Raffles will win and you will score the winner."

"Fuck off," Chris hissed.

"Come on ah, Chris. You're only doing what you're paid to do. You'll probably score the winner anyway, right? We just make sure it will happen and you score the only goal. Danny is out so your defence is much stronger, ha. Wee Kin is out so he cannot score. He was unlucky for you. We were going to use him, but things happen, never mind lah. So we hope you score, can? Near the end of the match, you will get a penalty. You will not be fouled. I watch you; you never dive, but your team will get a penalty. And you will score."

"Fuck you. I've never missed a penalty as a professional."

"And you won't miss this one. The goalkeeper will dive to your left, OK. Do not forget. The goalkeeper will dive to your left. He knows already. Just kick it anywhere to your right and it will go in, can or not?"

"I'm not *kelong*."

"I know lah. I'm telling you to score, not miss. You will score the winner so your team can keep the title lah."

Chris laughed loudly.

"You've got no fucking idea how football works have you? Do you know how hard it is to fix a football match? Do you know how many imponderables there are? How many things there are beyond your control? There are 22 players all making runs at the wrong time, mistiming tackles, missing open goals, scoring flukes from 40 yards, turning up offside, bumping into each other, losing their footing, tripping over their studs. And that's not even counting a hostile crowd, a shit referee, substitutions and even the weather."

"Or even the floodlights."

Tiger glanced at Billy and nodded towards Chris.

"He really doesn't know who I am, right?"

"What's that supposed to mean?" Chris asked.

"Forget it lah. Just remember to kick the penalty to your right. Anywhere to your right, on target, and you are the Player of the Year."

"So you only want one goal. Obviously, you're taking one goal for this match?"

"Just score your penalty and the match will end 1-0."

"What if I score before the penalty? What if I hammer one in from 40 metres? What if I score a hat-trick?"

"That cannot happen."

"Of course it fucking can. I've been scoring goals since I was five years old in Dagenham. How are you going to stop me?"

"I cannot, I'm not playing."

"So, what does that mean?"

"Ah, for fuck's sake, Chris, smarten up. If you score early on, he'll have your leg broken in a tackle or something," Billy said.

"Who the fuck's talking to you?"

Chris glared at Billy and Yati. He noticed Simon weeping on the sofa and Vince absentmindedly pushing the cocaine around the table with his finger. He suddenly felt light-headed. He took a deep breath and faced Tiger.

"Is that what's going to happen then? I score an early goal and then it's lights out for me?"

"Your girlfriend's other boyfriend seems to think so."

"And what happens if I miss the penalty? We'll still win the league."

"Yes, you will still win the league, but we'll email the video of these two fucking. Plus we'll make copies of this party video, we take out the sound first lah, and send it to the Premier League, the English Football League, the A-League, the S-League, all your old leagues, I think, and maybe all the other leagues. Oh, and one for your father, too."

Chris glared at Tiger and Ah Lian.

"So I'm fucked if I do and I'm fucked if I don't."

 **nineteen**

JIMMY Tan watched the Geylang shophouses pass the passenger's window in a colourful, neon blur. Siva was driving fast and the siren was blaring, but not fast enough.

"You driving for a funeral, is it?" Jimmy barked.

"No, sir," Siva said.

"Then put your foot down lah. I want to know what happened tonight."

"Yes, sir. So do I, sir."

"Oh, really? I've been working surveillance in narcotics for over 10 years and that has never happened before."

And it hadn't. Jimmy was there. He was standing beside the house of cards and had inhaled sharply. He was poised and ready to blow each of the grubby parasites down one by one. He was so close he could almost touch it, taste it, almost smell the victory. He stood with his team in the lift of Simon Jones' condo. That was how close he was. The lift doors had opened on Simon Jones' floor, and Jimmy had given the hand signal to fall in line and wait for his final order to break the door down. Jimmy always broke the door down. Other Senior Officers liked to follow protocol and give a solitary knock on the door, a quick shout to identify themselves and a single warning to open up immediately. But Jimmy was too Singaporean. He was *kiasu* and proudly so. In

Hokkien, *kiasu* loosely translated as 'scared to fail', which didn't do justice to him. He was mortified by the threat of failure. Why allow the suspects precious seconds to do a perfunctory clean-up? The drugs could still be sniffed out later, but why make the job unnecessarily difficult for forensics? Jimmy championed and cherished the tried and tested element of surprise. It was the most reliable weapon for a narcotics officer. Men like Jimmy did all the surprising. They abhorred being surprised by others.

The order was brief. It had to be. Jimmy was seconds away from smashing down Simon Jones' door. The order was as brief as it had been vague.

"Stand down immediately," a voice on the walkie-talkie screamed.

Jimmy had initially thought it was perhaps a miscommunication, a crossed line or a sick joke, and was prepared to ignore it. But the professionalism ate away at him. There were never miscommunications like this, not at that precise moment. Mistakes were made and far too often for Jimmy's liking, but not on major drugs busts like this one. Preparations were always meticulous. Preparation, preparation, preparation. Jimmy insisted on it before every crackdown operation. No margin for error was tolerated.

"This is a direct order for Senior Officer Tan," the voice barked again. "You are to stand down immediately. Do not enter the suspect's house. Do not engage the suspect. Do not alert the suspect to your presence."

That might be troublesome, Jimmy had muttered to himself. I'm standing outside his fucking door. Even though a raid had never been aborted at such a late stage before, Jimmy still clicked onto auto-pilot. Without speaking, he ordered his men to withdraw. No one spoke. There was barely a sound in the corridor. Jimmy signalled to his men to take the stairs. Modern

Singapore lifts with their fancy feminine robot voices made too much damn noise. He preferred the no-frills lifts in Singapore's older blocks. They never beeped and announced his arrival every time he stepped out into the lift lobby before a drugs bust. No one in Jimmy's team uttered a word until they were heading away from the lift lobby on the ground. That was not the time for words. Now was.

"Can you go any faster or what?" Jimmy yelled at Siva.

"Yeah, OK, OK. Sorry, boss."

Siva yawned as he checked his rear-view mirror.

"You're sleepy, is it? You want to be relieved, is it?"

"No, sir. It's just that it's nearly 4 a.m. and I haven't had much sleep this week."

"None of us has. And we're not going to get much sleep tonight either. Faster lah."

Jimmy picked up his mobile phone and dialled quickly.

"Hello, this is Senior Officer Tan," he barked. "I want to speak to the person who called off the operation. I don't care what his rank is, I don't care what department and I don't care what time it is. I want to see him back at the complex now ... Oh, really, oh, right ... er ... good. That's good."

Jimmy put his mobile phone back on the dashboard and stared out of the windscreen.

"Very strange," he muttered.

"What is it, boss?" Siva enquired.

"The idiot who called off the operation ..."

"Ya lah, idiot. You're gonna see him, right?"

"I don't have to. He's waiting to see me."

CHRIS couldn't sleep. The sofa in his living room was uncomfortable, but he wouldn't have slept in his bed either. Not that he was ever going to sleep in the bed again. That bitch had fucked that reporter in his bed—their bed—and it was soiled now. The entire apartment was contaminated and dirty, and Chris was eager to leave. Just one more game and he could. It would all be over in every sense.

Chris got out of the sofa and wandered across the warm tiles. The tiles were usually warm. He liked that. He rarely used air-conditioning. The idea of waking up in a cold bedroom reminded him too much of growing up in a council house in Dagenham, shivering in the hallway as he waited for the portable Calor gas fire to warm up. Money had been tight when the cutbacks started at Ford for his father. Money was no longer an issue and Chris didn't need to feel cold in the mornings any more.

Yati had told Chris that she preferred the breezy air that came from living on a high floor of a Singapore apartment block. Perhaps that was a lie, too. Perhaps the pair of them fucked like rabbits with Chris' air-conditioning units whirring in every room. No, of course they didn't. They had all the windows and doors open when that scumbag caught them on his mobile phone. They were captured, bang to rights. That wanker was shagging Chris' girlfriend, in Chris' apartment, in Chris' bed.

In any other circumstances, Chris would have happily knocked him out. Chris wasn't a violent man, but Billy Addis had broken every written and unwritten rule known to Man. He had crossed that line. Even Chris' father would have taken action. Tony Osborne was the most passive man Chris had ever known and it wasn't just because he was his father; everyone said it. Tony never raised a hand to anyone—man, woman or child. Except that one time. It was in the living room of their Dagenham council house. There was another man in the house. Chris and his father had returned home early one evening from football training and found them both in the living room together. It was the only time Chris ever saw his father lose his temper. The pair left the house and the incident was never raised again.

Chris leaned out of the window and stared at the Orchard Road traffic below. It was 4 a.m. and there were still fleets of blue, yellow and silver taxis patrolling the street, hoping to get lucky with that final fare of the evening—a disoriented drunk tourist, an American marine outside Orchard Towers, some locals after a KTV session or a prostitute with a customer.

Chris thought about his father. Would he be proud of Chris' behaviour so far? On balance, Chris thought he would. He had refrained from hitting Billy and berating Yati after Tiger and that wanker with the video camera had left. He was mentally exhausted. Tiger's threats had drained him of his anger and left him surprisingly empty. He lacked the energy to pick a second fight or row with Yati. Instead, he never said a word. He just left. He slipped on his shoes, opened the door and fell into a strange semi-conscious state. He wasn't fully aware of what he was doing again until he found himself paying the taxi driver outside his condo.

Without thinking, he picked up his mobile phone and dialled.

"Hello, boy, what are you doing calling me this late?" his father said down the line. "It must be early in the morning over there."

"Ah, I just couldn't sleep, Dad. Thought I'd give you a call."

"You're not nervous about the game, are ya? It'll be easy. Just do what you've been doing all season. You know you've got them beat for speed and strength. Just keep turning them with your first touch. You know that's your greatest asset."

Chris wiped the tears in his eyes and sniffed. Within seconds, his chuffed dad was talking football with his professional footballer son. He sensed the paternal pride down the line. Chris sniffed again.

"Yeah, I know that, Dad," he whispered.

"You all right, mate? Sounds like you've got a bit of a cold."

Chris held his hand over the receiver, sniffed a third time and took a deep breath.

"Nah, nah, I'm fine, Dad. Just a touch of allergy. You know what I'm like with allergies. The dust allergy is pretty bad over here."

"You'll be all right to play, though, right? They're relying on you, mate. Now you're playing up front on your own, they'll be looking to you, so you need to be a team player on Saturday."

"Yeah, I know, Dad."

"How's Yati doing? I'm looking forward to meeting her after the season."

"She's, er, she's fine, Dad. She's looking forward to meeting you, too."

"Bloody hell, have you warned her about Dagenham? After that lovely condo in Singapore, I think she'll be in for a shock when I take her for egg and chips up the Heathway."

Chris laughed as tears rolled down his cheeks.

"Yeah, I've warned her about your diet," he said.

"Hollow legs, mate. When you play as much football as I do, you can eat whatever you like."

"That's true, Dad. Here, listen, Dad, the reason I called is to find out if you've heard anything about some of the London clubs over there?"

"Well, I, er, I keep in touch with them, you know that, but I thought you told me to lay off a bit once you signed for Raffles Rangers. I thought you were having a great time over there. What's happening?"

"No, no, nothing, nothing. It's great here, Dad. I just thought it would be good to cash in now, you know. Top scorer in a rising Asian league, league champions, Singapore the best team in

Southeast Asia. Do you know Singapore recently beat Thailand and they are now managed by Peter Reid, the old Everton skipper?"

"Yeah, I know, but I thought you were settling there and they were even talking about you playing for Singapore one day."

"I know, but the season has gone so well that I thought I might have a good chance of cracking on with a London club. I've got some DVDs of my goals made up and I think something could be on the cards with Leyton Orient."

"Really? I've never heard anything from them."

"No, I know, but do you remember Trevor Bonds?"

"Yeah, yeah, Trevor Bonds ... good little fullback at Newcastle, played a few times for England I think."

"That's him. Well, he's over here doing a bit of TV work with Danny and he's got some mates at Orient and he fancies my chances there."

"Really? Right, well, OK then. I'll look into it, if that's what you want. But I think you should be focusing on this Saturday for now."

"Yeah, I am, honestly, but I'm taking a long-term view of my career, Dad."

"Don't be a sarcastic little sod."

"I'm not. I'm just thinking we should take advantage of the season I've had quickly."

"All right, I'll phone them once your season is over. So Trevor Bonds rates you, does he? That's great. Have you been on any of Danny's shows with him?"

"Nah, I haven't done too much of that lately."

"No, you're too busy playing, not like that lazy bugger Spearman. How he gets away with it I'll never know."

Chris stared at the shimmering lights of the cranes working off Marina Bay, building a casino, another gambling fortress, another free ATM for men like Tiger. He thought about his father's words. During the row with Tiger and Billy, Chris had forgotten about the mighty Spear. As two gangsters ordered a Raffles Rangers striker to fix a score line and demanded that a reporter swallow any conspiracy theories, Danny Spearman had sat quietly by the see-through coffee table. The biggest mouth in Asian football hadn't said a word.

JIMMY marched briskly along the corridors of the Central Narcotics Bureau complex. Siva struggled to keep up. Jimmy stopped periodically to peer inside offices before marching on.

"Where is he?" he demanded. "Where's the big shot who called off my undercover operation?"

"Sir, maybe you should stay calm," Siva interjected.

"I was calm at the raid. Now I'm angry. Where is he?"

Siva's mobile phone rang. He stopped in the corridor to answer as an impatient Jimmy strolled on.

"Ya, OK ..." Siva said. "Sir, he's waiting for you in the interrogation room."

"That's the best place for him," Jimmy shouted back.

Jimmy threw open the door to the interrogation room. Internal protocol insisted that all CNB officers, regardless of rank, knocked before entering the interrogation room. What went on behind those closed doors went on behind closed doors for a reason. Jimmy had no time for protocol now. He stormed into the room and saw a young, scruffy Chinese man sitting on a wooden chair with his hands placed nonchalantly behind his head and his feet up on the table. He wore ripped jeans and a grubby white singlet. Jimmy was appalled by his appearance, but vaguely recognised him. He had seen him around, but couldn't quite place him. This idiot was hardly a high-ranking officer, if Jimmy was unable to put a name to the familiar face. This idiot can't be the reason why three months' worth of work had all been wasted in one evening, he thought.

"Who the hell are you? What department do you work for? And who gives you the authority to pull the plug on my CNB operation?"

The Chinese man smirked at Jimmy. Jimmy wanted to strangle the smug bastard.

"Good morning. I am Detective Low and I work for the CPIB," he said slowly.

Jimmy was surprised by his accent. He spoke in perfect English. It was flawless. Clearly, this idiot had been educated overseas.

"The CPIB?" Jimmy scoffed. "Please lah, this is a CNB operation. We had a dealer supplying cocaine to all the big shots in Singapore. We've been following the dealer for three months already. Who gives a shit about CPIB? How the hell can CPIB pull rank on CNB?"

"We didn't, I'm afraid. The order to abort your raid came from the Home Improvement Ministry. The CPIB is working on a particularly sensitive case with international connections. We have been meticulously tracking one of the world's biggest match-fixing syndicates and we are almost ready to move in. We couldn't risk it for a few *ang mohs* and Singapore celebrities getting high at parties. You've been following a dealer for nearly three months? I've been undercover on this case for nearly two years. My alias is Ah Lian."

twenty

JIMMY watched Detective Low sip his latte. The guy looked like an *Ah Beng*, called himself Ah Lian and had the refined taste of a barista. The mind struggled to comprehend what the eye saw. But then nothing this young detective said made much sense.

"So what you're saying is, Low …" Jimmy began.

"Please call me Ah Lian," he interrupted.

"You want me to call you Ah Lian, is it?"

"This really is good coffee, you know. Do you know where the best coffee in the world comes from? You'll probably say Brazil, right? Everyone says Brazil. But it's not. It's Ethiopia. That's the home of the Arabica tree and that's the tree that produces the berry that contains the coffee bean. Did you know that?"

"I don't give a shit about coffee, Low. I want to know …"

"Please, really, call me Ah Lian. It's important to be consistent."

"It sounds ridiculous."

"I know, but it stops me from getting confused. When you're undercover for so long, you get called Ah Lian from the moment you open your eyes until the moment you close them again at 5 a.m. I ask everybody to call me Ah Lian; then there is less chance of me making a mistake and blowing my cover."

"But why did you pick Ah Lian? It's such a lousy alias."

"I didn't. My target, Tiger, did, because he said I looked like a skinny little girl gangster."

"That's our target, too, remember. We've been tracking Tiger, too, you know."

Ah Lian smiled at Jimmy. His CNB counterpart was clutching at straws already.

"No, that's not strictly true, is it? You were following Vince the Mincer, our rapper friend. He's just our idiotic Falstaff. You knew he bought from Tiger, but you had no real idea who Tiger was, what he did or where he got the cocaine from. I've been working with him for two years."

"So who is he then, ah?" Jimmy snapped.

Ah Lian's cool demeanour irritated him. He was part of the new generation of Singaporean police officers raised on computer games and undercover cop movies like *Infernal Affairs*. These young kids always performed a role, pretending to be Andy Lau or a character in *Grand Theft Auto*. Every undercover operation was a game. Jimmy was too long in the tooth to play games.

"Tiger has probably been involved with every major match-fixing case in Singapore, if not the region, since the S-League started back in 1996. He has links with Asian syndicates in Malaysia and Hong Kong, and even has ties at the highest level with some Chinese crime organisations in the UK. But we haven't made that final connection yet. We don't know how far Tiger's reach goes. But we do know that they are planning to fix the final game of the S-League season. We have to see that through. That's why we couldn't let your drugs raid happen at Simon Jones' premises. We had to allow Tiger the chance to set the ball rolling, as it were, and hope that the *kelong* players on both Raffles Rangers and Orchard FC do the rest."

"There are *kelong* players on both sides?"

"Of course. Tiger leaves nothing to chance. There is too much money riding on this game. His runners have been working for weeks to tilt the market in Orchard's favour. Everything is now in place. Everyone has been fixed. Now we need to maintain a calm exterior until after the game when, hopefully, all hell will break loose."

"What will happen after the game?"

"Well, if it's a low-scoring game, particularly 1-0 to Raffles Rangers, then there will be payouts. Syndicates across Asia must be paid their winnings and Tiger organises all the transactions. They are in cash obviously and he may even ask me to make some of the deliveries, wherever they may be—Singapore, KL, Kowloon, Macau, Bangkok. I don't even know how many syndicates Tiger has got on board. But all we have to do then is follow the money trails. I might as well turn up with the money in one hand and the handcuffs in the other."

"Can't you just arrest Tiger after the match?"

"There's no point. The man hasn't spent a single day in prison. He's a wily operator with deep throats everywhere. Do you know how many officers gamble? And most of them play outside. They don't play with Singapore Pools. They play outside because they get better odds. Where do you think they go to play? Besides, Tiger doesn't even know all of the people he's working for. I'm pretty sure of that. He takes a lot of calls from runners like me working overseas, but he doesn't know all the bosses. But this is a big one because he's been given a lot of money to bankroll the operation. That's how you got involved."

"Me?"

"Well, you and the CNB. Tiger doesn't really deal drugs. He doesn't need to. Compared to football, the returns are small and the risks are too high. Everyone knows Vince the Mincer. He's an idiot, but he's a useful link. He thinks he's a gangster. He plays the rapper tough guy. But he's just an English-educated, middle-class Singaporean-Indian from the housing estates who wants to be liked by the right people. He wanted to convince his celebrity friends that he was a real player on the street, and Tiger knew that footballers turned up at these parties and he needed an edge. The cocaine did the rest."

"And I nearly messed up the party for you all."

Ah Lian giggled as he sipped his latte and spilt some on his chin.

"Whoops sorry about that," Ah Lian coughed. "I don't mean to be disrespectful, but I saw your unmarked car outside Simon Jones' condo weeks ago. I was happy to let you scramble around and build your case because I didn't expect any raids before the end of the season. You moved faster than I expected."

"Oh, I'm so sorry," Jimmy said sarcastically.

"No, no, my sincere compliments. Your operation must have been prepared meticulously. I only found out about the raid by luck. I asked a colleague to do a routine check on Simon Jones' condo before I went in there with Tiger to make sure there were no security booby traps I didn't know about. And it popped up in the computer that the place was under surveillance. We quickly worked out the rest. I'm really sorry, but I had to make some calls to stop the raid. The Home Improvement Ministry is monitoring our progress closely. They are demanding results."

"The Central Narcotics Bureau demands results, too," Jimmy sniffed.

"And you can have them, by all means, and with our genuine gratitude, too."

"Please, lah, we didn't go through with the raid. We need scapegoats too, you know."

"And you will have them, but you've just got to wait until after the match. Let's get the match out of the way. Let's not make anyone suspicious. When the match is over, we'll both have enough scapegoats to keep the ministry happy. You will have your magazine editor, your pop star dealer and perhaps even a prominent female journalist if you want. I think those three will certainly send the right message."

"How lah? We've got no evidence."

Ah Lian smiled and stood up. He walked over to a shelf and picked up a laptop. He placed the laptop on the table in front of Jimmy and pulled up the screen.

"Watch this little home movie of mine," he said. "It was produced by Tiger, but I think you'll love my direction. After you've seen it, you and the rest of the CNB team will be giving me a large red packet for Chinese New Year."

DANNY Spearman trudged slowly towards his car. He had struggled to find a space in the car park earlier. The Tanah Merah Golf Club was packed on a Friday at the best of times and a charity round sponsored by the Super Soccer channel always brought out plenty of the old boys from the Padang and the Singapore Polo Club. His game had been a disaster. He was 12-over on the front nine and even Trevor Bonds, who'd never played a round with Danny before, knew something was wrong.

"What did you take after I'd left that party?" Bonds had asked.

"Nothing, nothing, I just had a skin-full, that's all, and hardly any sleep," Danny had replied.

The answer appeared to satisfy Bonds, but the Super Soccer channel director and producer who made up their flight didn't look convinced. Rumours had circulated the studio for weeks. The Spear was injured. The Spear was going to miss the title run-in with his old ankle injury. But The Spear's ankle never let him down when he went out with the studio lads to CHIJMES and danced with the local groupies at 3 a.m.

Secretly, Danny was delighted to be out of the spotlight. There was too much heat on this one. Even by Tiger's elaborate standards, that party video was an audacious move. There must be serious money riding on the final game. Danny had the easy job—sit in the dugout and publicly cheer on his team-mates and privately pray that they didn't win by more than a solitary goal. Had he been playing, then the finger would surely be pointed at The Spear, especially by that prick Billy Addis. Danny had to admit it. He could've kissed Tiger at the party. Getting Billy involved had gotten him off Danny's back.

Everything was down to Chris now. As long as that Cockney wide boy kept up his end of the bargain, then Danny was in the clear. His job was done. He had steered clear of discussing Raffles Rangers' final match on air and he had avoided giving any interviews to the media, despite the daily requests. He had even distracted Billy when he was poised to go in for the kill at the party. Billy had said no one escaped the CPIB after questioning; charges were always laid. A CPIB interview always led to a match-fixing charge and an eventual conviction. What a naïve prick. Billy knew nothing. The Spear missed nothing.

Danny reached his car and deactivated the central locking system. He liked showing off his Lexus at the golf club. God knows, he had earned it. Danny heard footsteps behind him.

"*Aiyoh*, your back swing damn lousy one."

Danny turned and sighed.

"Hello, Ah Lian," he muttered.

Ah Lian mimicked Danny's wayward drive.

"I watch you from behind the fence, damn funny lah you," Ah Lian giggled. "Cannot focus, is it? You drunk, is it? *Wah lao*, your ankle very pain, is it?"

"Yeah, OK, very funny. What do you want?"

Ah Lian checked the car park. Apart from a Chinese *towkay*

squeezing the backside of his mistress as he led her towards the clubhouse, the car park was empty. Ah Lian edged towards Danny. Danny flinched.

"I am growing increasingly tired of your antics," he whispered in flawless English. "You almost jeopardised the entire operation."

"What are you talking about? I did what you told me to do," Danny replied. His high-pitched whine betrayed his nervousness.

"Don't piss me off, Danny. We made it with seconds to spare. Fucking seconds. You were seconds away from six years. Is that what you want, Danny? Do you think you could handle six years with the drug couriers and the molesters? Do you want to be a celebrity prisoner in Changi? Do you want to be the next Nick Leeson? Do you think you could live off the royalties of your prison memoirs? I've got to be honest here, Danny. I cannot see The Spear's autobiography having the same international appeal as *Rogue Trader*. And I can't see Ewan McGregor playing you in the movie either."

"I did what you wanted," Danny pleaded, looking over his shoulders for other golfers returning to their cars.

"You were supposed to message me when everything was in place and all the main players were seated around that damn coffee table. I told you to get them drunk and keep them there until everyone else had gone so we could go in."

"I did."

"Fuck you," Ah Lian raged. "You went into the kitchen and forgot all about it because that reporter was giving you a hard time."

"It wasn't like that."

"Really, what was it like then? Did you message me because Billy Addis had you by the balls and you needed us to burst through the door in our superhero capes and rescue you, just in case your feeble, intoxicated brain said something that you'd later regret in court?"

"No, no, of course I didn't," Danny mumbled.

He stared at the floor. They both knew that that's exactly what he did.

"You're lucky. I really don't think you realise how lucky you are because I really did save you and your cokehead pals that night," Ah Lian said.

"How do you mean?"

"That's none of your business."

Ah Lian glared at Danny contemptuously. The so-called mouth of Asian soccer, the mighty Spear who always hit the target was a pathetic little man.

"So is he going to do it on Saturday?" Ah Lian asked.

"Er, yeah, I think so. Well, I hope so. I guess he has to really. There's no other alternative, is there?"

"Well, he had better to do it, for your sake. Believe me, I'm the least of your worries. If the match doesn't go the right way, then I'll be forced to come out and round them all up. But Tiger will be a hard man to find and put on a leash."

Danny shuffled his feet uneasily.

"Can't you just arrest him at the game?" Danny asked.

"He won't be at the game, will he? It doesn't matter where he will be. All you need to know is if your boy doesn't deliver from the penalty spot, then the syndicates will come for Tiger. So he will have to come for all of you. There has to be reprisals."

"Can't you protect us? Stick us in that witness protection thing or whatever you call it?"

"Oh, certainly, Danny. That's exactly what we'll do. We hadn't thought of that one. We'll hide the most recognisable *ang moh* face in Southeast Asia and the most popular striker in the country in a government apartment in Toa Payoh. You'll just disappear after the biggest game in the S-League's history. And then we'll say you both had to disappear for your own safety after being blackmailed by a major crime syndicate at a cocaine party into fixing the biggest game in the S-League's history. We could hide you, Danny, I suppose, but you might have trouble getting a job washing dishes at a *roti prata* stall once it's safe to come out."

"So what can I do?"

"Nothing. Keep your mouth shut and encourage your friend to do what he is supposed to do and then leave us to pick up the pieces. We might be able to save you an appearance in court, but that depends on what we get. Make sure you have a nice shirt and tie just in case."

"What happens if the game doesn't finish 1-0?"

"Ah, that's easy, isn't it, Danny? Just hope that we find Tiger before he finds you."

 twenty-one

CHRIS wanted to be sick. He could taste the vomit at the back of his throat and fought the temptation to wretch. The greatest day of his life had become his worst through no fault of his own. From the moment he gave up the pretence of trying to nap in the afternoon and hauled himself up off the sofa, the day took on a dream-like quality. He had washed, shaved and dressed, waved good afternoon to the Indian security guard who always asked for betting tips, and stepped into the taxi he had called for earlier. He found his way to Stamford Stadium. He felt like a stooge in a hypnotist's routine. He was there, but he wasn't really present.

But Chris felt the atmosphere on the way to the stadium. He could sense it—a surge of electricity that shocked him out of his trance. There was singing, lots of singing, which wasn't commonplace in Asian football, but wasn't unheard of either. This was different though. They were singing outside Stamford Stadium. Hundreds, perhaps thousands of voices, all chanting in unison, chanting in the street. They were singing and dancing in the street. Chris had never seen this in Singapore before. He had only witnessed such a collective singing and dancing routine once, and that was at the National Day Parade. But that had been coordinated. Every clap, cheer and whistle was rehearsed. Chris had chuckled at the spectacle from the VIP enclosure, as a guest of the Minister for Home Improvement. It was loud and stirring, but thoroughly manufactured.

The Raffles Rangers fans were spontaneous and real. Just like West Ham fans. West Ham fans could be uncouth and downright offensive to former players, but they were also funny, original and unique. They had made Chris feel alive when he was a child. When he had held his father's hand as they walked down Green Street together, Chris had never wanted the walk to end. In those moments, he wanted to live in Green Street forever. When Chris raised his hands above his head, along with thousands of others, and sang "I'm Forever Blowing Bubbles", he felt like he was at the centre of the universe. He belonged.

For the first time since he signed professional forms with Harry Redknapp at West Ham, Chris belonged. He belonged to Raffles Rangers. He belonged to the Raffles Rangers fans. He was one of them now. As he made his way through the crowd towards the main stand, he was barely aware of all the backslapping and the handshakes. He hardly noticed the toddler who was lifted up for him to kiss on the cheek or the teenage girl who had forced him to pose for a photograph on her mobile phone. But the voices made him stop. The voices made him listen. They were chanting his name, hundreds of them, outside the stadium. He stopped outside the door marked "Staff Entrance" and turned around. He watched hundreds of fans stand before him, raise their hands and applaud. He tried hard to focus on their singing. He loved them for their singing; it was a temporary distraction. It took him away. For a few, glorious seconds, there was no Tiger, no Yati, no *kelong*, no Ah Lian and no video. There was only football. He was back at Green Street and the collective sense of anticipation was building. Footballer and fan were briefly united in their shared excitement. In that fleeting moment, nothing else mattered apart from the game itself.

Chris found himself raising his arms to the crowd, encouraging them to sing louder. He knew the words, but he needed to be reminded.

"There's only one Chris Osborne," the crowd cried. "One Chris Osborne ... There's only one Chris Osborne ... One Chris Osborne!"

Chris raised his arms again, demanding more voices and more volume. He had to remember this moment. They had to remember this moment. He wanted the crowd to remember that there really was only one Chris Osborne; that Chris Osborne's goals and assists had helped to bring them here; that Chris Osborne had made the S-League fashionable again; that Chris Osborne was the reason why so many of them stood before him and chanted his name outside Stamford Stadium.

Chris Osborne the Raffles Rangers fan was desperate for them to cherish those memories and appreciate his contribution to the club because Chris Osborne the Raffles Rangers footballer knew he was about to betray every one of them.

Chris took a deep breath, waved to the fans and went through the players' entrance. He walked down the long, concrete corridor as familiar faces came at him from every open doorway—stewards, the fan club secretary, medical officers and even the bloody mascot. They either applauded or slapped his back, but they demanded the same thing—goals and victory.

In the dressing room, Chris noticed his team-mates all huddled together and tasted the vomit at the back of his throat again. They were on their mobile phones, either text messaging or speaking softly in Malay or a Chinese dialect. They smiled briefly at Chris and then quickly turned away. Chris was no mug, not anymore. They were placing bets. They were placing bets on their own match with illegal bookies—their own fucking match. They mostly took one goal. One goal would obviously pay the most.

Raffles Rangers were the highest scorers in the S-League by some margin. They averaged 2.4 goals a game. Chris alone accounted for almost a goal every game. No one outside the inner circle seriously expected this game to be determined by a solitary goal. Chris realised why his team-mates hadn't bothered to conceal their illegal betting from him. They already knew what he had to do. He was one of them now.

Chris dashed to the toilet and spat out the vomit at the back of this throat.

Danny walked into the dressing room with Michael Nielsen. The other players put away their phones. Chris noticed that Danny was agitated, but their coach appeared to be the most relaxed man in the dressing room and that pleased Chris. Michael Nielsen was untainted.

Danny stood in the middle of the dressing room as the players laced up their boots.

"Right, lads, as club captain, you know I'd give my right ball to be out with you boys today," he shouted. "But whatever happens, I expect to be joining you on the pitch after the game to lift that trophy with you again. It's all about the result today, boys. Nothing else matters now. I know we've been playing some pretty stuff this season, but Orchard FC get stuck in. So don't give the bastards any time on the ball. Be careful how many players we commit forward because they'll hit us on the break. Remember, they need the three points, we don't. So if we can just hold them and sneak a win, then they're fucked and I'm poor because the beers are on me tonight."

The players cheered. Chris laughed to himself. Bloody hell, Spearmint, he thought, why didn't you just bring Tiger in to deliver your little captain's pep talk?

"Anyway before you guys go out there and rip these bastards apart, someone wants to wish you good luck."

Danny opened the door and Mr Teck walked in with the Minister for Sports (Land and Water). The players all applauded, including Chris. He liked both men.

"Hey, don't applaud us, we should be applauding you," Mr Teck said. "Look, you boys know I can't do all the blood and guts speeches like The Spear and Michael can. But I will say that I couldn't be happier. We won the title last year and we can do it again this year. In fact, I know you boys will do it again this year."

The players all cheered.

"So all I will say is go out there and just do what you've been doing all season. We've got the best crowd of the season out there, we've got the TV cameras out there, and most importantly of all, I've already got the sponsors lined up for next season so your wages are all taken care of. So if that's not an incentive to deliver, then I don't know what is. Good luck, lads."

The players laughed and applauded as Mr Teck and the Minister for Sports (Land and Water) left. Michael shook hands with them both and closed the door behind them. He turned and smiled at his players.

"Boys, there really is nothing left for me to say at this stage," the coach said calmly. "So I'll just say this. In Denmark, we have a phrase which I think sums up everything which is beautiful about my country's football philosophy. It translates as, 'go out there, boys, and rip their fucking heads off!'"

The players roared in unison, jumped up and applauded each other as their coach led them out of the dressing room. Danny stood by the door and patted each one of them on the shoulder as they went out. Chris lined up at the back of the queue. Danny nodded at him.

"Good luck, Chris. Have a good one," Danny muttered.

"Fuck you," Chris whispered.

PARANOIA dominated Chris' game. His team-mates didn't pass
to him. On the rare occasions when he did find himself with the
ball at his feet, three Orchard players immediately surrounded
him and denied him any space to turn. Chris wasn't sure if
desperate defenders always hunted him in packs because of
his reputation or because they had been advised not to let him
shoot. Chris had no idea who was bent and who was straight.
When offside decisions went against him, he wasn't sure if the
officials were *kelong* or he had mistimed his runs. When he found
space outside the box and wasn't picked out, he wasn't sure if his
midfield hadn't seen him or they had seen him and were worried
he would leave them in trouble with their bookies.

Surely the fans could sense something was awry? Chris glanced
up at the crowd, but they appeared to be oblivious, still chanting
his name and getting the party started early. Chris looked across
at Billy Addis sitting behind his laptop in the VIP area. That
bastard knew something was amiss, Chris thought. He could see
it up there from his ivory tower, but he lacked the balls to do
anything about it.

But Chris had balls. He was one of the good guys. He was
sure of it.

The second half followed a similar pattern to the first. Chris
was denied the kind of service that he usually took for granted and
his team-mates at the back were comfortably handling Orchard's
uncharacteristically toothless attack. Both sides appeared content
to play out a goalless draw, which made no sense. Any half-
educated football fan could see that. Orchard needed a victory,
nothing less than three points would do. They were not playing
for pride; they were playing for the title. The pattern of play was
all wrong. Chris thought about his father. Tony Osborne was
no mug. He would've spotted the incongruous pattern of play
immediately.

Games of this nature were not played this way. Orchard had to come out and pummel Raffles at the start of each half to unsettle the home side and quieten the crowd. Orchard's only chance was to plant a seed of doubt, snatch an early corner, or narrowly miss a free-kick, or force the keeper to make a reflex save from a snapshot. Chris' father would have made them watch videos of Arsenal's title win at Anfield back in 1989. That early Alan Smith goal in the second half stunned Liverpool, had them questioning their own invincibility and marked the beginning of the end of their empire. And while the Gunners had needed to win by two goals at Anfield, Orchard just needed to win at Stamford Stadium.

But Orchard were not chasing the loose balls with the level of tenacity expected for a team in their position. Chris could see that and even the crowd began to sense the lifeless performances on the pitch in the second half. They detected the lack of urgency on the part of both teams. Chris heard one or two boos from the Orchard supporters, which only further fuelled his paranoia. Were they booing their team for not taking the game to their arch-rivals? Or were they in on the bet?

Chris was in on the bet, but not by choice and he could still fuck it up for everyone. If his timid team-mates would not feed him the ball, he would go and get it. Chris looked up at the clock on the electronic scoreboard. Just under 10 minutes left. Perfect. There was more than enough time to score—more than enough time to score two against these cowards. Fuck Tiger. Chris would win the game for Raffles Rangers, but only on his terms.

Chris dropped back into midfield and stole the ball from his own dithering winger and spun away from a fullback. He cut inside from the left flank and sprinted towards the penalty box. He was no Ryan Giggs, but he had pace—more than enough to get away from these *kelong* wankers. Where are my three shadows now, Chris thought, as he closed in on the area. I'm the pied fucking piper and I'll dance to my own tune.

But his run was too easy. Chris sensed something wasn't right. For over 80 minutes, he couldn't sneeze without one of his three markers blowing his nose for him. Now he had space and time and the ball at his feet. Oh well, tough shit. They had their chance, Chris thought, now I'll take mine.

Chris shimmied his way into the penalty area and lined up his shot. This was Sunday morning park football all over again. He was playing for Dagenham Schoolboys and waltzing past confused defenders with his dad quietly analysing proceedings on the touchline. Orchard's keeper advanced quickly, his instinctive reaction to narrow the angle perhaps overriding any other instructions, and Chris was forced to change direction and shift the ball onto his left foot. No problem. Those months spent standing in the middle of Parsloes Park wearing a Darth Maul slipper and feeling a right dickhead were about to pay off. Chris Osborne was poised to win his first league title as a professional footballer with his weaker left foot—a low curler would do the trick, around the keeper, bottom left-hand corner, easy, men against boys.

Chris spotted the raised boot out of the corner of his right eye. Where did that come from? He never saw the defender. Not yet. Just the raised boot aimed at his right calf. Chris was surprised by his first reaction. That's got to be a straight red card, he thought, and such a stupid time to do it, too. And then he saw the defender's face. He was smiling. He was smiling at Chris and everything became clear. Chris had done the job for them. It was time for the penalty and he had handed it to them with an honest run into the box. Just under 10 minutes left. Perfect. There'd be little time left for a second goal. The penalty would kill the contest. That's what Billy Addis could say in his report. The decisive penalty took the wind out of Orchard's sails, he'd write. That made perfect sense. Every informed reader should buy that. The betting-obsessed, conspiracy theorists might cry "*kelong*", but no one ever took those gambling addicts seriously. A late penalty often settled a nervous, cautious game. It happened on countless other occasions in legitimate matches so no one would question Orchard's commitment when their players inevitably curled up in the corner for the remainder of the match.

Chris made a valiant attempt to evade the raised boot, but it was a futile effort. The foul had been timed quite brilliantly. It was enough to send Chris tumbling and maybe leave a bruise on his calf, but it was no leg breaker. It couldn't be. Chris had to take the penalty.

The referee blew his whistle and stopped play. Chris didn't bother to look up to see if the man in black had pointed to the spot. It wasn't the referee's decision to make. Chris pushed himself up off the ground and brushed the blades of grass off his shirt. He scooped up the ball and squeezed it between his palms in front of his chest. He wasn't superstitious, but he had always performed this little ritual before a penalty. He wasn't even sure why. Chris squeezed the ball several times and then threw it to a team-mate and glared at the Rafffles Rangers dugout.

"I'm not taking the penalty," he said to no one in particular.

"Oi, what are you doing, Chris?" Michael screamed from the bench. "Get that ball and take the damn penalty. You haven't missed all season. Now pick it up and get this over with."

Chris peered across at Danny, who sat at the other end of the dugout. Danny cupped his hands around his mouth and mouthed the words, "Take the penalty, go to the right". Chris looked up at Billy Addis in the VIP area. The journalist nervously bit the skin on the top of his thumb. That's right, Chris thought, I'll make you bastards sweat it out for just a few more seconds.

"Right then, give me that fucking ball," Chris said finally.

The referee handed Chris the ball and smiled.

"OK, are you ready?" the referee asked.

"Just give me the ball."

Chris placed the ball on the penalty spot and adjusted the tongue on his right football boot. He tightened the laces on both boots, another ritual he couldn't really explain. He glanced up at the goal and saw his father standing between the posts. He peered down at the ball again, picked it up and re-placed it on the penalty spot, and smiled as his father's voice goaded him.

"You're gonna miss, you're gonna miss, you're gonna miss."

Chris stood up and stared at the goal.

"You're gonna miss, you're gonna miss, you're gonna miss."

Chris blocked out the sound of the crowd and the encouragement of his team-mates, and took his usual three steps backwards.

"You're gonna miss, you're gonna miss, you're gonna miss."

Chris stood with hands on his hips. He took one last look at the goal and then he trotted towards the ball.

"You're gonna miss, you're gonna miss, you're gonna miss."

But Chris did not miss. He never did.

He knew that his father would be really proud of him as he watched the ball sail over the crossbar.

twenty-two

AH LIAN was easy to spot in the partying crowd. He was the only spectator sitting down. He held his head in his hands as the Raffles Rangers fans danced around him. A slender, bespectacled Malay man in a Raffles Rangers shirt leaned over Ah Lian, grabbed his arms and tried to pull him up, encouraging him to join in the celebrations. Ah Lian glared at him. The fan did not try a second time.

Ah Lian looked down at the pitch and watched the Raffles Rangers squad parade the S-League trophy on their lap of honour. He stared at Chris Osborne. The Londoner raised his arm towards the journalists in the VIP area and fist-pumped. Ah Lian chuckled. He admired the *ang moh*'s courage if nothing else, because there really was nothing else worth celebrating. Good for you, Ah Lian thought, but very bad for me.

His mobile phone rang. Ah Lian pushed the phone hard against his right ear and squeezed his left hand tightly against his left ear. The voice was barely audible, but it made no difference. Ah Lian knew who was calling and what he was going to say.

"Ya, hello!" he shouted. "Very difficult to hear lah."

"Fucking bastard," Tiger's voice screamed. "Why the fuck he never score ah? You're watching lah. How come he never score?"

"Please lah, how can I make him score? You ask me just to

watch him play, make sure everything OK."

"You think everything OK, is it? It's not OK. Everything is fucked up, man."

"Ya lah, that's why I told you, right? Should use Poh Wee Kin. Singaporeans better, much more scared. Got nowhere to go. This *ang moh* can go back to England, what."

Ah Lian meant it, too, both as a bookies' runner and as an undercover officer. He had expressed his reservations to Tiger about Chris. Caucasians thought they had freedom of movement, freedom of choice, freedom of expression and all those other personal freedoms they took so seriously in the philosophy classes Ah Lian had to sit through at the London School of Economics. Chris Osborne would consider his principles. He would believe he had a choice. Poh Wee Kin was the safer, more reliable option, both for Tiger and the undercover operation. If only his dick had been a little more reliable, then neither Tiger nor Ah Lian would be in their current predicament. But the Government had taken care of Poh Wee Kin. And they were lumbered with a free-thinking fuckwit—a footballer with principles.

"Balls to you," Tiger raged. "I'll fix him before he goes back to England."

"*Aiyoh*, cannot kill him lah."

"Eh? You watch too many Hong Kong movies again, is it? Who's killing anyone? Talk cock lah, you. I'll fix him. Must see how first, but I'll fix him."

Ah Lian sighed and stared at Chris as he danced along the touchline and hugged Michael Nielson and Mr Teck. He peered across the pitch and saw Danny Spearman standing by the dugout. He clapped along with his team-mates, but the distance was obvious. The Spear no longer looked so mighty.

"And Spearman also?" Ah Lian asked. "Can see him here. You want me to fix him also?"

"Ya lah, go smash him next to the TV cameras. Make sure everyone can see. You're an idiot! You and Spear, both idiots. He told me this *ang moh* would score lah. Never mind. I fix him also."

"So how? You want me to make collection?"

"Collection for what? There were no goals. We lost. You want to collect broken bones, is it?"

"No lah, maybe I speak to them, explain."

"Explain what? That we lost their money, is it? You want to see them lose face, is it? If they lose face, then you lose face. You want to keep your face?"

"OK lah, I come and meet you."

"Cannot, must wait first. I don't know what to do yet. Shit, this thing so fucked up lah."

Tiger hung up. Ah Lian watched Mr Teck shake each of the Raffles Rangers players' hands down on the pitch. He glanced over his left shoulder and spotted a dazed Billy Addis in the press box staring over the top of his laptop. For the first time, Ah Lian had to agree with Tiger. This thing was so fucked up.

Ah Lian glanced down at his phone. He had to do something. He dialled quickly.

"Hello, it's me," he said.

"Oh, hi. Ya, very difficult to hear, so much shouting on your side. I was thinking about you. I just saw the match on TV," Jimmy Tan said.

"Yes, well, then I'm sure you can appreciate my predicament. I've got an operation with no end result, no payouts to syndicate bosses, and a pissed off bookie who's hiding somewhere and planning to hospitalise every famous footballer in Singapore."

"So, what do you want to do now?"

Ah Lian paused.

"What would you do?"

"Seriously, you're asking me, is it?"

"Why not?"

"I don't know anything about CPIB and match-fixing."

"Yeah, so what? I know everything about CPIB and match-fixing and look where it's got me. You know all the key suspects involved."

"That's true, but I don't know, man. Well, I suppose you cannot find your prime targets and we know where my targets are. Let me round up my scapegoats and see if they know anything about your scapegoat."

"That's such a long shot."

"Hey, I'm in the Central Narcotics Bureau. We never gamble at the Central Narcotics Bureau. We're not interested in odds lah."

Ah Lian laughed.

"You're right, Jimmy. I've got nothing. Nothing at all. Round 'em up."

SIMON Jones sobbed uncontrollably. The dishevelled, unshaven magazine editor looked like a cover shoot on the homeless. He sat opposite Jimmy at a bare table in a sparse interview room. There was a video camera at the top right-hand corner of the room pointed down at the table. A second officer sat at the back of the room, typing into a laptop. His face glowed in the laptop screen's light. The wall on the left side of the room was covered with a one-way mirror. Ah Lian stood on the other side of the mirror, giggling at the proceedings. He had interviewed more bookies, gamblers and footballers than he could remember, and they had never wept like this before.

"I'm so sorry, I'm so, so sorry," Simon cried, wiping the snot away from his upper lip. "I never meant for any of this to happen."

"You never meant for any of this to happen? Please lah, you've been holding these parties for months, some of our sources say for years," Jimmy replied.

"No, no, it wasn't like that. No, no, my first few parties were not like that. We just had a few drinks. We never had any of that … stuff."

"Cocaine. It's called cocaine. And here in Singapore, if you're caught with more than 30 grams of cocaine in your possession, you will be hanged. You know that."

"Please, God, no," Simon wailed. "I never did anything like that. Vince. He got me that stuff. Vince the Mincer. And it was never in those kinds of quantities. It was for personal usage. Well, personal usage for me and my friends."

"Ah, you see lah. If you are buying with the intention of supplying to your *ang moh* and famous party guests, then you are a supplier."

"No, you can't do that. Please, I'm just a magazine editor, that's all, trying to provide for my wife."

"Please lah, everybody knows that your marriage to your Filipino maid is a sham. We have sources. We know what goes on at your parties. That can be another charge, too, if you want."

"No, no, please. I have an elderly mother living in Brighton. She's retired, lives in a little bungalow by the sea."

"Do you think I give a shit about your mother? Do you know how many people I've arrested at Changi Airport, hiding cocaine in their surfboard bags? I've caught young people, much younger than you, Australian backpackers with cocaine hidden in their socks. I send them to the hangman. That's my job and I sleep OK every night. No problem. Everybody knows the risks about drugs in Singapore. Everybody. It's no secret. They knew the risks and so do you. But people like you think you are above the law, right? People like you buy your cocaine and have your private parties and switch off the TV when the news says another backpacker is hanged for smuggling, right? I arrest another Vietnamese kid with heroin in little condom balloons shoved up his ass and you don't care, you just change channels. And then he gets hanged and his crying mother breaks down on TV, and you change channels again. You're not interested in these people. You don't live in their world. You have all your famous singers and actors and TV stars at your house and you all think you are so smart and so clever and so Western, right or not? And Singaporeans are so boring and so safe and so conservative in their little concrete government apartments, right or not? And you make fun of us in your *ang moh* magazines, saying we are dull and we never wear the right clothes and we never watch the right movies and we never have enough sex, but we are safe. That's why you come, because we are safe. But you are a hypocrite. Because you know that your countries which are so sexy and so exciting are not safe. So you come here. And you are safe and rich and respected. So you have your parties and you have your drugs and you laugh at us for being so boring. Well, I am boring. I am a boring, boring policeman with a boring, safe family, and I like it. And you are an exciting, famous *ang moh* with a sexy Western lifestyle, but you, Mr Jones, you are going to hang."

"No, please, it's OK. I know everything. I have many friends who can help me, who can speak to you. I spoke at residents' committee meetings for politicians. They're my friends."

"Not anymore. You won't have any more Singapore friends. Not now. You bought drugs to distribute to others, you are a drugs supplier. It's over."

"No, please, I beg you, please. My wife doesn't know anything about the parties, about the stuff, about the games. She doesn't know anything."

"She will soon. This will be a good story for the Chinese

newspapers. Those boring, safe Singaporeans love sexy stories about big shot *ang mohs*, right or not?"

"No, please, I can help you, right? That's why I'm here. I can help you, right?"

Jimmy looked up at the one-way mirror and smiled. He faced Simon again and glared.

"Tell me about Tiger."

Simon felt nauseous. He wiped his eyes and swallowed hard.

"Tiger? You want to know about Tiger?" he asked, looking around nervously at the other officer in the room.

"No more party games, eh, Simon? We've seen the video."

Simon's mouth dried up. He coughed uneasily.

"The video? How do you know about … I mean, no one was … how can you …"

"We've got it. That's why it's all over. This is a very easy case for me. All I can do now is testify to the judge that you were helpful. Who's Tiger?"

Simon started weeping again.

"Simon, this is your last chance. I'm not bluffing now. Your apartment, your property, had more than 30 grams of cocaine on the premises, much more. That's more than enough. It's your apartment so it's your cocaine. I'm your only hope now. After this question, I leave and I won't be coming back. Who is Tiger?"

"I don't know. I really don't know. He just turned up at the party," Simon whimpered.

"You must know him. You don't know where your cocaine comes from? Cocaine is not cheap, you know."

"I don't know, I swear to you I don't know. He turned up at the party with another slender Chinese guy and that was the first time I had ever seen him. He deals with Vince the Mincer. You have to ask Vince. Yeah, talk to Vince. He must know him. You must talk to Vince or maybe talk to the other Chinese guy.

Find the other Chinese guy. He works with Tiger. He can help you. Please find him, please, he'll tell you about Tiger. See, that's helpful, right? If you, yes, if you find that Chinese guy, he will lead you to Tiger. That helps you, doesn't it, right? I mean, that will help you find this Tiger, right?"

Jimmy glanced up at the one-way mirror and sighed.

"Is that OK? I mean, can I ... you know ... please ... I don't know what else ... I mean ... What happens to me now?" Simon mumbled.

Jimmy faced the *X-Pat* editor and smiled.

"Two things will happen, Mr Jones. I will have my high-profile scapegoat to feed to the media. That's you. And you will be hanged."

JIMMY led Vince the Mincer along the corridor and stopped outside the interview room.

"I told you, bro, I don't know why you bring me here. I got nothing to say, man," Vince said, pushing out his chest.

"I think you'll talk when we go inside. Someone is waiting to see you," Jimmy answered softly.

"Hey, is it my new record producer? That's the bomb, man."

"No, it's an old gangster friend, I think, *man.*"

Jimmy opened the door slowly and led Vince into the interview room. Ah Lian sat on the other side of the table, with his hands behind his head and his feet up on the table. He rocked backwards and forwards on the chair.

"Hey, 'brudder', it's Vince the Mincer. The number one gangster in Singapore, JB and some say Batam," Ah Lian said.

Vince eyed Jimmy nervously.

"Why is he here?" he said slowly.

"Who? This guy? He said he's a gangster friend of yours, right or not? That you do some work together on the street and you go to some parties together," Jimmy replied.

"No, no, I don't know him. Well, I don't really know him," Vince stammered.

"*Aiyoh*, why you so nervous?" Jimmy mocked. "You don't sound like a, how you say ah, a gangster rapper now."

Jimmy smirked at Ah Lian and headed back towards the door.

"OK, I leave you two *kakis* to talk," Jimmy said. "Have fun."

Jimmy closed the door behind him. Vince the Mincer stood still. Ah Lian glared at him and gestured towards the chair opposite him.

"Sit down, big shot," Ah Lian said. "Come lah, you sing about being a big time Singapore gangster. This is what gangsters do lah. Come. Sit."

Vince The Mincer glanced around the room. He pointed at the one-way mirror.

"I know what that is, can't fool me," he said quickly. "That's one of those mirrors, right? You can see from the other side. See, I know. That cop on the other side … Hello, Officer Tan, can you see me? … This is just like a recording studio. That's the control room, the producer is up there and I'm down here, man, doing my thing, this is my studio, man, give me a microphone, man."

"Wah, you do the gangster thing good, man. Damn *shiok*, I tell you. Almost cannot see you are bluffing. But I can see. You not a gangster one. Can see your head, man, sweating, it's raining up there, bro. You never been here before, 'brudder'? You watch the Hong Kong movies and then play gangster, right?"

Ah Lian laughed, partly because he considered Vince to be a fraud, but mostly because he sounded like Tiger.

"Please, I know why you're here, man. You got arrested, right, yeah, must be, got arrested after that party, got caught, and now you are the rat," Vince rambled. "I'm not the rat man, bro. I've got no video, man. I've got no phone. I don't know anything about that coke at the party. It was just there. I don't know nothing about that, man. I know you got that video, so what. Watch it, man. I'm doing nothing. I'm smart, man. Watch the video. I'm touching nothing on the table, man, nothing. That's it, man. You got caught, too bad, brother, but you cannot catch me, man, cannot catch Vince the Mincer."

"Oh, we caught you several months ago, my friend. We intercepted the mighty Vince the Mincer a long time ago and we've had you under surveillance for many weeks," Ah Lian said slowly in flawless English.

Vince didn't move. His eyes widened.

"Who are you?"

"I'm like you, Vince the Mincer. You see, we really are brothers. Like you, I make my living pretending to be a gangster."

Ah Lian took out his wallet and opened it up for Vince to examine. The rapper read the name beside the photograph. Detective Low. He scanned the other words. They surprised him. The Corrupt Practices Investigation Bureau. The infamous CPIB.

"What the hell is going on?" he asked

"I really think you should sit down now," Ah Lian muttered.

Finally, Vince did as he was told.

"You see, I wasn't really interested in you," Ah Lian said. "I knew all about the drugs, the parties, but I really wasn't interested. Officer Tan and his team at CNB will take care of small fry like you. I'm happy for them to have their celebrity singer scapegoat. All I am interested in is Tiger."

"But I don't know …"

"I don't mean to interrupt you there, gangster man, but time is really against us. You see, Tiger has anger management issues, as I'm sure you can appreciate. Certain events were supposed to transpire at that match and they didn't. Money has been lost and he will go after the culprits. He will consider every one of those party guests to be a culprit."

"But I'm just a …"

"A lowlife peddler, dealer and the occasional rent boy, pimp, I know all of that. I've read the file. Don't worry about that, Mr Mincer, Senior Officer Tan is a meticulous, respected drug-buster. He has enough on you to earn you at least 10 years. That's a foregone conclusion. You're going to Changi, if you're lucky. If Tan proves that you've passed on more than 30 grams at any one time, gangster man, you will get the rope together with your expatriate party host."

Vince felt a burning sensation in this throat. His eyes filled with tears.

"But I'm supposed to be recording my new album. I've got appearances lined up on Channel 5," he croaked.

"No, that's not going to happen now, tough guy. At best, you're going to prison. The wheels are in motion, nothing can stop them now. It's true the government does have a sense of humour when it comes to crime and punishment. Maybe they'll make you a poster boy for their drugs campaigns. Maybe you'll be spared prison in return for a lifelong contract hosting all those televised charity gigs. Although having seen those TV charity appeals, you might be better off in Changi. Either way, all I can do is stand up in court and say that you fully co-operated with the police and then leave it up to the judge."

"But I don't know anything about Tiger, really," Vince whimpered.

"OK, then, big shot, thanks for your time."

Ah Lian stood up to leave.

"No, no wait, wait, er, I must know something, wait," Vince cried. "Er, let me think. I met Tiger through Spear some time last season. He told me that Tiger was a big fan of Raffles Rangers, one of their biggest fans. This Tiger told me he was a taxi driver and his son was a big fan of mine."

"You really are a deluded pop star, aren't you? Tiger doesn't even have a son."

"I'm telling you that's what he said. He 'bigged me' up."

"He did what?"

"Tiger 'bigged me' up, told me that his son and all his teenage friends said I was as good as 50 Cent and Eminem, told me I was going to be a big star. And I got excited and a bit over-confident. We talked for a while and Spearman told Tiger I was going to a party where there were lots of footballers. Tiger got really excited about that. Spearman said Tiger could help me out, he said that I liked to dabble a bit and that I had unreliable sources. So Tiger and I chatted a bit and he said his source was reliable and cheaper."

"So you bought cocaine from Tiger."

"Yeah, but that's it. Whenever we met after that, there was no small talk. You know that, sometimes you were there, right? Sometimes Tiger sent someone else to meet me. But I had a number to call. I called the number before Simon's parties and collected and that's it."

"What did he say when you collected?"

"Nothing. nothing. Oh, he might ask me what footballers were going to a certain party, but that's it. That's it."

Ah Lian glared at Vince.

"You really are a naïve prick, aren't you?" he hissed. "You're just a pampered middle-class kid with a chip on his shoulder. You can't even keep up your 'hoodie' street accent in here, can you? We're done then. There's nothing left to say. Officer Tan's team will take over now."

Ah Lian pushed his chair under the table and headed slowly for the door.

"Please, please, don't go," Vince sniffled. "Please, stay here. We can talk some more. Please. Don't go. Let me talk."

"I've got nothing else to say to you because you're a tough guy, right? So you're not going to tell on all your friends, right? You're going to take your punishment like a big man, right?"

"No, no, please, I can tell you more, I know so much. Wait, wait, you said you wanted scapegoats, right? I can give you them, I can give you them. I know so many. Whatever you want. I've seen them all take drugs, at parties, orgies, photographs, video cameras. I've seen everything."

"You're going to prison, Vince."

"No, no, wait. I've seen it all, cocaine, Ecstasy, everything. All of them. Actors, singers, dancers, deejays, swimmers, writers, journalists, I've got all of them. I can give every name you want. What else do you want? I've got the ones who read the news and sport in the morning, the ones on the night-time news. I've got people from the news on the radio side. Actresses from the Chinese dramas. I can give you all their names, no problem. Please, don't go, wait. Give me some paper, I'll write them all down for you. All the famous people in Singapore. I've seen all of them taking drugs. I'll give you all their names."

"Goodbye, Vince."

"No, please, wait, don't go, I can … Oh, fuck, fuck, fuck."

Ah Lian heard a dripping sound. He stopped at the door and turned back. He smiled as the urine trickled off the bright white Nikes and formed a puddle around Vince the Mincer's feet.

JIMMY and his colleagues laughed as they watched Vince wet himself on the other side of the one-way mirror. Ah Lian quickly joined them.

"Well, I think our big-time gangster is going to give you plenty of your coveted scapegoats, once he's finished pissing himself," Ah Lian said, gesturing towards Vince.

"Oh, this is going to be wonderful. The ministry will love this. There'll be another anti-drugs campaign up and running before the end of the year and maybe more funding for us, thanks to this. Sorry we couldn't be more helpful with your case though."

"Ah, what to do? It was a long shot anyway. We both knew that."

Officer Siva opened the door and hurried over to Jimmy.

"Siva, how many times have I told you? Knock first lah," Jimmy said.

Jimmy raised his eyes at Ah Lian. Ah Lian smiled.

"Sorry, sir, but I was told to interrupt and tell you and, er, Ah Lian immediately."

Ah Lian and Jimmy looked at each other.

"Tell me? Tell me what?" Jimmy asked. "What's happened?"

"Chris Osborne has been assaulted outside his condo. His legs have been smashed," Siva said quickly. "His attacker was wearing a black balaclava. The security guard at the condo claims he didn't see anything else."

"I know the security guard. I'll make him give a statement, but it won't make any difference," Ah Lian sighed. "We all know it's Tiger. He's already been given his orders."

"What are you going to do now?" Jimmy asked.

"I don't know. I'll have to speak to the ministry. I know what they'll say though. Calm exteriors. Sweep up as many as you can and hide them under the carpet."

"How will you do that?"

"I don't think we'll have to. Tiger will do it for us."

 **twenty-three**

DANNY Spearman stood on the steps outside the hospital and peered up at the low, grey sky. Bloody Singapore rain, he thought. He spotted his Lexus in the hospital car park. The distance wasn't far, but it was far enough for a thorough soaking. There was nothing worse than meeting a fan and looking like shit. Danny had already signed the plaster cast of that Xavier kid and a couple of doctors had clearly recognised him in the corridor. Danny liked to keep up appearances with his show's viewers. That hadn't been a problem with Xavier. Danny had been comparatively upbeat. But the haggard, ghostly pallor of Chris stayed with him. When those two doctors had nodded to him on the way out, Danny barely mustered a smile. He couldn't stop thinking about Chris' eyes. The boy was understandably angry, but his eyes gave the game away. He was still scared. Danny recognised those eyes. He saw them in the mirror after Simon Jones' party. That's what Tiger could do.

Through the rain, Danny noticed a skinny Chinese kid hovering around his Lexus. That's all he needed—a teenager scratching his most prized possession. He dashed through the drizzle, avoiding the bigger puddles in the car park.

"Hey, mind the car, mate," he shouted. "You're too close to it, you'll set the alarm off. You can't afford to scratch that car."

"Hey, it's you, right? You're the *ang moh* footballer on TV, right?" Ah Lian replied.

Danny stopped running and walked slowly towards his car.

"Oh, it's you," he mumbled.

"Of course, it's me. You're lucky it's me, too. If it was any of my colleagues, you'd be in prison. And if it was any of my *other* colleagues, you'd be in a bed beside Chris Osborne."

"What do you want?"

"Luckily for you, and sadly for me, I don't really want anything. There's nothing else I can get from you at the moment. For now."

Danny wiped the rain from his forehead.

"So I'm going to be arrested then," he muttered.

"No, not yet. There's nothing I can really arrest you for, is there? We both know what a slippery bastard you are. You sell out your football team to a loan shark, you sell out a young singer to a drug dealer, you take a young footballer under your wing and then encourage him to fix the most important game of his life and you even try to set up a decent journalist who was trying to expose you. All so you can make enough money to live the kind of lifestyle you think your average football deserves. I'm still not sure why. I've read all about you. You were an honest footballer in England. You weren't very good, but you were honest and the fans respected that."

"I'd die for those fans in England," Danny whispered.

"What's that supposed to mean?"

"They were fans. They supported their team. Their local team, no matter how shit they were. I played for teams worse than Raffles Rangers and Orchard FC in England, but they still got over 5,000 local fans every week, whatever the weather, whatever the standard of football. And then I come here, and everyone wants every game fixed. Everyone believes the game is *kelong*. All they talk about is gambling. Gambling, gambling and fucking gambling. Do you know I played for a Singapore Selection side against Manchester United?"

"Yes, I know. I was at the game."

"You talk about Chris Osborne's greatest game. Fuck him. That was against Orchard FC. Who are they? I was born in Yorkshire. It was my dream to play the old enemy in Lancashire and give them the game of their life. I knew we couldn't win, but I was ready for the battle. And what happened? We laid down for them and let the superstars take the piss out of us. They played their goalkeeper outfield and the crowd laughed at us. They showboated and the crowd laughed at us. And when they scored, the crowd, *our* crowd, a Singapore crowd, cheered against us. That game was shown across Asia and on MUTV. All my family watched it in England. And we were a joke, a laughing stock. I've been called many things in my career—fat, too slow, no pace, no passing range, but no one ever questioned my commitment. I never bottled a challenge and I was never called a joke. That game meant everything to me and all the fans cared about was making money off the back of it. All they wanted to know was how many goals in each half, should they buy the handicap, should they play low goals, should they play high goals. No one gave a shit about the actual game itself, about the 22 players who had sweated blood for the fucking game since they were 10 years old. Those gamblers made me stop caring about a game I loved and I'll never forgive them for that. So I thought, fuck it, if you're only worrying about making money off me, then I'll only worry about making money off you. I'll take their money from Tiger to set up my clinics. And then I'll take their money again when their kids come to my clinics."

"That's a really touching story, Danny, but Chris Osborne and Poh Wee Kin still wanted to play the game they loved, and

Billy Addis wanted to expose scumbags like you ruining the game that he loved. And I think, and I choose my words carefully here, you're the most selfish prick I've ever met who doesn't give a shit about anyone but himself. I'd personally drop you off at Changi Prison if it was up to me, but I can't."

"Why not?"

"Because, Danny, ironically, your ugliness may be your salvation. The ministry are having enough trouble dealing with corruption in football and do not want your grubby little tales feeding the *kelong* beliefs of all those Chinese newspaper readers in the housing estates. Not without an end goal, at least. If we pick up Tiger and, hopefully, one or two of his paymasters, then we'd be happy to drag you off to court. We know how much you love a microphone and an audience. But we've got no Tiger and no syndicates, which means we've got no case in court yet, so it's all about calm exteriors for now. But the investigation is ongoing. We will find Tiger's bosses and when we do, I will personally send you down."

"So I'll just carry on as before."

Ah Lian glared at Danny and then laughed. Danny looked away.

"Don't be ridiculous, Danny. This is Singapore. Haven't you read your Dostoevsky recently? We believe in crime and punishment. The ministry has declared that your unstable ankle can no longer be risked at the highest level. Your playing career is over. Wait for Chris to be discharged from hospital and let him go back to England first. When he's been there for a few weeks and the *kelong* rumours die down, you will announce your retirement."

"But, I can't, I mean, that'll only kick-start the rumours again."

"Yes, but then the rumours will only be about you being

corrupt. The ministry and the CPIB, and me in particular, have no problems with that."

"But how can I do the Super Soccer channel stuff with all those rumours flying around?"

"Good point. You can't. Your contract with the channel ends when all the European leagues finish their seasons."

"But that's my main source of income. That's how I … I mean, I can't just …"

"You've got 24 hours to tell them. Or we will tell them for you. We will release a statement to the media that you are suspending your work with the Super Soccer channel to further help the CPIB with the enquiries."

"But I need a bit more time."

"It's not a request. The ministry has made the decision and moved on."

"But what will I do in Singapore?"

"Fulfil your dream. Work full-time on your football clinics. You paid a high price to set them up, don't you think?"

PETER Chan straightened the sports editor's plaque on his desk and took a deep breath. He picked up a file marked "Raffles Rangers" and took out several newspaper cuttings. He laid out the major headlines across his desk: OSBORNE ATTACKED; CHRIS MISS DOUBT; RAFFLES REJECT RUMOURS; TECK BACKS CHRIS,; WE'RE CLEAN: NIELSEN; and OSSIE ON THE MEND. Peter flicked back his hair and examined the bylines on each of the stories. None of them were written by Billy Addis. He sighed and picked up his phone.

"I'm ready for them now," he said softly. "Yes, please send them both in."

Peter swivelled his chair and adjusted the framed photograph on the wall behind him. It was his favourite photograph—the one of him standing side by side with Cassius Clay. He stared at the photograph and smiled. Happier, simpler times, he thought.

"Shall we sit down?" Billy asked nervously.

Peter turned back. Billy and Yati both stood in front of his desk. They looked tired. Peter noticed that Yati's eyes were red and swollen. She had been crying.

"Er, yes, please, yes, sit down," Peter stammered.

Their dishevelled appearance had caught Peter off guard.

"You, er, may be wondering why, er, I asked to see you both alone, rather than bringing in your lifestyle editor, Yati," Peter continued, slowly regaining his exposure.

"I think we all know why," Yati mumbled. "I think everyone in the office knows."

"Oh, it's not about you two. Please, we've known about you two being together for ages. This is a vibrant newsroom, of course we know. We're not supposed to condone it, but you two have been discreet. You're both adults and I assume that the relationship is between you two and Chris Osborne to sort out. No, this is about something else."

Billy held Yati's hand tightly under the desk.

"What's it about then, Peter?" Billy asked slowly.

"Have a look at these newspaper headlines. They're all decent, relevant stories. I mean, look at the first couple. Chris Osborne hasn't missed a penalty all season, knocks them in for fun and then, finally, in the most important game of the season, he misses one. Not only does he miss it, he sends it so far over the crossbar that the ball must have landed with snow on it. But you never really picked up on the rumours in your copy ..."

"No, wait, I did say that ..."

"I know you did. You said that the pressure of the big occasion got to a young footballer playing for his first major trophy. I accept that. But you didn't even raise the question, you of all people. All season you have been probing the S-League and Raffles Rangers in particular, picking up on every *kelong* rumour. You wrote all those follow-up stories about Danny and the CPIB and you were in my office every five minutes, justifying expenses for bills in KTV lounges, coffee shops and bars."

"Yeah, but the thing is …"

"And I paid them all. I paid them because I saw a hunger in you. You were one of the best rookie reporters we've ever had. You worked long hours and established great contacts, and I think you really were on to something. And then the best player that this league has ever known gets his legs bashed in and you write nothing."

"No, I wrote the news story."

"Please, it was so straight, one of my interns could have done it. Where was your colour, the comment pieces, the follow-ups? After a season of digging, you finally strike gold and then you throw it back for all our rivals to pick up."

"Maybe I was too close to the story."

"No, maybe you were threatened at that party at Simon Jones' place."

Billy and Yati glanced at each other.

"How do you know about that?" Yati blurted.

"My editor told me about it."

"How did he know about it?"

"How do you think? Who do you think we work for? I told you when you first stepped into my office, Billy, that the most important aspect to Singapore life is its image. That's all the powers that be are looking for. They have enough things to worry about. Being a tiny multicultural island surrounded by the biggest Islamic nation on the planet is one; dealing with so many races and religions in a little city is another. They know that everything is not as harmonious as we like to pretend. They know there are racial concerns, religious issues, political dissension and foreign talent complications. They also know that they are building two massive casinos in a country that is addicted to gambling. So as long as they can maintain an image of calm, we can all just about live and work together. A country this small must maintain the status quo. But we cannot have calm if we have conspiracy theorists getting excited about fanciful match-fixing plots involving some of the country's top footballers, pop stars, editors and journalists."

Yati wiped her eyes and stared at her shoes.

"But we were only there. We didn't actually do anything," she mumbled.

"You see, that's where we have a problem. You didn't do anything. You are right. You were only there. As I understand it, you had no direct role in any daft schemes or match-fixing allegations, but you were there and you never reported it, never went to the police and never did anything. In many respects, you failed the first principle of journalism—report the events as they unfold."

"Maybe she was scared," Billy said.

"Maybe. Or maybe she had her head full of cocaine at the time."

Yati lifted her head and wiped her tear-stained face.

"You know about that?"

"I don't really know all the details. Neither does my editor. The ministry only ever tells us what they think we need to know, so we don't challenge their final decision."

"What decision?" Billy asked

"It's your lucky day. You're both going to become sub-editors. The editor here wanted to fire you both, and I agreed with him, but we were both encouraged to see the bigger picture. Sacking you both so soon after Chris Osborne's attack would raise even more questions. So Yati, you're going to learn how to lay out simple pages at our home decorating magazine. It has a terrible circulation, but the pages are always pretty. Billy, as you're on a fixed expat contract with us, you're going to review books and CDs for our smallest men's magazine until your contract expires, and then you're going back to England. I don't know how that will affect your relationship. That's for you two to discuss. But I've been advised to inform you, Billy, that any future visa applications to Singapore will be rejected."

Yati sobbed quietly. Billy stared at the photograph of Peter Chan and Muhammad Ali.

DANNY looked up at the main stand outside Stamford Stadium. In the darkness, he could still make out the top of the stand and the rectangular frame of the floodlights. He was surprised that sentimentality had brought him here. He had watched Ah Lian disappear through the rain at the hospital car park and then sat in his car staring at the rain trickling down his windscreen. He had picked up the phone. He had even dialled the studio a couple of times, but ended the call before anyone had a chance to answer. It wasn't right. Even Danny's conscience told him that. He was too close to Chris Osborne's hospital bed. So he had switched on the ignition and allowed his subconscious to make the decision for him. It had taken him to Stamford Stadium.

He peered down at his mobile phone and pressed redial.

"Er, hello, it's The Spear here," he muttered. "I guessed there would be no one at the studio and it's probably easier to do this on answer phone and then we can chat more in the morning. I've been giving it a lot of thought this week about the show and I do feel I'm getting a little stale. I've been caught up with worrying about Raffles' title race and to be honest, the ankle injury is really starting to take its toll and I just can't focus on anything until

I've got it sorted out once and for all. So I think I'm gonna have major surgery on it and then see where to go from there. The clinics are taking off as well, so I don't know if I'll have the time next season. Anyway, so what I'm saying is, I'm thinking of taking a break next season, just to get my ankle sorted out and spend a bit more time on the clinics. Sorry to hit you with this so suddenly, but, you know what The Spear's like, tell it straight and no bullshit. I'll come in tomorrow and we'll talk more about it then. Bye."

Danny put his phone in his pocket and stood back a little to take in the entire main stand of Stamford Stadium. For a Southeast Asian football league, it really was a lovely little stadium, Danny thought. He realised now how much he had loved the early days—leading the boys out every week, the banter in the dressing room, the heckling from the away supporters, getting stuck in and hearing the local crowd roar. Those early days had been quite special. Maybe some of the supporters might remember those early days when Danny announced his retirement. He certainly hoped so.

Danny heard footsteps behind him. He felt the fear rising. The fear he saw on Chris' face in the hospital, the fear he saw in the mirror after Simon Jones' party, but he shouldered it, tackled it, kicked it into touch. Danny Spearman still had bottle, even now.

Instead he glanced up at Stamford Stadium one more time and smiled.

"Hello, Spear," Tiger said softly.

 twenty-four

CHRIS rested on one of his crutches and stared out of the window. He watched an elderly Indian labourer in a straw hat tend to the hospital's beautifully manicured gardens. The morning rain had dried up and the orchids dazzled in the sunlight. Chris turned unsteadily, hobbled slowly and dropped onto his hospital bed. He checked his suitcase again. The club had kindly picked up some clothes from his condo, packed them and dropped them at the hospital, but they were mostly the wrong clothes for the English climate. Chris didn't care. He didn't want to go back to the condo. He wanted to go home.

"Is my little soldier ready to go home?" Rosito asked.

Chris looked up and saw Rosito, the wonderful, kind Rosito, walking along the corridor. Chris grinned. The Filipino nurse always made him smile.

"Hey, you, not so much of the little," Chris joked. "I know you've changed my dressing down there, but there's no need to be personal."

"Please. I'm far too professional for that," Rosito insisted.

Well, she usually was.

"Now you're going to let me email you, right?" Chris asked. "And these Facebook details are correct? There's nothing worse

than looking for a pretty nurse on Facebook and it turning out
to be a 50-year-old computer geek living at home with his mum."

"No, no, it's definitely me. I've got to keep an eye on my
patient, haven't I?"

"Absolutely. And I may be back next season so you might be
able to keep an eye on me up close and personal. What do you
think?"

"Maybe."

"Yeah, maybe."

Chris and Rosito giggled. They both knew they would keep
in touch with each other.

"Now, I do not wish to rush you, Mr Osborne, but we need
your bed."

"Ah, that's charming, isn't it?"

"So I've got two messages for you. First, we have called a taxi
for you and it should be here in five minutes. Will you need
a wheelchair?"

"No, no, I'm fine with the crutches, Rosito. What's the other
message?"

"That's from your father. He called reception and insisted
that we give the message exactly how he said it."

"What did he say?"

"He said, 'If that silly bugger thinks I'm going to get
sentimental with him on the phone then he's got another thing
coming. But I will meet him at the airport and I'm glad he didn't
miss the penalty' … Do you understand that?"

"Yeah, I do," Chris laughed.

"But I thought you did miss the penalty."

"I know what he means. Now, can you help me to the taxi
stand so I can give you a big hug in front of all the ambulance
crew?"

CHRIS held on to the door handle as the taxi driver swerved across two lanes of traffic on the East Coast Expressway.

"It's OK, mate. I've already checked in online. I'm not in a hurry," Chris said.

"No lah, this idiot in front driving damn slow," the driver replied.

He stared at Chris in his rear-view mirror.

"Hey, you're that footballer, right? The one who got whacked, right?"

Chris grabbed one of the crutches beside him in the back seat and waved it in front of the rear-view mirror.

"Nothing gets past you, right?"

"No lah, I recognised your face what, from the newspaper. I knew it was you outside the hospital. I watch you on TV, you not bad, man."

"I had my moments."

"So you feeling better now already?"

"Not bad lah. Still painful, but can walk with the crutches."

"Not bad ah, your Singlish, not bad."

"Have to, right? If not try, then how?"

"Ya lah, that's true … Hey, you don't mind ah, why you *kena* attacked, boss? Was *kelong* right? Someone fix you, is it? That's what I heard. The match fixed, right?"

"No lah. Cannot always believe what you read in the papers. It was just a mugging, I think. The guy saw an *ang moh* outside the condo and must have thought I was rich. He obviously doesn't know I play in the S-League so he attacked me. Luckily for me, I was going to training so I only had my taxi fare in my pocket."

"Ya, I suppose so lah," the taxi driver muttered, clearly not convinced.

Chris saw the Changi Airport tower lit up at the end of the East Coast Expressway and felt a surge of relief. He was almost there.

"Which terminal ah?"

"Er, Terminal 3, I think. Singapore Airlines."

"Ya lah, SQ, mostly Terminal 3. That's good lah, you go Singapore Airlines, the best."

"I hope so. The club's paying for me, so it should be OK."

"You fly business class, is it?"

"No, I play in the S-League, remember."

"So the S-League not *kelong*, then?"

"I don't think so. Hope not. I scored a lot of goals last season. They were hard work, those goals."

"Ya, but you missed that penalty right? In the last game?"

Chris gritted his teeth. The forthright attitude of taxi drivers never usually bothered him. During the season, he had been asked how much rent he paid for his condo, how big his apartment was, how much money he earned and how sexy his girlfriend was, and he had swatted them all aside. But this question grated.

"Why do you think I was *kelong*? Because I missed the penalty? Great players miss penalties. Baggio missed a penalty in a World Cup final. Players do miss penalties, mate," Chris said.

"OK, OK, sorry ah. You were just unlucky."

"That's right, I was just unlucky. But we won the title and I finished as the season's top scorer, so maybe I wasn't too unlucky, but I played the game my way. No one told me what to do. No one fixed me, all right, mate?"

"Ya, ya, OK, sorry."

The taxi driver glanced up at Chris in the rear-view mirror and then looked away quickly. They headed towards departures when his face brightened suddenly.

"Hey, you used to play for West Ham, right?" he asked.

"Well, sort of. I never played for the first team," Chris replied bluntly.

"Ya, ya, but you know the players, right?"

"Most of them, I suppose. Why?"

"This weekend they got Man U at Old Trafford. You think Man U can score more than two against West Ham? That Robert Green quite good, right? He might save a few. Can or not? How much you think? You think 500 can? Need to win this week, lost quite a bit on Liverpool last week. That match at Anfield definitely fixed. You think West Ham got chance at Old Trafford? How much you think? Maybe 1,000 bucks can?"

"We're almost there," Chris muttered.

CHRIS sat in the departure lounge and tried to ignore the stares and the whispers around him. He saw passengers nod towards his crutches and mutter their disapproval. It didn't help that the flat screen TVs hanging down from the ceiling at his gate were repeating a speech made earlier in the day by the Minister for Home Improvement. He had dismissed rumours of corruption in the S-League, emphasising yet again the need for players, coaches and fans to remain vigilant at every level.

Chris had no issue with the Minister. He had enjoyed their lunch together and accepted that the oblivious Minister had to churn out the same old bullshit to appease his superiors. It was the news report's insistence on showing footage of Chris' penalty miss and the ambulance crew wheeling him into hospital that pissed him off. Surely, the juxtaposition of those images in a report on match-fixing was libellous, Chris thought. Oh well, fuck them and fuck everyone else staring at him in the departure lounge, too. He knew the truth. His conscience was clear. He had taken his punishment from Tiger like a man and he would play again. The doctors had assured him, but he had already suspected as much. He could sense it. Trevor Bonds had promised his father a meeting with Leyton Orient, and he would be ready. Chris tapped his passport softly against his bandaged knee. He was free.

"Hello, Chris. Do you mind if I join you?"

Chris looked up and smiled.

"Of course you can join me. What are you doing here?"

Mr Teck sat beside Chris. He looked immaculate in a pair of faded jeans, a Ralph Lauren shirt and a Hugo Boss jacket. He rested his Samsonite briefcase between his legs and smiled at Chris.

"I can't lie, Chris. I have some business in London and when I heard the club had booked you on this flight, I booked myself on the same one."

"That's good of you, mate."

"Don't be silly. It's the least I could do after all you've done for us this season. I just wish we could've done more, really."

"No, you've done enough. The hospital bills, the flight, the packing. The staff have been great. I'll always be grateful."

"And so will the club. We'd give anything to have you back here next season, but I think, you know, it's the right thing to do after that terrible business outside your apartment. There was no need for that. Maybe it's better if you have a fresh start in England."

"I think so, yeah, but I loved my time at Raffles Rangers."

"And you're now going back as a top scorer and the official S-League Player of the Year. That's got to look good on the résumé when you go for your meeting at Leyton Orient."

Chris blushed. Mr Teck smiled.

"Oh, don't be silly. I'm pleased for you. You're a professional footballer looking out for your best interests and, ultimately, that's what we do—we look out for our best interests. There's no shame in that. Michael Nielsen told me about Leyton Orient."

"I hope you don't mind."

"How can I mind? You'll be a free agent soon anyway. It was only a one-year contract and things didn't pan out exactly how we had hoped, but that's life."

"Yeah, I suppose so. So why are you off to London?"

"Ah, the same old thing. Construction. Most of our big projects are in Europe now. As you know, we do work on sports stadiums. We nearly got some contracts for London 2012, but the British Government were quite fussy in their stipulations. I'm going back to examine some renovation and expansion projects on a couple of stadiums over there. I've got a couple of Asian contractors in there because I like to give jobs to people in the region and I trust their work ethic, but they're not getting things exactly right."

"Oh, that's a bit of a pain."

Mr Teck stared straight at Chris.

"It can be. Sometimes you just cannot get the personnel to do exactly what they are told. That only makes more work for me because as the boss, I have to soothe the clients. Reassure them that their projects are in the right hands. Don't get me wrong, Chris, I have some sympathy for them. We all make mistakes. But a global construction company needs major investment constantly to remain competitive in a cut-throat industry. When we make mistakes, we can lose money for clients in many different countries. Sometimes we get the dimensions wrong, the seating wrong, the roof wrong, or we just use the wrong materials. Sometimes we can't even do something basic like make the floodlights switch on and off at the right time. You wouldn't believe how many times we've got something as simple as that wrong. Do you know how embarrassing that is, when the lights go out at the wrong time in a big game when all my clients are watching?

"Ah well, what to do? My staff do miss the odd open goal from time to time, Chris, as I'm sure you can appreciate. But my job is to be there for them. When the smelly stuff hits the fan,

I can't delegate anymore. I have to be hands-on. That's why I'm flying to London. I like to remind my staff that even though I'm based in Singapore, I can still be there for them. I can still keep an eye on them and know what they're up to, even when they're in London. Do you know what I mean?"

"Yeah, yeah," Chris whispered.

"Oh look, I think they're about to call Raffles Class passengers. I love flying Raffles Class. It always feels strangely apt, don't you think?"

"Yeah, I suppose."

"Anyway, I'm sure I'll see you again at Heathrow, but if I don't, good luck at Leyton Orient. If you have any problems in London, I've got staff there who can always help you out. I've told them all about you. They know who you are. They know you're coming."

"Yeah, OK."

Mr Teck stood up and headed briskly towards the plane. Chris watched the chairman of Raffles Rangers Football Club hand his Raffles Class ticket to a member of the ground staff before disappearing down the boarding bridge. Chris looked down at his passport and ticket.

His hands were shaking.

THE Minister for Home Improvement stood on the balcony of the Singapore Cricket Club and peered down at the lush green turf of the Padang. There was no better turf anywhere else in Singapore. Leading cricketing nations, top rugby sevens sides and even Liverpool Football Club had all played or trained at the Padang. Several signs along the edge of the field reminded Singaporeans to keep off the grass.

The Minister for Home Improvement sipped his cognac and watched the steady stream of traffic pass the Old Supreme Court on his left. Such a majestic, classical building, he thought. The

British know nothing about a successful public housing policy, but the old empire had undoubtedly left behind some classical architectural gems.

The Minister for Sports (Land and Water) joined his Cabinet colleague on the balcony. He adjusted the belt on his trousers, pulling them even higher.

"Sorry about that," he said. "But I never had a chance to go after all those meetings this afternoon."

The Minister for Home Improvement handed his old friend a cognac.

"Yes, it has been a lousy business, very troublesome," he said. "I've had to make one anti-corruption speech after another in the last couple of days. I've dealt with them all—the CPIB, *The Newspaper* editors, the S-League and even your damn Raffles Rangers."

"Hey, did you see the match? Your side didn't exactly cover themselves in glory. No one tried in that game, no one, except poor Chris Osborne."

"Yes, that was terrible, wasn't it? There was no need for it to end that way."

"Is it all settled now? I heard about the journalists, that expatriate editor and the irritating singer. But are you going to pursue it any further with my club? My conspiracy-obsessed constituents are already demanding an inquiry."

The Minister for Home Improvement stared at his glass and swirled the ice in his cognac.

"Do you know High Teck Construction accounts for almost 10 per cent of the private construction industry in Singapore? Do you know that the company is practically recession-proof? When the Asian currencies all crashed back in '97, they still kept building. They also kept going through the SARS virus crisis and will keep building through this recession."

"They do have a great work ethic at the company."

"It's much more than that. They have one of the best public safety records and meet all building regulations no matter how stringent. They honour every payment and deadline, and offer the best accommodation and wages to our foreign workers. That's important. That strengthens our relations with our regional neighbours."

"They are a great economic asset to Singapore."

"We're lucky to have them."

"So it's settled then."

"I think it has to be."

The ministers sipped their drinks and gazed at the Marina Bay hotels overlooking the mouth of the Singapore River. The Minister for Home Improvement glanced across at his colleague and smirked.

"Come on then," he said. "Get the gloating over with."

"What are you talking about?" the Minister for Sports (Land and Water) replied, feigning ignorance.

"You know perfectly well what I'm talking about."

The Minister for Sports (Land and Water) slowly put down his glass and started cheering.

"There's only one Raffles Rangers," he chanted softly, raising his arms in the air. "One Raffles Rangers, there's only one Raffles Rangers. Come on then, cough up. Your boys lost again."

"At least we took you to the last 10 minutes of the season this time."

"Ah, don't start with the lame excuses. I won, you lost, now cough up."

"Yes, yes, all right. Savour it while it lasts."

The Minister for Home Improvement opened up his wallet, counted out some coins and handed them to his friend.

"Is that it? Is that all you're giving me, three lousy bucks?" the

Minister for Sports (Land and Water) asked incredulously.

"That's what we agreed upon. One plate of chicken rice to the winner."

"I'd love to know where you buy your chicken rice. Still, a win is a win. My boys delivered, once again, and it's back to the drawing board for Orchard FC."

"We'll finish above you next year. Don't worry. I've got a secret weapon up my sleeve."

"I know you have. You rejected Chris Osborne's application for permanent residency, didn't you?"

"I had to after all that nonsense at the party."

"Please lah, I checked. You rejected the application before the final match and before the party."

"Yes, well, he was having problems with his local girlfriend and he wasn't keen on starting a family here. The population unit needed a Caucasian pin-up and he didn't fit the bill. We may use some white guy in the Singapore side instead."

"It was a sneaky way to try to win your bet, wasn't it?"

"What did you expect? Osborne couldn't stop scoring."

"Still a bit cheeky though, considering what you did with the other guy."

"Please. That Poh Wee Kin was sentenced as soon as he threw the punch. I actually thought the sentence was too lenient. Five years for a serious assault? Where does that judge think we are? Australia? We'll have to speak to him about that."

"Either way, I've lost two strikers now, haven't I?"

"Ah, never mind. There's always next year. Let's make it 10 dollars next season."

"Yeah, sure. I've heard Raffles Rangers are giving trials to a couple of Africans in Bencoolen Street. These Africans are unique. They can actually play football."

"Right, then, you're on. Ten dollars it is for next season."

The ministers raised their glasses and toasted their new S-League bet.

They sipped from their glasses as a warm breeze blew across the balcony. The Minister for Home Improvement peered down at the Padang and noticed a couple of teenagers passing a ball to each other on the famous turf.

"Look at these two idiots," he said. "Don't they know they're not allowed to play football here?"

the author

In 1996, Neil Humphreys left Dagenham, England, to travel the world. He got as far as Toa Payoh, Singapore, and decided the rest of the world could wait.

His 10-year sojourn in Singapore saw the publication of three best-selling works: *Notes from an Even Smaller Island* (2001), *Scribbles from the Same Island* (2003) and *Final Notes from a Great Island: A Farewell Tour of Singapore* (2006), and the omnibus *Complete Notes from Singapore* (2007).

Neil then headed south for Victoria, Australia, where his fifth book, *Be My Baby*, was conceived and gestated in 2008. He writes for several magazines and newspapers in Singapore, Australia and the UK. He still watches West Ham and believes Billy Bonds could get a game for them.